THE FIRE THIEF

ERIN ST PIERRE

GWYNN WHITE

4XOVERLAND

FOREWORD

Thank you for purchasing *The Fire Thief*. We really appreciate it and hope you love Stasha and her world as much as we enjoyed writing it. If you'd like to know more about her world, please sign up to receive our newsletter at: https://www.gwynnwhite.com

CHAPTER ONE

"Three iron coins says the scrawny kid eats dirt!"

Stasha just made out the shouted bet above the icy rain that pelted her, Klaus, and the other orphans streaming into the fighting pit hidden deep in the Wryrors Forest.

Her stomach churned. A year ago, almost to the day, she'd sworn never to step into another fighting pit. But here she was, about to bet her last few coins on the most important fight of her life.

If she won...freedom for her and Klaus.

But if she lost—

That wasn't an option.

She tossed her wet golden-blonde braid over her shoulder and stood taller in her soaking gray tunic, threadbare gray leggings, and worn-through boots.

No one could see how much coming here today cost her—and not just in coin.

The crowd lurched forward, carrying her and Klaus through the rickety wooden archway into the pit.

Klaus grunted against the surge of bodies pressing into him. His questioning eyes bored into her. "Stasha, why are we here?"

She quickly looked away.

Focus. Focus on what I have to do.

A wet, misshapen hat perched on a wobbly table in the middle of the muddy walkway. She dropped two of her four precious irons into the hat to buy her and Klaus entry into the pit. They tinkled against the other irons already tossed in by the crowd.

A big hand reeking of wet sheep grabbed her arm. She grimaced.

Only one person around here smelt that bad. Feral Fox, the grizzled fighter who ran the pit. Tall, rangy, and dressed in a filthy sheepskin jacket and loose-fitting burlap trousers, Feral Fox shot her an almost toothless smile. "Been a long time, Stasha," he yelled above the cheering, laughter, and banter coming from the pit. "Glad to see you back." He clapped Klaus on his skinny shoulder. "You too, lad."

"Good to know I was missed." She dropped into a flamboyant bow, letting her fingers almost touch the churned-up mud.

As soon as she straightened, Feral Fox said, "Always, Stasha. We miss Tarik too. But no matter what the fae did in Teagarten, this is still your home." He waved vaguely at the crowd. "And we are still your people."

Feral Fox didn't know how wrong he was. Thanks to the murdering fae, Klaus was the only person left in the world whom she called family.

"I've come to win a whole lot of coin off my people," she yelled back, keeping her voice light. No need for him to know her true intentions tonight.

"Still fancy the underdog?"

She threw her head back and laughed. "What a silly question."

Feral Fox chuckled. "Then you're in luck." He dragged her and Klaus closer and whispered, "I'll keep the betting open long enough for you to have a really good look at him in action." A final smile and Feral Fox moved on through the crowd.

Typical of Feral Fox to offer her a welcome-back gift. His kindness made her chest burn. She swallowed hard and squared her shoulders. She had to remember why she was here.

She had no idea what his real name was; no one did, but like her and Klaus, he'd once been an orphan who had miraculously outlived the two-faced god and his servants, the Kňazer and the Martka's best efforts to sling him into an early grave.

Feral Fox now ran the pits to help other orphans survive. The entrance fee would go to the winner of tonight's fight. If she took his advice and betted wisely, she and Klaus could scoop up all the coins betted at her table. Hopefully, enough coins for them to escape Askavol in the morning.

Feral Fox would walk away with nothing but the satisfaction of knowing he'd taught desperate orphans like her how to survive. Not surprising that Feral Fox was the only person from the pits she'd missed in the last year since Tarik's murder.

She clawed at her leggings. Don't think about Tarik. Not now, or she wouldn't see this through.

She forced a smile and swayed her hips as she elbowed her way through the crowd. Behind her, Klaus stumbled. Her heart dropped, and with it, her fake smile. She lunged for him and yanked him back to his feet before his spindly right leg buckled him into the mud.

It was her fault Klaus was crippled.

Ten years before, she'd snuck away from the wool loom, where she worked, to visit with Klaus in the wood mill. One of the rusting chains heaving the trunk of a pine tree to the saws snapped. The massive log had whipped around so fast, she hadn't even seen it coming.

Klaus had.

He'd darted into its path to push her out of the way. The massive log had struck him and pinned him to the stone floor. In her nightmares, she still saw his mangled leg poking out from under the trunk and heard his screams. For weeks after the accident, she'd pleaded with the two-faced god to heal him. Her prayers had proved just as useless as the Kňazers' joy-killing piety, and the Martkas' salt rituals.

She would never forgive herself for hurting him. Or the gods for being so powerless—and so uncaring.

She conjured her elusive grin. "Careful, you clumsy brute."

Klaus shot her an uncertain look. "You didn't answer my question. What are we doing here?"

She shrugged. "An early celebration of my eighteenth birthday."

She wasn't ready to tell him the real reason for this visit. If she stayed in Askavol beyond her birthday, the Kňazer and Martka would conscript her into accepting an acolyte's robes as a servant of the two-faced god. If she refused, she'd be sold as a wife to some stranger, who'd pay the Kňazer a tithe for her hand.

Why anyone would want her—or any of the starved orphans in Askavol—as a wife was beyond her. Surely, skin and bones, and, in her case, a bad attitude weren't qualities men looked for in a wife?

Neither choice was an option for her. She had to leave Askavol.

If she were to leave Klaus behind to rot, may darkness devour her.

Crippled as Klaus was, he was too weak to travel. For months now, she had avoided the impending doom. With her birthday just days away, time had run out.

Winning on tonight's fight was nonnegotiable.

To complicate things, no one here could know—or even suspect —her plans. If the Martka and Kňazer discovered they were leaving and that someone here had failed to report it—

She shuddered at the thought of flayed backs and broken fingers.

So much to hide. So much to lose.

Just keep smiling. And laughing. Be the old Stasha back in her favorite haunt....

She sauntered to her old betting table. Goul and Ivan were the only boys she recognized out of the crowd milling about.

Her heart sank. Goul had found Tarik's broken body in Teagarten. Had led her to him. He was the last person she wanted to run into today.

She dug deep and gave him a mischievous grin. With luck, it hid the unease she was sure burned in her eyes.

Goul's pinched face beamed back at her. "Stasha!" he yelled above the clamor. "Long lost, but not forgotten!"

"Hello, Goul," Klaus muttered, his face a pale shade of green. He'd also been in Teagarten that morning.

Goul barely spared Klaus a look.

Her fists clenched. But she wasn't here to fight. She forced them to relax, then pushed the bravado, both for Klaus and Goul. "I figured it was time to come back and strip you of some of your coin." She leaned provocatively against the betting table.

Ivan, Goul's idiot friend, laughed. "Brave words, Stasha. Do you even know who's fighting?"

"Still working on it." She looked at the ring to find Feral Fox's underdog.

Vlad and Matthias stood in fighting stance in the center of it. She knew them both by sight from the orphanage but had never seen them fight.

"Matthias is a giant compared to Vlad," Klaus whispered. "No wonder Feral Fox called Vlad the underdog."

Now there was a truth.

"Size doesn't always count," she whispered back. Hunger and desperation often drove winning punches. "Do I have to remind you of all my many, many celebrated wins?" She shot him a grin. "The ones when I beat boys much bigger than me."

Klaus rolled his serious tawny eyes. "Spare me." He'd never understood the allure of the pits.

She chuckled. A real one this time. "What are the odds?" she asked Goul while twirling the end of her braid. Any coin would be shared between the lucky few who bet on the winner.

Goul shrugged. "Matthias is bigger. Heavier. But neither of them have fought before. So toss in your coin, and let's see who wins."

She looked back at Matthias and Vlad circling each other, waiting for Feral Fox's signal to fight.

Klaus was right. Anyone with half a brain would bet on Matthias. Only someone with their *entire* brain intact and functioning would bet on Vlad.

She was just such a girl.

"Get those bets in," Feral Fox yelled from a splintering, ramshackle dais overlooking the pit.

"Matthias to win." Idiot Ivan slammed his coins onto the scarred wooden table, proving that he did indeed have half a brain. No surprise there.

The rattle of coins beneath his pounding fist set her blood pounding. A few more of those and...

Four of Ivan's equally stupid friends tossed their coins onto the pile in agreement.

Her lips twitched. Twelve irons would buy food for ten days if she and Klaus were frugal.

"Fighters!" Feral Fox yelled. "On my signal. One. Two. Three." A piercing whistle cut across the din.

Matthias slammed his knee into Vlad's stomach. Vlad doubled over, coughing through gritted teeth. He tried to retreat. She frowned.

The low wooden fence circling the ring stopped him. Someone leaned over and shoved Vlad back toward Matthias. Vlad stumbled and nearly fell into the slick mud. It wouldn't have made a difference. He was already covered with the stuff.

Perhaps her brain had failed her too, and this wasn't the fight she should risk her precious coin on.

Yet, Feral Fox was rarely wrong about the orphans who fought in his pit. And, true to his word, he hadn't yet called an end to the betting.

She shoved her way to the wooden fence and watched Vlad for any sign of hidden strength that could change the game.

Vlad swung a fist at Matthias, who caught it and flung it back. Matthias followed it up by crunching his elbow into Vlad's nose. Blood splattered on both of their filthy tunics.

She snorted sourly. Feral Fox had misread this one. Vlad was a hopeless case. She was even worse. A year ago, she would not have assessed a fight so badly. She started to turn away, then stopped, hooked by a flash in Vlad's eyes.

Fury raged behind Vlad's tears.

She knew that look. She'd burned with that same fire while throwing punches in the pits.

Lips tilted in a triumphant smile, she swung back to the betting table. "A week's wages say the little thing puts Matthias on his ass." She slammed her two iron coins down. They left new scratches on the scuffed pine.

"What?" Klaus gasped. "Are you insane? Stasha, take it back."

His outrage wasn't misplaced. Vlad was getting a royal ass-kicking from Matthias.

Heart pounding as hard as one of the Martkas' beatings, she glanced at Feral Fox. He nodded at her and smiled.

Feral Fox had never failed her before.

"Just trust me," she hissed under her breath to Klaus.

"But—"

She turned away to watch the fight. Two more boys calling Matthias's name tossed coins onto the table. How long could Feral Fox keep the betting open?

Klaus grabbed her elbow and pulled her closer, leaning all his weight on his able leg. "Are you insane? We're about to lose all the coin we own on a kid who'd have better odds facing a *fae.*" He grimaced at the word and clutched the hilt of the schorl blade strapped to his waist, the only weapon known to ward off fae.

She yanked away, grinning like a wildcat to soothe his fear. "Just you wait, my friend. That kid will pull through."

Matthias's roar spun her back to the pit. He delivered a crushing kick to Vlad's stomach. The smaller boy gagged, spitting blood. And perhaps a tooth from an earlier punch.

"Your money's mine now, Stasha." Ivan loped over to her. Instead of looking at the fight, his eyes roved up her long, mud-speckled legs and stopped at her chest. He didn't meet her hard stare.

What he found to interest him, she didn't know. There wasn't much of her to ogle at, being barely more than skin and bones.

"Maybe next time we'll make the bet a little more interesting," Ivan purred.

She wanted to gag. Instead, she twirled her braid while pillaging his lanky body the same way he had hers. Only instead of leering with lust-hazed eyes, she merely smirked. "I would take you up on that, Ivan, but that would imply there's something interesting about you."

She slid her gaze, hopefully sultry and sly, to the irons on the table. Enough for her and Klaus to eat for two weeks. And still no closing-bet whistle from Feral Fox. She grinned. "And I do believe that the swell of my pockets after this fight will be a lot larger than anything you could possibly offer me."

Ivan's buddies roared with laughter.

"There's the inappropriate comment I was expecting," Klaus murmured, lips twitching while his brow crunched into a frown. How anyone could look concerned and relieved at the same time, she didn't know, but Klaus always pulled it off with ease.

A sneer replaced Ivan's grin, and he finally met her stare. "I'll remember you said that when your pockets are empty later and you're without food. A nice snack for traveling fae soldiers. Just like your boyfriend, Tarik."

A breath hissed through Klaus's teeth, the only sound in the unnerving silence at her table.

A haze of heat settled over Stasha's head. Red clouded her vision. "That's it! You don't walk out of here tonight." Fist raised, she charged at Ivan.

"Stasha, no." Klaus grabbed her balled hand before it rammed into Ivan's stomach. "We all know that Ivan is about as sharp as a marble," he hummed calmly and so softly only she would hear. "Don't let the moron rile you."

Stasha gaped. "Did you not hear what he—"

"I heard." Klaus didn't relinquish his grip on her fist. "He's a real prick. No question about it. But don't give in to him."

Klaus was right. Too much was riding on the fight in the pit to tangle with Ivan. She glowered and spat a curse at Ivan but dropped her fists to her sides.

Goul punched Ivan in the kidney hard enough for Ivan to flinch and squeal like a four-year-old. "That was sick. Even for you."

Ivan flushed pink and jerked a thumb toward the ring. "That tiny thing isn't walking out of here in one piece. Say goodbye to your bet, Stasha."

"You think I'm as stupid as you are?" she spat. "Vlad will come through."

"I'll take that bet too." A voice rumbled across the pit like thunder before a storm. Low, thrilling, and intimidating, it made every hair on her body stand at attention.

She turned to the speaker.

Tall, powerfully built, he had inky-black hair that tumbled around an intense, handsome face, dominated by shockingly blue eyes framed by long ebony lashes.

She'd never seen him before—not in the pits, or in any of the nearby villages. She would have remembered him if she had. No one in the pits looked that well-groomed. Or fed.

"Two coins say Vlad wins." The stranger tossed two *silver* coins on the table.

"All betting is now closed."

She barely heard Feral Fox and certainly couldn't keep her jaw from dropping. *Two silver coins.* The boys at the table gaped. Goul gulped, and Ivan swore. If Vlad pulled himself together and won, she and Blue Eyes would share that pool.

More money than she'd ever seen in her life, let alone dreamed of having. What could possibly have prompted Blue Eyes to wager so much? When Vlad won and she and Blue Eyes shared the bet, he would be out of pocket. More fool him.

One silver coin would get her and Klaus safely to Ruepa, the capital of the Kingdom of Atria, her homeland.

Now, *two* silver coins would set them up properly in the city. Lost in the crowd, the Kňazer and the Martka would never find them. They'd finally be *safe*. With her fighting skills and savvy, and Klaus's gentle wisdom, they could build a new life for themselves.

But first Vlad had to win—and she had to wheedle that second coin from Blue Eyes without being impaled on the fancy sword hanging at his side.

Hands shoved lazily into the pockets of black trousers trimmed with gold thread that matched his tunic and jacket, Blue Eyes ignored them all and watched the fight. His drenched clothes hugged rippling muscles. Expensive clothes that poorly concealed a fighter's body.

She pulled her attention away from him, back to the fight.

Arms wide, exuding confidence, Matthias skipped from foot to foot. He had a lot to be cocky about. Blood poured from Vlad's nose and mouth. It mingled with the mud coating his face and clothes. Still, he circled Matthias with a predatory gleam in his fiery eyes.

Was Vlad playing the crowd? Hoping to build a reputation for himself as the kid who came from nowhere to win?

It's what she would have done.

While she applauded his motives, she still tapped her icy fingers impatiently against her leg.

Come on, Vlad. Just flatten him. You know you want to.

Vlad struck a fist straight into Matthias's unprotected stomach. Matthias's roar turned to a yelp, and he buckled. Vlad skipped around and planted his boot heel square into Matthias's groin. Matthias howled and hit the mud with his knees. His hands clutched his goodies.

A wild laugh burst from her lips.

Vlad jumped away and landed one last kick on Matthias's back. Matthias toppled and landed face-first into the mud.

Fight over.

She leaped over to Klaus and hugged him hard. "We did it! He won!"

Klaus hugged her back. "Still not exactly sure what we did, but you're happy, so that makes me happy."

"Silly brute." She pulled away from him to enjoy her victory.

The crowd had gone wild. Hands slammed on thighs, and fists pummeled the wooden fence as everyone chanted, "Vlad, Vlad, Vlad!"

Vlad burst into hysterical laughter. He wiped his ruined nose and blinked at his adoring audience. Vlad, the scrawny, dirty kid who'd whipped Matthias's butt, would walk away with a title and a pouch filled with coin. If he were smart, he'd eat for a month from tonight's fight.

She had her own winnings to collect. Winnings that offered a brand-new life she could almost taste. With all the bets on the table forfeited, all she had to worry about was the blue-eyed stranger—and his two fabulous silver coins.

The rules said that she split the winnings down the middle with him.

The rules be tossed! She was leaving Askavol, so it no longer mattered what she did as long as she and Klaus escaped.

Her gaze ran up the stranger with the inky-colored hair, crushing blue eyes, and fancy clothing. Just his silver ring with its fancy sigil could have fed her and Klaus indefinitely. He'd likely never been hungry in his life. He could afford to sponsor her and Klaus's escape. And then some.

She tossed her braid over her shoulder and sauntered back to the betting table. Pointedly ignoring Blue Eyes, she fluttered her thick lashes at Ivan. "Look at how fat my pockets are about to become." She placed her hands on either side of the coins, daring anyone to touch them. "But don't worry, Ivan. I'll be thinking of you tonight ... while I count my money."

Ivan glowered. Klaus laughed; a wild and relieved sound, it filled her with joy.

"Not so fast, pit princess."

Her gut wrenched.

Hands still in his pockets, the stranger watched her through piercing eyes. The rest of his brutally sculpted face was equally as challenging. "Half of this money is mine."

Klaus stilled. His hands clamped on her arm.

Uh ... of course. She needed a plan.

It helped that she had the upper hand here. Yes, Blue Eyes was undoubtedly bigger than her. And his well-fed body, with its taut, lean muscles showing through his stupidly expensive clothing, was menacing.

Not to mention the black ink that swirled on the sun-kissed skin beneath his sleeves and collar.

His power to intimidate showed in Klaus trembling behind her, and Ivan's circle of friends all backing off to watch the encounter from a safe distance.

But he also wasn't from these parts; that much was obvious.

Maybe not even from the Kingdom of Atria. Blue Eyes knew nothing about her.

Also, he was farther away from the table, and thus at a less advantageous angle. She had a clear route to the exit.

And she needed that money more than he possibly could. None of the people here would betray her if she stole a coin from him. That wasn't how the pits worked. They may have fought and wagered against each other like ravening fae, but when it came to them versus the spoiled rich, they had each other's back.

Always.

And if it came down to it, she had her schorl knife strapped to her belt.

The only thing that could slow them down was Klaus's bad leg. She'd have to carry him. If he caught them....

How could she refuse such an opportunity?

Time to go for broke.

She dug her boots into the mud to stop her knees from shaking and forced a smug smile. "Of course it is, *my lord*. Let's divide it, shall we?" She lowered her stance—a predator on the prowl—and picked up a shining silver coin. Now, like a traveling magician, she ran it from finger to finger. "One silver coin." At least her hands weren't shaking. Well, not too badly.

Holding the coin high so Blue Eyes couldn't mistake it, she snatched up the second coin and slid it into her tunic. The cold metal stung as it scraped against her warm amber pendant hidden under her clothes. "Two silver coins."

Ivan and all his buddies' eyes followed the coin down her cleavage.

Blue Eyes didn't.

She held her breath and flipped the second coin into the air. As it sailed up, all eyes on it, she swiped her hand across the tabletop. The pile of irons shot off the table and landed in the mud—her gift to Blue Eyes.

A thrill ran up her spine as his eyes met hers just as the second silver coin landed on her open palm. This heist was going to work.

Laughing against her pounding heart, she flipped the table into the mud as well.

Blue Eyes stumbled back to avoid the spray.

She had about five seconds to make her getaway.

"Don't argue," she yelled at Klaus as she dragged him across her shoulder.

"Really, Stasha?" Klaus protested, but he still clung to her like a tick on a dog.

She thrust through the crowd, shoving and pushing until they burst through the wooden archway into the ancient pine forest surrounding the pit. She didn't stop to check if Blue Eyes followed.

Under her weight and Klaus's, her breath rasped, and her chest ached. She slithered across ankle-deep wet pine needles. The two silver coins jingled as she jumped ditches of half-frozen muddy water and mossy fallen branches sprinkled with frost.

If Blue Eyes caught her and reported her to the Kňazer, it would be a week of solitary confinement in lockup, at least. That punishment would be followed by a fate that would make lockup seem as sweet as honey cake.

He would have to catch her first.

CHAPTER TWO

A HATED PLACE

*T*he sounds of the fighting pits fell away and then faded to nothing. The icy rain abated too, leaving swirling mist in its wake. Dusk had fallen. All the better for hiding. Still carrying Klaus, Stasha slowed to a trot and then a walk.

Klaus slipped off her shoulder and stumbled to stand in the slick pine needles.

Breathing hard, she rubbed a painful stitch in her side. Aided by cold starlight, she stumbled through the mist to a fallen tree. It had probably broken in one of the many earth tremors that had wracked the district since that terrible night in Teagarta when she'd lost Tarik. They could sit for a minute, just to let Klaus regain his strength. Resting wouldn't hurt her either. And then she would tell him everything.

"Are you crazy?" Klaus hissed.

She smirked. "No. Just rich." The last thing she wanted was for him to worry. Not with the news she had to impart.

"Rich and dead." Klaus sat on the log next to her. His knee bounced like a leaf in a breeze.

"Seriously, Klaus, can you shake any more?" she joked. "We haven't had an earth tremor in at least three days, and I'm sure we could use one."

Once, she'd thought that if it hadn't been for Klaus's lame leg, he should have enlisted as a fighter in the pits to toughen him up. But after a lifetime of friendship, she no longer believed his peaceful nature could be changed. Gentle kindness was in his bones, as much as stubbornness and trickery were in her blood.

Unfixable.

Although the Kňazer and Martka had certainly tried. They hated that Klaus was the light to her darkness. She would not change that for all the silver coins in the world.

Klaus looked at her owlishly. "I'm serious, Stasha. He could report you to the Kňazer. You're already on thin ice with them. And if he does, you'll spend days in lockup."

Lockup: a dark, dank room little bigger than a cubbyhole, furnished with hay that reeked of mildew and horse manure. She'd be offered no food and very little water for as long as she remained there, forced to fast until the Kňazer deigned to forgive.

"Lockup is nothing compared to what's coming." She jumped up and looked at him through the drifting mist. "I was called into Martka Alonya's study today."

Klaus's face darkened "Of course. Your birthday." He bit his lip, then moaned. "What are they planning for you?"

She kicked the tree. "The same as everyone else. Marriage or acolyte."

"Marriage? Who?" Klaus demanded, voice hard.

"Some stranger she's dragged out of a swamp, I assume." She started walking through the forest. "We have to leave. Hence my bet."

Klaus lumbered to his feet. "I've no problem with that, but the practicalities—" He stumbled on his injured leg to match her pace.

She stopped to let him catch up. Her fault. She'd done this to him. How could she take him on this crazy escape?

But, equally, how could she leave him when all that waited for him on his eighteenth birthday was more slavery in the mill? A mill that would see him in an early grave.

She stood tall and stared him down, daring him to defy her with his "practicalities."

As usual, he did just that.

"What about the fae? We're bound to run into their patrols." Face bleak, he fingered the schorl blade hanging off his belt

"I *hope* one of those animals attack," she gritted out. "I'll stick my blade right into its heart."

After Tarik's murder, they had both saved for months to buy schorl blades. She was just itching for a chance to use hers.

Klaus snorted. "Nice sentiment. You're human. They're ... something else."

A shiver ran up her spine, colder than the frost clinging to the trees. "We're going to Ruepa."

Klaus barked a humorless laugh. "You want to risk fae attacks and head north with winter coming? We have no coats or food. And don't deny it; your boots have holes in them. You'll have frostbite within a week." Despite the cloying mist, sweat pricked on his temples.

She had no time to coddle him.

"Hence my fabulous victory tonight. We have two silver coins. They'll give us everything we need." She flashed him a grin. "I could get those red boots I saw in the shop window. They really are gorgeous."

"Practical boots, Stasha, not—" His head cocked. Listening.

She froze.

A twig cracked, the sound muffled in the mist.

It could have been anything. Or it could have been Blue Eyes. Her heart thudded so loudly, she was sure Klaus could hear it.

She grabbed his hand and whispered, "Move your butt before he finds us."

She scurried with him across the pine needles. There were two possible routes home. The Eastern Road was quicker but infinitely more exposed than the other—a secluded path through dense forest. Trouble was, the little-used track took them past Teagarta, another place she'd sworn a year before never to visit again.

She could defend Klaus, her two silver coins, and herself against the usual vagrants and thieves that looked for easy pickings on the Eastern Road.

Blue Eyes was another matter altogether.

Being a stranger, he was unlikely to know about the Teagarta track. Even if he did, it would be easier to shake him off if they took that long-abandoned route.

Teeth gritted, she veered off toward the ruined town.

Klaus scowled. She couldn't blame him. Not when they were so close to a place of such savagery and pointless destruction.

The place where Tarik had died at the hands of fae.

They crept through the trees in silence, her ears keyed to sounds of pursuit.

Nothing.

At last, through the frosty mist, a broken cobbled road loomed at the edge of the forest. It had been busy once. But a year on from the massacre, it was overgrown with brambles and snakeweed.

No one came here now. Not unless they had to. Some out of fear of the fae, others out of respect for the many who'd been lost. Whatever their reasons, the world had abandoned the once proud town of Teagarta in the heart of the Kingdom of Atria.

A cold wind swept past them. It carried the scent of rain, frost, ashes....

And death.

How many storms had there been since the massacre? Yet none had been cleansing enough to wash the smell of broken bodies from the fire-blackened stone. No doubt, the storms had also failed to fade the casually carved firebird crest the fae had left on a marble boulder at the far edge of town ... a crest that claimed their kill with pride.

Her calloused fingers scraped a thick, ugly white scar that crossed her palm. She had ripped it open trying to tear that crimson-marble boulder off—

"Stasha. This is a bad idea." Klaus slowed, his limp deepening. "We shouldn't be here. Let's go back and take the Eastern Road." Washed with worry, his eyes flickered to her icy face. "Anything could be lurking in these woods. In the ruins. Watching us."

He was right. She'd made a mistake in coming here. An exceptionally stupid one. She wanted to curse at herself, but the effort of speaking was too much. Her shoulders hunched, and she hugged herself for comfort.

If something sinister indeed lurked here and Klaus was harmed, she would never forgive herself.

Just as she would never forgive the sacking of Teagarta.

She stumbled on a loose stone. Crimson marble streaked with gold lines and pumpkin-colored flecks glinted in the starlight breaking through the mist. The marble had once been part of the beautiful onion dome that had roofed the town hall. In a world where everything else was constructed of pine and drab gray stone, Teagarta was the only truly beautiful place she'd ever seen, even if green moss had stuck to the shingles, the color stark against the brilliant red and orange domes.

She had blanked out Teagarta. All she could remember of that terrible morning was finding Tarik. And after she'd found him....

She hadn't cared enough to look at the dome. She hadn't cared about anything.

Now she looked. And looked. Her chest squeezed painfully, and she swallowed the burning lump in her throat.

The front of the once lovely town hall had been ripped away as if the giant marble blocks had been mere pebbles. Those boulders were strewn on the ground, moss and mushrooms creeping up the sides. The marble was no longer beautiful. Now, it reminded her of blood. The grand door, exploded off its hinges by fae, lay in splinters across the overgrown town square.

The inside of the building was worse. One broken wall, which had survived the attack and earth tremors, was stained black with soot. Lengths of charcoal, all that remained of the wooden rafters from the vaulted roof, littered the broken flagstones, where rosewood benches had once stood. The stained-glass window was gone, and in its place a dark maw devoid of beauty.

Her favorite shop across the street—one that had once sold delicious pastries—was nothing more than crumbling foundations. Fire had scorched the bricks, just like every other home and business in the town.

Fae had done this.

Pyreack soldiers invading Atria. Locked between the coast and the land to the south claimed by the Kingdom of Zephyr, Atria crawled with both humanoid fae with their hideous pointed ears, and monstrous faeries, creatures born of nightmares and terror.

After the centuries-long war between the four fae kingdoms, the king of Pyreack seemed to be winning—if Teagarta was anything to judge by. Not that she cared about fae victories and defeats, not when staying alive from day-to-day took all her energy.

Klaus's hand brushed against hers.

She'd stopped walking. They weren't far from the spot that used to house the fighting pit. She cleared her throat and forced her stiff legs to move toward the marble boulder that had crushed Tarik's torso. Tossed so carelessly by the all-powerful fae, it still lay on the side of the road where Tarik had died.

Shoulders pulled back, she kept her neck taut. It was the only way she could stop her head from turning, unbidden, to look at it.

Would his blood still stain the boulder?

Klaus whimpered beside her. He'd looked.

She wrapped her scarred hand tightly around his. They had both lost someone that day, not just her. Sometimes, she allowed herself to forget that.

That didn't mean she could speak. Neither of them could, she knew. But she could give him this, at least. His trembling fingers steadied as they wound through hers. She held on tightly. No matter what the Martka and Kňazer said when they arrived back at the orphanage, she would never let go of Klaus.

A bird cawed.

"A raven," Klaus hissed.

Her stomach knotted. "Where?" she choked out.

A streak of glossy black shot through the ruins and landed on a burnt roof. Undoubtedly a raven.

Klaus's fingernails bit into her palm, and her hand trembled. Ravens were an omen of punishment, or so the Kňazer and Martka insisted.

Seeing one—especially after dark—was a warning. Seeing two, an omen. Three meant the threat was no longer coming. It had already arrived.

She ground her teeth and turned away from the bird. She had enough problems without adding the Kňazer's silly superstitions.

Trouble was, she couldn't shake her dread that her life was about to change.

CHAPTER THREE

CAUGHT RED-HANDED

Stasha would never risk taking their winnings back to the orphanage in Askavol. The Martka searched daily through her and the other orphans' meager belongings for "vanities"—their word for pretty things. They claimed that anything pretty or frivolous was an affront to the two-faced god, and the person who owned it should be punished. Any money found would be heavily tithed. So she and Klaus stopped at the wool mill, where they stored their stash.

A wooden shutter hid a small window at the back of the building. It was too high up for her to climb into on her own.

Klaus squelched down in the mud, propped his injured leg up on a sodden woodpile, and offered her his clenched hands. His face blanched as she hopped on his palms and stretched to open the shutter.

Once, she'd argued with him to climb in first so he could use her as a step. He'd insisted on helping her up before him. It had been the only time he'd ever argued with her. She'd relented; it couldn't be pleasant to always be helpless.

"Sorry, Klaus," she murmured as she wrestled with the sash window. It always jammed in the rainy weather. Below her, Klaus trembled. She gritted her teeth and wrenched. A judder followed by a screech of swollen wood, and warmth poured out the window. She breathed in the musty, sickly sweet odor of damp woven wool and grimy sheepskins. Comfortable and rough.

"Stop enjoying the view. My arms are breaking."

It wasn't Klaus's arms she worried about. Nevertheless, she said, "Then you should exercise more. Build up those puny muscles."

She pulled herself up through the window and thudded onto the floorboards. In the pale light cast by the torches in the mill, she scrambled over to the bales of wool and fished out the frayed rope they kept hidden for just such eventualities. She tossed one end out the window and, holding the other end, braced herself for Klaus's weight.

Klaus tugged on the rope first. Typical.

"Just climb before Blue Eyes catches you."

He scowled up at her. "Not funny, Stasha." He probably said that ten times a day.

"Then haul your skinny ass up here. I'm hungry."

He pulled the rope taut. "Don't drop me," he growled.

"That was one time." She flashed a fiendish grin. "It was an accident."

"Sure it was." He struggled for grip while his right leg dangled uselessly. She grabbed his outstretched hand and pulled him inside. He collapsed on the floorboards in a cloud of dust.

She dropped to her knees next to him and fumbled for a familiar knot in the floorboards with numb, frozen fingers. Her fingernails slipped into it, and she prized the boards apart. A small hidey-hole gaped. Years ago, she and Tarik had carved it to hide their fighting-pit winnings.

Now, it was empty except for a single length of red ribbon. If the Martka found it, they'd toss it in the fire and her into lockup.

She would die fighting before that happened.

Tarik had given her that ribbon as a reminder to have hope. He'd also said while hope was vital, without action, it was wishful thinking. That's why they fought in the pits, so they'd be free. Freedom brought choices, he'd said. Not to mention food for the belly and finery for the heart.

She hadn't had much to hope for since his death.

His gift would definitely go with her when they ran. A constant reminder that she needed to have hope if she were to carve a better life for Klaus and her.

Careful not to crush the ribbon, she thrust the rope into the hole.

She kissed the two shiny, warm silver coins before dropping them in too.

Klaus helped wedge the floorboards back into place. "What if that man is waiting for us at the orphanage?"

If Klaus had a failing, it was that he could never let things go.

If she had a failing, it was an abiding obsession to keep him from worrying so much.

She rose and made a show of brushing dried mud off her leggings. "Tell me; have you ever seen him around here before?"

Klaus's brow knitted. "No."

"Me neither. He's a stranger. He has no idea who we are, or if we're even from Askavol. For all he knows, we come from Drueya or Shoiland. Or any other village for miles around."

Klaus's scowl deepened.

"Come on, Klaus. I thought you were the smart one. Why haven't you put this together?"

"He's unlikely to be stupid enough to forget two silver coins."

"It is a lot of money, isn't it?" She beamed, trying to shake off the weight of the day and the challenges tomorrow would bring.

"I'm serious, Stasha."

Her shoulders slumped, and she sighed. "What else could I do? We didn't have enough. I had to take the risk."

Heavy footfalls echoed on the wood floor. Her head jerked up. The sound came from beyond the dark stone archway that led to the looms and spinning wheels.

Martka Gabika, judging from the stomping. She always walked like she was trying to bring down a mountain.

"Who's down there?" Martka Gabika called.

"We need to leave tonight before they—" Klaus whispered urgently.

"Shh!" she snapped, giving him a warning look. Her mouth dried, but it was too late to leave now. Their only choice was to play ignorant. "It's me, Martka Gabika. Stasha."

Martka Gabika rounded the corner. The old woman was dressed in a black gown trimmed with perfect white embroidery depicting the cycles of the sun and moon. Back-lit from the torches in the mill, the artistically twisted veil covering her hair cast a shadow over the stark ritual scarification on both sides of her leathery face. On her left cheek, a knife had scored ugly stars that drooped into teardrops. These had been blackened with ink to create the illusion of a weeping, deathly black night. On her right cheek, the violent scars depicted the sun. The rays, cruel and ghostly, had been filled with chalk-white ink.

She honestly didn't know which was uglier: the facial scarring or the black raven feathers tattooed on the Martka's hands and arms. They were a constant reminder of what awaited the disobedient.

The same scars and tattoos would be carved into Stasha's face and body if they trapped her in an acolyte's rough robes.

Martka Gabika's eyes widened. "What are you doing?" Spittle flying, she stormed down on them. "Stasha! Alone with a young man after dark?" Spit flecked Stasha's nose. She grimaced and only just resisted the urge to wipe it away. "Martka Alyona has already chosen a husband for you. What will he think? Do you want him to call you a harlot?"

The plans had gone that far? She clawed at her leggings.

Better not to let the old woman know how terrified she was. She gritted her teeth. "We were just talking, Martka. We're friends."

Martka Gabika knew that. Everyone knew that.

"That doesn't matter." Martka Gabika grabbed them both by the arm and hauled them out into the silent mill. "You can't be friends with a boy."

Klaus winced and stumbled on his lame leg, but Martka Gabika ignored it.

It took all of Stasha's self-control not to punch the woman. That would land her in lockup. Neither she nor Klaus would benefit from it.

"You know better than to be alone with a man who is not your husband," the hateful woman continued.

Nothing about Blue Eyes?

That was good news. Also, Martka Gabika hadn't seemed to have noticed their muddy, wet clothes.

For show—and because Martka Gabika would expect it—she kicked the closest loom. "Why am I the only one in trouble? He was alone with a girl."

"Don't talk back to me." Martka Gabika let go of Klaus—who had regained his balance— and smacked Stasha on the side of her head. Her head jerked to the side. Pain sliced from her neck down her shoulder. Her amber pendant flicked out of her tunic. She slipped the pendant back under her clothing before Martka Gabika saw it.

Klaus threw her a scowl. A silent warning not to do anything foolish. He knew her well.

Martka Gabika dug her fingernails into Stasha's arm and marched her through a row of looms to the main entrance. The great pine door, wide enough for a horse and cart to pass through, stood open to the icy night. A long, thick line of salt was drawn across the doorway. Salt supposedly kept fae, fairies, and other nasty creatures from crossing.

What had brought Martka Gabika here looking for them, if not Blue Eyes? Perhaps the hateful woman was leaving it to the Kňazer to deal with her. Martka Gabika pushed her out into the biting cold, as if to confirm it.

She shivered. The first snow flurries would be on them within days. Klaus was right; they needed warm clothing. That meant a trip to Drueya. Bigger than Askavol, it had the only shop for miles around that sold quality clothing.

The shop would be closed now, another reason to delay their departure until morning. Just as long as nothing happened during the night to upset their plans. She refused to even think about that raven.

"Go to the dinner hall. Both of you. It's the Hiding of the Moon, so expect a feast." Martka Gabika slapped their backs.

Feast! She snorted. The stale brown bread, gray stew and thimble of milk they received once a month on the Hiding of the Moon would do little to help them on their journey.

Still, it was something. For the rest of the month, meals at the orphanage had to be bought out of their earnings. Sadly, no one earned enough to buy a meal a day from the Martka. It seemed they and the two-faced god didn't want orphans surviving into adulthood.

"Just because the moon goddess hides her face tonight doesn't mean she can't see your wickedness, Stasha." Marka Gabika wagged her finger. "She sees all. You're lucky the fae didn't come for you too."

Another reference to Tarik that she had to let slide. Her icy skin burned hot.

Legend said that, centuries before, on the Hiding of the Moon, the hated fae lord responsible for starting the war that still ravaged the continent of Zathryth, and which had left her and Klaus and so many others orphaned, had disappeared, never to be seen again. Once a month, the moon goddess covered her face, to allow humans to hide from the ravening fae in her shadow.

Stasha had never believed the stories, although she was grateful for the morsel of food they provided. All she knew for certain was that before the war, humans and fae had ruled side by side.

Now, humans were little more than prey in the game of war the four fae kingdoms waged against each other. Unable to fight against fae magic, human cities and towns had been turned into nothing but fae army camps and war bases. Her people had become loose ends in the conflict.

Martka Gabika slapped her. "Don't let me catch you alone with Klaus again, or it will be lockup for you."

Hips swinging provocatively—just the way Martka Gabika hated —she sauntered across the quad to the orphanage.

It was a decrepit building of three floors, roofed with wooden shingles and a rickety wooden onion-dome, nothing like what had once existed in Teagarta. It housed nearly two hundred orphans.

Like so many others, she had arrived at the orphanage as a baby. Unlike so many others, she had carried something with her—her teardrop-shaped amber pendant. For reasons she'd never fathomed, the Martka had not taken it from her. As long as she kept it hidden under her clothes, she seemed to have silent permission to wear it.

Strange, she'd always thought. But she wouldn't risk losing it through questioning them.

As to the mysteries of where she'd come from or who her parents were, she had no answers. Like most of the waifs she shared her home with, she had no idea if her name had been given to her by her missing parents or by the Kňazer.

Her necklace gave her hope that her parents had named her.

Not that it really mattered. Tarik and Klaus were her real family—the only people in the world whom she loved. Whoever her parents had been, how much impact could they really have on her life? No one was alive to remember them. No one even knew where their bodies lay.

Probably in a mass war grave.

There were dozens of orphanages, just like hers, spread across Atria. They all had their mills or farms where orphans were given jobs with little or no pay and in return were expected to serve the two-faced god and their deities with unquestioning obedience.

The Kňazer never let them forget how much they owed. How little they gave. What burdens they were. How they should beseech the two-faced god for forgiveness for even being born.

Since Tarik's death, Stasha had no time for such nonsense.

It was one of the reasons she could never accept an acolyte's coarse robes. That, and the mutilation of her face and hands.

She and Klaus reached a pockmarked door—like everything else in the orphanage, it needed a lick of paint. A fresh line of salt lay across the threshold.

Klaus leaned in. "This is it," he whispered. "If he's here, we've had it."

She refused to indulge his fears. "Just relax. We'll be fine." But as she creaked the door open, she held her breath. Was the dark-haired stranger with the achingly blue eyes indeed waiting for her?

She scanned the long, narrow room with its scarred trestle tables and rows of buckled benches.

A dark-haired man stood with his back to her at the head of the room. He was talking to Martka Alyona, who listened intently with turned-down lips.

Icy dread chilled her to the core. Maybe Klaus had been right, and she shouldn't have stolen the coin. There was nothing left but to face her accuser. She swallowed the nausea rising in her throat and prepared for the worst.

CHAPTER FOUR

RAVEN'S WINGS

Stasha's stomach churned, and her chest locked up. The man shifted to face her. Boring brown eyes stared blankly at her. A new male acolyte. She huffed out a breath, and a knot of tension vanished from her shoulders.

She nudged Klaus. "See, all that energy spent worrying—wasted."

He snorted and stepped into the hall.

She followed. The familiar reek of kitchen grease, sweat, old pine, and firewood stung her icy nose. She rubbed her hands together, blowing on them to warm her numb fingers as she weaved through the lines of tables to their favorite seats near the fire. Its limited warmth was welcoming.

The table was already crammed with people desperate to get some hot food before the long month of fighting for scraps began after the feast. That made it impossible to discuss her plans with Klaus.

She flopped down onto an unforgiving bench and grabbed a bowl of stew. Gray and unidentifiable, at least it was warm. She slurped a spoonful of the greasy saltiness—and earned a disapproving look from Klaus, probably for forgetting to thank the two-faced god.

"Eat your food, or I'll have to pour it down your throat," she joked as he bowed his head and prayed. She dug her spoon into the glutinous mess, ready to ladle another mouthful.

He shoved her arm. "Gratitude is never misplaced." He smiled. "And I don't inhale food like you do."

She rolled her eyes and scarfed the mouthful. She'd barely finished swallowing when the floor rocked beneath her feet. The table rattled. Even though earth tremors were commonplace, the younger kids still screamed as dust rained down from the low wooden ceiling.

"Earthquake drill!" one of the Martka yelled.

Almost as one, Stasha, Klaus, and the other orphans clambered under the tables.

They were well practiced.

Stasha's long limbs splayed out awkwardly in the small space. Klaus wrapped his arms around her shoulders, pulling her close while wooden bowls tumbled onto the floor, and milk splattered. His hot breath warmed her ear.

She clamped a sweaty hand on his arm as his grip tightened around her. It wasn't all fear that made him clutch her—he had her back just the way she had his.

The quake moved on, cascading down the valley like a wave. The ground shuddered one last time and then stilled. A few of the younger children whimpered in the sudden calm. Food and milk dribbled from the tabletops onto the cracked flagstones. Someone was praying, reciting an old verse she'd heard a million times over in a tongue she'd never deigned to learn.

"The quakes are probably caused by fae," Klaus whispered. "The Pyreack are coming for us here in Atria. Not even the moon goddess can save us."

"Been reading the Kňazer's newspaper again?" she whispered. Klaus had taught himself to read years before from a book he'd saved from one of the Martka's many pyres. He'd insisted on teaching her and Tarik their letters. If she took it slow and concentrated really hard, she could have read the newspaper too. She left that kind of thing to Klaus.

He leaned in close. "I saw it today. I should have told you...." He sighed. "Too much else going on. According to the paper, it isn't enough that the fae kingdoms have stolen all the territory in Zathryth —Pyreack wants more. Everything."

People were moving, and it would seem odd if she and Klaus stayed under the table, but she had to know more. "Then not even

Ruepa will be safe. What are we supposed to do? Where should we go?"

"The Kňazer said the answer is to pray." Even Klaus sounded dry.

She snorted. No doubt when Pyreack had conquered Ocea, Atria's easterly neighboring kingdom, all the humans who had been ripped to shreds had been praying too. It hadn't done them much good. "All the more reason for us to leave. We can decide what to do once we're on the road."

He nodded, but his eyes flickered to the bustle around them. "We need to move, or Martka Gabika will be on us like bugs in summer."

She grabbed his arm before he could scramble away. "Tomorrow, let's go to Drueya after work, before the shop closes. We'll get what we need and then head into the forest. No one will notice we've gone until morning."

Brown hair hanging in his tawny eyes, Klaus squeezed her hand. "Try keeping out of trouble until then."

After clutching his hand one last time, she climbed out from beneath the table and looked around.

At least the walls and ceiling were still intact. That had been a mere shudder, as earthquakes went.

One of the younger Martka knelt beneath the statue of the two-faced god. It stood in an alcove carved into the wall in the front of the room.

Sadly, it too had survived.

The two marble figures shared legs and hips but were separated at the torso into two distinct bodies. One wore a delicately carved cloak that draped like wet silk over the effigy's pure-white skin. His hood hung over his shoulders, revealing a beaming face crowned with laurel leaves. The same sun tattoo the Martka wore was engraved into his forehead. He represented purity—the good, submissive worshipper.

His face was patronizing.

The second looked as though it had been dipped in black ink. The dark stone was rough like old wool. His hood was up, hiding his eyes and nose. Only his thin, frowning lips and the stars and tears tattooed into his neck were visible. A raven perched on his shoulder, claws digging in sharply. His downward pointing fingers were skeletal. Death. Disgrace. Chaos. A stupid threat for naughty children.

More Martka knelt at the statue, their cloaks pooling out like dark water.

Martka Gabika pulled handfuls of salt from the pouch tied to her waist and tossed them across the buckled floor. She muttered something unintelligible.

Stasha's stomach rumbled. Her bowl had also toppled onto the floor. She groaned and pouted, crossing her arms over her chest.

Another hungry night awaited.

Wizened as a piece of sun-dried hide, Martka Alyona scrambled up a set of wrought-iron stairs to a small pulpit, used only by herself and the Kňazer. "Boys and girls," she called from the top. "Come, lay yourselves before the two-faced god. Plead for protection and forgiveness."

As dumb as the notion was—surely they should evacuate the building in case of aftershocks?—the little children ran to obey. The older ones took a little longer to comply, some grumbling their reluctance.

Darkness would swallow her before she'd deign to join them.

"I'm going to bed." She brushed Klaus's shoulder with tender fingers. "Until tomorrow." She shoved her way through the sea of children surging to the statue with pleas on their lips and eyes brimming with tears. Maybe she was as dumb as everyone else for staying inside, but it had been a long day, and she wanted to be alone in her dormitory for the last time.

"What about dinner?" Klaus called after her. "Maybe they'll give us some bread, if nothing else."

"I've lost my appetite." She didn't look back to see the hunger in his eyes.

Before she could push through the throng to the open hallway door, Acolyte Inna grabbed her arm. Just turned eighteen, Inna had once been beautiful. Now, engulfed in heavily twisted gray robes, and with her dark hair severely pulled back, it was impossible to tell. The scars on her face were freshly scabbed in unnatural colors. Newly mutilated.

Inna stabbed a tattooed finger at Stasha's pendant. "You shouldn't be wearing that. It's an affront to the two-faced god." Inna wiggled her fingers, fluttering her raven's feathers. "Hand it over."

Stasha palmed the stone and tucked it beneath her tunic. It must have fallen out as she'd climbed beneath the table. "The necklace stays with me. Everyone with a bit of authority around here knows that."

Inna's eyes narrowed, and she winced; it must have pulled the skin on her face. "The two-faced god frowns on you for your arrogance and vanity." Her obvious pain did nothing to soothe the harshness in her voice. "Forsake the necklace and be forgiven." She jerked her hand again, fully expecting Stasha to submit.

Glare unwavering, Stasha crossed her arms. "I dare you to try and take it." She allowed a coy, challenging smile to twist her lips.

Inna lunged for her throat.

She sidestepped. Her fist swung up, but she stopped it an inch before connecting with the stupid acolyte's chin.

Inna gaped but didn't try that stunt again. "Forsake the necklace and your ungodly vanity," she wailed, "which has wrought such calamity." She pulled out her salt pouch and tossed a handful at Stasha. "Forsake it all," she moaned as Stasha darted away to avoid being pelted. "Or spend the night in lockup."

Stasha's spine stiffened, and her lip curled back. "Go speak to Martka Gabika or Martka Alyona." Her voice was thin. Sour. "They'll tell you that this necklace is *mine.*"

Inna looked around. No doubt unsure how to deal with disobedience.

Stasha pushed past her, but Inna grabbed her arm. The acolyte's gaze darkened. "The two-faced god frowns upon you, girl." Her voice dropped to a rasp that sent a shiver up Stasha's spine. "Allow yourself to open the sacred doors to meet the two-faced god."

Stasha froze.

"Accept what gave you life and purpose." Drool collected at the corner of Inna's mouth. "Put away things of vanity and pride. Cast aside your ungodly selfishness." Her voice spiked with fervor. "Accept the keys of his majesty, and he will forgive and protect you."

Stasha yanked her arm back. This time, Inna didn't try to stop her. Clearly touched in the head, the acolyte stumbled away and sagged to the floor amid the spilled food.

Stasha's lip curled as she turned away. If her supposed groom rejected her for being a harlot, they wanted her to become one of those.

Never in a fae lifetime.

She stomped to her dormitory.

It was deserted. Red coals flickering in the potbellied stove in the long, narrow room gave off the only light as she weaved past the other girls' beds to her straw pallet in the alcove off the main room. She sighed with relief as she plunked down on her gnarly mattress and pulled off her worn boots. She plunged a finger through a hole in the sole. It had leaked water, drenching her foot. As Klaus had observed, new boots were a necessity.

The calf-high, bright-red boots in the shop window in Drueya were fabulous.

And red was her favorite color, mainly because the Martka and Kňazer had outlawed it for its rampant frivolity. If priced the same as the boring brown boots, she'd snag them. She grinned, her icy rage at Inna melting away as she tossed the broken boot to the floor.

The small stove wasn't enough to prevent the cold from pricking her skin as she wriggled out of her tunic and leggings. Everyone's nightgowns had been shaken off their hooks on the wall and lay in a tangle on the floor. She scrambled through them until she found hers. Quickly, she pulled it over her head, balled her damp clothes for a pillow, and dove onto her pallet with them. Snuggled down under her blanket, she rolled the glowing amber between her thumb and forefinger.

Had one of her parents given it to her? They must have. The Martka and Kňazer would never do such a thing. Did that mean she had been loved, however briefly?

She let the stone drop against her chest. None of that mattered. Tomorrow she and Klaus would be free. With nothing behind them and everything ahead of them, they could re-carve their lives into what *they* wanted them to be.

Pity she had no real idea of what that was.

Footsteps clattered into the room. The person stopped and tsked disapprovingly. It sounded like Hathrine. The youngest, quietest girl in the dorm, Hathrine never spoke unless spoken to, and even then, she was painfully shy.

What had upset her?

Stasha pulled her head out from under her blanket.

Hathrine stood in the doorway, a candlestick in hand. She glanced at Stasha, placed the candlestick on the windowsill and then began straightening up the other girls' beds.

Stasha's cheeks flushed. How had she not noticed that the earthquake had shifted all the beds?

Hathrine even shook off the blankets Stasha had traipsed hardcaked mud over.

She was getting up to help set the room right—

"Lenka died that day too," Hathrine said.

The blood drained from Stasha's face, and she slumped back onto her bed.

There was no doubt about what day Hathrine referred to. It was on everyone's lips. She vaguely recalled seeing Hathrine in Teagarten that morning. Hathrine had held someone in her arms. It had to have been Lenka, the pretty girl with the curly chocolate-colored hair and smooth dark skin. Lenka and Hathrine had been inseparable.

After wallowing in her own grief and fury over Tarik's killing, a whole year had passed without her noticing that Lenka was gone.

Hathrine picked up an armful of nightgowns. "I know what you feel, Stasha. The pain. The anger. The sorrow that never goes away. But I think it's better not to give in to it."

Was Hathrine making excuses for Stasha's lack of awareness? If so, Hathrine was kind and too generous. She should have thought about the other girls and tidied the room before diving into bed. She was the eldest, after all. Why was she so blind that she could only think of herself or Klaus? She leaned across her pallet and snatched the nightgowns from Hathrine. "I'll hang them up. You get ready for bed."

Hathrine hesitated.

The doubt did nothing for Stasha's self-esteem. She shoved the girl aside, clambered out of bed and gathered the nightgowns.

Hathrine moved to the window and retrieved her candle. Her startled intake of breath snagged Stasha's attention.

Eyes wide, face pale, Hathrine couldn't have looked more shocked if she'd seen a fae.

Or a dark-haired stranger with chilling blue eyes.

Stasha dropped the nightgowns and loped to the window.

Only mist swirled in the quad below.

Still, her skin crawled with frightening presentiment. She swallowed and forced a smile. "Seeing ghosts now?"

Hathrine shook her head. "I—I'm not sure what I saw, but he was —" She shivered. "He's gone now." A last look out the window, then Hathrine turned to pick up the discarded clothing. But even the mundane task of hanging the nightgowns could not lift her pallor.

Stasha frowned, searching for whatever had frightened the girl. Nothing moved below her window. She was about to give up when she spotted a raven perched on a stunted tree at the end of the quad.

A second raven.

She hissed and balled her fists.

The bird cawed as if it heard her. Impossible. Yet it fluffed its wings, discomposed.

She tsked at herself for her foolishness. It wasn't an omen. It was just a bird. She forced herself away from the window, ignoring the persistent voice in her head that insisted she run *now*.

It's just a bird. Nothing more.

Still, hand trembling, she took the nightgowns from Hathrine and placed them on their hooks. Grateful to hide, she climbed back into bed and pulled her blanket over her head.

If Hathrine had seen the stranger, why hadn't he come to the door looking for her? Why stand under her window like he knew she lived in this dorm? And if he didn't want his money, what did he want?

She closed her eyes tight, channeling Klaus with all this worrying. As soon as their work was done, she and Klaus would get their supplies and flee. But that didn't stop an unwelcome thought pressing on her mind: It's too late to run. Too late. Far, far too late.

She scowled into the darkness until she fell into a restless sleep.

She dreamed of raven's wings.

*O*rphanage rags left in a heap in her dorm, Stasha strode along the cobbled road to Drueya. She was dressed in a set of well-worn, slightly too-small fighting leathers Feral Fox had given her on her sixteenth birthday. Tarik's red ribbon, tied in her braid, flew proudly in the cutting wind.

Klaus, hobbling next to her, had no other clothing other than his orphanage uniform. That would change when they got to the shop in Drueya.

Work had dragged like an eternity. She'd messed up her spinning at least a dozen times daydreaming about freedom. The Martka in charge of her section had finally shooed her out before she could mess up yet another order. She'd been only too glad to escape and had even enjoyed the challenge of collecting her ribbon, their winnings, and the bit of frayed rope undetected. She'd also filled a knapsack with steaming-hot brown bread, hard cheese, a foot-long salami, and a dozen apples stolen from the Martka's private kitchen. It would last them a week, maybe two if they were careful.

Klaus also toted a knapsack jammed with a blanket, which they'd share. It wouldn't offer much protection from the cold, but it would have to do.

And speaking of cold....

Late-afternoon ice nipped at her, a warning that the shop would soon close. She ticked off a list of prices in her head for new boots and a warm cloak for her, and a pair of thick leggings, a tunic, and a heavy coat for Klaus. Never before had she imagined buying so many things at once. It would eat into one of the silver coins tucked into her pocket. It couldn't be helped. Keeping warm was a top priority. She smiled, strangely glad to be parting with the money if it fed her hope.

Klaus frowned. "You make me nervous when you smile like that."

She huffed a laugh. "Everything makes you nervous. How long do you think it will take us to get to Ruepa?" They'd decided to continue on that course, regardless of what Klaus had read.

His brows crumpled. "A month. Maybe more."

Trust Klaus to know that. "Do you think we'll need transport?" She glanced down at his mangled leg. It was always worse in the winter.

Another thoughtful sideways glance from him. "Only horses around here."

She sympathized with his concern—orphans weren't taught to ride—but she brushed it away with a wave of her hand. "How hard can it be?" Her chin tilted defiantly. "You sit on it, hold tight, and dangle a carrot in front of its nose."

Klaus snorted. "I'm sure there's more to it than that." No mention of how difficult it would be for him to stay on a horse with his leg. Maybe he wanted to cultivate hope too.

"We'll figure something out. The important thing is, we're finally escaping.

He cracked a wan smile. "And we'll be together."

"Exactly."

The gray stone wall surrounding Drueya rose ahead of them. They sped up as the open gate drew near. She skipped through it into the market town. Eyes watchful, she led Klaus down the main street until they reached the dried-up fountain in the center of the weed-ridden and decaying town square. It was just the way things were in Drueya and all the surrounding villages.

A flash of inky wings flapped in the corner of her vision.

Her stomach looped painfully.

A raven swept through the buildings and perched on the fountain. It cawed, claws scraping the gray stone as it stared at her.

A third raven.

She turned away, refusing to acknowledge that disaster had arrived.

A woman and her child crossing the square must also have seen the raven. They both cried out and backed away from the bird.

Refusing to be intimidated, Stasha set her mouth into a hard line and grabbed Klaus's hand. "Through here."

They scurried through a crumbling archway to a line of sagging buildings, housing a variety of shops. Gone was the black lettering that proclaimed this was the clothing store. In its stead, shadowy imprints stained the cracked blue door. She tugged the handle, and the door squealed loudly as it swung open.

Given the lateness in the day, the store was empty of customers. An old crone sat at a cluttered table at the back. She squinted at her sewing, not even bothering to look up as they entered.

Stasha shoved Klaus toward a rack of coats and leggings. "Can I trust you to pick your own?"

He glared at her. "I'm not an idiot, you know."

"No, just a clumsy brute." She shot him a tender smile. "Choose warm things."

Her fingers trailed along shelves crammed with tunics and leggings in all colors, bright coils of ribbon, cards of lace, and jars of pearly buttons as she made her way to the rack of boring, sensible brown leather boots. Meanwhile, the startlingly red boots in the window shouted *hope*.

She turned on a heel and strode to the red boots before she could change her mind. She'd eyed them often enough to know they'd fit her. And even if they didn't, she'd put up with her feet rattling around in them or the leather squeezing her toes.

She snatched them up. Every stitch was perfect. Even better, the cobbler had threaded strong leather laces up the front. Her hand dipped into one of them, and she cooed. It was lined with thick, warm sheepskin. Ideal for the coming winter. And much, much nicer than any other boot she'd ever seen. She flicked over the price tag and hissed. Two coppers more expensive than the brown boots.

They could spare the coin.

Well, not really, but she was going to indulge anyway.

Eyes twinkling, she waved the boots at Klaus. He was trying on a very plain gray coat. "Look how pretty they are."

Klaus huffed a laugh and shook his head. "You'll stand out like a fae's ears in those." His hand drifted to the schorl blade strapped to his belt—something he always did at the mention of fae.

She ran an eye up the gray coat he'd selected and shook her head. "Not that one. You need pockets."

"I guess you're right." He looked lovingly at a fine, ankle-length black coat with two big pockets, then sighed. He tugged the lapels of the boring one. "This was cheapest."

She leaned in. "Let's do this right," she whispered. "Don't scrimp."

He shuffled to the black coat. Leaving him to enjoy his shopping, she turned to three wooden mannequins. Each was draped with a wildly different cloak. Almost drooling, she fingered a red one first. Velvet as soft as lamb's fleece slid between her fingers. If Klaus thought her red boots conspicuous, he'd have a seizure if she bought this. Or the bright-blue satin draped next to it.

Lips pulled into a responsible line, she fingered the black serge cloak on the last mannequin. While not as flamboyant and stylish as the other two, it was warm and had a voluminous hood.

Sensible.

She took it off the mannequin and turned to find Klaus.

Dressed in a new pair of thick, black leggings, a black woolen tunic, and the black, ankle-length coat adorned with large pockets, he waited for her near the saleslady.

Arms bulging with her selections, Stasha was about to join him to pay when a basket of woolen scarves and mittens snagged her. A set like that would be perfect for Klaus. She opened her mouth to ask him what color he fancied but snapped it closed—a bright-red set was squished at the very bottom of the pile. She yanked it out and dangled the scarf and mittens under his nose. "Perfect. They'll match my boots and my ribbon. The final snub to the two-faced god."

Before Klaus could comment about her extravagance—or her irreverence—she plunked her shopping onto the sales counter.

The old lady's lips pursed. No doubt preparing to say, *You can't afford all that, girl.*

Stasha slapped the silver coin down on the table first.

The woman's eyes widened behind her half-moon glasses. "Where did you get that, girl?" The sewing dropped into her lap, and the needle pinged on the wood floor.

Stasha shrugged, trying for an innocent smile. "I saved. For a long, long time."

Klaus coughed loudly behind her. He excused himself and headed across to the display of scarves and mittens and picked up a gray pair.

Rolling her eyes, she snatched them from him and tossed them back on the pile.

He needed some hope too.

The shopkeeper's lip curled, but she wouldn't turn away the money. In fact, the crone's hand trembled as she counted out the change—two handfuls of irons and a few coppers.

Stasha winced at how little of the silver coin remained. The purchases had been necessary. They had a hard journey ahead, and they needed all the advantage they could get. But from now on, they'd have to be as stingy as the Martka were at dinner time.

The saleslady didn't need to see her worry. She slipped the change into her pocket and bobbed a bow—as if she could afford to throw money around. "You have an excellent day."

She swung the cloak over her shoulders and headed for the door. Klaus's coughing followed her.

Not wanting to swap her boots in the cold air outside, she stopped before going out. Stepping out of her old ones was easy. She passed them to Klaus, who leaned against a wall for support. Just the short walk from the mill to the store and then a bit of shopping had tuckered him out.

She pushed her fear for him aside as her feet sank into her new boots. A perfect fit, her toes snuggled down into the soft fleece. She spun in a half circle while he surveyed her. "What do you think?"

Klaus swallowed. "They're ... very nice." He shifted his weight, careful not to fall over. "And very noticeable."

"And very warm. Now hold out your hands."

He frowned but dropped her old boots to obey.

She slipped the wildly conspicuous red mittens onto the fingertips of each of his hands and draped the scarf around his neck. "Happy birthday to me. And screw the Kňazer and Martka."

His eyes widened. "For me?"

"For you." Over her shoulder, she added, "The world awaits us."

She opened the door and then stopped dead.

Blue Eyes stood on the other side of the street. His tattooed hand rested on the hilt of his fancy sword. Crushing blue eyes seared into hers.

"Where's my money, pit princess?"

Chapter Six

BLUE EYES

Stasha didn't move. Didn't blink. Didn't breathe.

Neither did Blue Eyes. He watched her with predatory focus. The same threat she'd often used in the fighting pit when she'd known she'd win.

Moving slowly so as not to provoke him, she sloughed off her knapsack and dropped it at Klaus's feet. "Go back to the mill," she murmured. "I'll meet you there when I'm done here. Wait for me."

Klaus bounced on his able foot. The silent question—*What about you?*—floated between them.

She nodded once, internally cursing him for not moving at her first command. She didn't want to take care of him while dealing with Blue Eyes.

Klaus finally squeezed her arm. He stumbled off, nearly tripping over his bad leg.

She fought a wince.

Blue Eyes didn't bother looking after him. He tipped his chin at her new boots. "It looks like you're wearing my half of that bet."

She caught a glimpse of the swirling black lines on his hands. Just another layer to the predator. The cat's stripes designed to keep it hidden in the long grass.

Despite the churning in her stomach, she was no mouse.

She pulled herself to her full height, threw her shoulders back, and pasted on a, hopefully, convincing smirk. "Half of that money was mine."

"It's the other half I'm worried about, pit princess."

She rolled her weight onto one hip, trying to look bored with the conversation. "It's not like you'll miss your half. Why else would you have bet so much coin on someone like Vlad?"

He snorted. "I bet on that kid because I knew he'd win. I don't make hopeless investments."

"Everyone else watching that fight said the exact opposite."

He arched a perfect eyebrow. "Not you. You bet a week's wages. You knew the quality of the bet. And the odds." He sauntered forward, then stopped. "You knew he would win. Just the same as I did."

Her spine locked up. She rolled onto the other hip, trying to relax. "So what if I like an underdog?"

He took another step closer. "And would you say that you're the underdog right now?"

A spark lit in her blood. Long-forgotten excitement shot through her. The standoff before the first punch was thrown. "Not a chance."

He took the last step, closing the gap between them. His breath warmed her chilled face. "Then let's see what you're worth in the fighting pits. See if you can actually win that coin in a fair fight."

She smirked at his ignorance. "Fights are booked a week in advance."

"Not when you have silver to flash around." A lazy smile. "Feral Fox? I think that's his name. He was only too happy to fit us in." His inked fingers flicked between them. "Unless you don't have the guts?"

"Of course I've got the guts," she snapped. Part of her wanted to stomp over to the fighting pit right now to finish him off for his arrogance. Even better, when she won, she'd collect all the entrance fees.

The sensible part told her to refuse. She and Klaus didn't have time to delay their escape from Askavol.

She bit her lip. Not going with Blue Eyes was just as risky. He'd tracked her with ease. Unless she played along with him, he could either drag her to the Kňazer—she would not get another chance to escape—or he could stalk her all the way to Ruepa. Risking their freedom was not a bet she was willing to make.

She pasted on a defiant smile. "You're on."

CHAPTER SEVEN

Stasha sauntered into the fighting pits, flaunting her new cloak, new boots, and Tarik's red ribbon in her braid. She tossed an iron into Feral Fox's hat at the entrance. If the fight went as she planned, she'd be winning it straight back, along with all the other entrance fees.

The dimly lit spectator area already teemed with people. Their excitement, laughter, and tension crackled like lightning. Just what she'd always loved about the pit. But as exciting as it was, she intended to win this fight as quickly as possible so she could rejoin Klaus at the mill for the start of their new life.

Too warm in the crush of bodies, she sloughed off her new cloak and leaned against the wooden fence between the ring and the spectators to center herself. She'd never liked talking before a fight. Best to stay in her head until the very last moment.

Her head wasn't a happy place tonight.

A year had passed since her last fight, and now she was forced to think about why that was. Not only that, the stakes in this fight were higher than ever. After buying their supplies, the second silver coin was their only salvation. If she were to lose it—

Not. Going. To. Happen.

She scanned the crowd for Blue Eyes.

He was nowhere to be seen.

That meant nothing. A man that arrogant wouldn't back down. Just as he probably didn't doubt that she'd show up too.

Time to move.

She drew in a deep, steadying breath and pushed her way

through the crowds to her betting table. As usual, Goul and his friends monopolized the space. They were drinking from a shared mug.

Goul took a swig, wiped his mouth with the back of his hand, and called, "Look! Stasha dressed in fighting leathers."

"Fighting leathers?" Ivan blinked his shock. "Is this your way of avoiding the betting? Scared to take me up on last night's offer?" He winked at her.

She tossed her cloak on the table to keep it clean and snatched the mug from Goul. The mouthful she gulped tasted like piss. Cheap, watered-down ale. "Oh, I intend to bet *and* fight. It's my birthday in a few hours, and I have some money to win. For the second time."

She caught a glimpse of Blue Eyes on the opposite side of the ring. Hands shoved lazily into his pockets, he nodded at her.

She ignored him. But her fingers clawed the mug. She forced them to relax.

Ivan took the mug out of her hand, eyeing her warily. "Who's the unlucky sod?"

"Him." Stasha pointed across the ring. Blue Eyes' astonishing gaze fixed on her. Assessing. Evaluating. Looking for weakness.

He probably saw plenty. A year had passed since she'd fought in the pit.

This wasn't the time to show fear or weakness. She tossed her shoulders back, although her insides clenched. Blue Eyes was no starving orphan boy, here for a few knocks with his friends. Dressed in black leather from head to foot, he looked even more intimidating now than he had the previous evening.

"Seriously, Stasha?" Goul nearly choked on his own spit. "You're good but not that good."

She appreciated his shock. It mirrored her own disbelief that she was getting into the ring with that predator. But Goul didn't need to know that. Languidly, she twirled her ribbon and tilted her head. "Care to bet on that?"

Goul's eyes darted between her and Blue Eyes. She could have sworn Goul's fingers trembled as he pulled a coin from his pocket. "An iron says Stasha loses this one."

Good. Let the whole pit think she was about to get her butt kicked. That way, when she won, she'd clean up the betting at her table. More money to fund her and Klaus's great escape.

"You're on." Ivan chucked his coin down too. He huffed a nervous laugh through crooked teeth. "It's a shame, Stasha. I hate to see your pretty face messed up. Imagine what it's going to do to your insufferable confidence."

"You'll like my face a lot less when I'm smirking at you and taking your money." One hand braced on the table, she pulled the silver coin out of her pocket and flashed it in the torchlight. "One silver coin says I win."

If she lost to Blue Eyes, he'd have to sort out ownership of his precious coin with the people at her betting table.

If she won—however unlikely—then she'd truly have earned the coin. Goul, Ivan, and the rest of them would replace a little of the money she'd blown on supplies.

Either way, Blue Eyes would hopefully stop stalking her and Klaus.

She dropped the coin on the table.

A shockwave of *oohs* and *ahs* reverberated around the group.

She sauntered into the ring and stopped at the entrance. The muddy circle and buzzing crowd that surrounded it were achingly familiar. Only one vital piece was missing. Tarik. In her memory, he laughed through split lips, just as he'd done the last time she'd seen him alive. Her muscles turned to mush.

She hissed and shut her eyes. Now was not the time for grief. Look to the living. Look to Klaus. Tarik was beyond her help now.

She gulped a couple of breaths, opened her eyes, and stepped into the ring.

Yesterday's mud had congealed into a gooey jelly. It squelched under her new boots, and she winced. The crowd cheered, so she rewarded them with a flourishing bow. None of them needed to know that her ears were burning or that her throat ached hot and dry at the incredibly high stakes.

Blue Eyes joined her. He didn't raise his fists, didn't drop into a fighter's pose like her opponents usually did. If anything, he looked disinterested. Bored. Except for a slight twinkle in his eyes. Clearly, he was enjoying the game.

Bastard.

Even though they'd probably all bet against her, the crowd chanted her name. They were her friends. They'd watched her fight since she was twelve. They knew how many times she'd lost and won. And they knew why she'd avoided the pit for a very long year.

She rolled her shoulders and fixed Blue Eyes with her own gaze. "The crowd knows my name. Don't you think they should know yours too? You know, to mark on your gravestone once I'm done with you."

He arched a perfectly sculpted eyebrow in what looked like genuine amusement. "Averin."

The crowd hissed Averin's name. Coin hitting betting tables boomed through the pit.

She grinned. Any moment now, she'd mess up Averin's perfect eyebrow. She pushed the notion away. Using her fists on men's thick heads was both painful and a waste of energy. They would always be stronger and bigger than her. She had to be stealthier and use their weight and strength against them.

She balanced her stance, ready to grab Averin and fling him to the floor.

His fist slammed into her stomach.

She doubled over, gagging.

But instead of following up on his advantage, Averin stood over her, chuckling.

Not just a bastard, but a patronizing one too.

Winning now wasn't just about the silver coin—she had to wipe that self-satisfied smirk off his oh-so-pretty face.

She jumped up, pivoted and landed her boot solidly on the back of his knee. She braced for him to fall—

His leg barely buckled.

What in the darkness was he made of?

He grabbed her collar and scooped her into the air as if she weighed no more than a kitten. A small, exceptionally annoying part of her was impressed with his strength and resilience.

She struck upwards and slammed her palm into his nose. Lovely red blood splattered her hand and shot across the ring.

Averin yelped. But instead of dropping her, he rammed his head into her face.

Pain exploded through her jaw, and her lip split. "Nice one." She gave him a bloody smile.

Averin dropped her into the mud. She fell back against the wooden barrier with a jarring thud.

He wiped his hand across his nose. A bloody smear trailed along his cheek. "Glad you approve, pit princess. Now, should we finish this?"

He was waiting for her to stand? Why the gallantry? Anyone else would have leapt at an opportunity to win. Maybe he did have more silver coins than he needed and was happy to make her work for the one she'd filched.

Elbow leading, she leaped to her feet and lunged for him. He blocked lazily. Her elbow found its mark, juddering to a stop against abs as hard as a schorl blade. Pain jarred up and down her arm. Not in five years of fighting in the pits had she hit an abdomen as toned as that.

All advantage lost, she barely managed to dodge his grabbing hands. She twisted away sharply and smashed the side of her hand into his neck. He stumbled back. She followed up with a sharp elbow jab into his solar plexus. Despite his rock-solid torso, this time it was he who dropped to the floor.

A quick pirouette followed by a leap and she drove her boots into his back. A satisfying crunch—and pretty Averin, with the gorgeous blue eyes, sprawled face-first, into the mud.

She grinned wildly, then spat warm blood. "Fight over." Had he let her win? Who cared? The coin was hers. She and Klaus could now leave without the fear of being followed or hunted.

The crowd went wild. "Stasha! Stasha! Stasha!" People stood on the betting tables and stamped in tune to the chant. Others beat their fists against the wooden barrier.

Arms waving, she twirled her hips and chanted with them. Her victory dance spun her toward Averin. He'd pulled himself to a sitting position and was grinning at her. "Congratulations, pit princess. The coin is yours."

"Now was that so hard to admit?" With a flourish befitting the show she was putting on, she offered him a hand to help him up. "You could have saved yourself an ass kicking."

Averin accepted her hand and let her pull him up to full height. He was only a couple of inches taller than her. He fixed those piercing eyes on her, and her stomach swooped deliciously. "Maybe I like getting my ass kicked by a pit princess. Now, I believe you owe me a drink."

Still reeling from her unexpected reaction to him, her mouth opened and closed lamely.

Humiliating.

She could fight him, but she couldn't talk to him?

Way to be pathetic.

Another of Averin's low, throaty laughs. "Go get your winnings, and I'll meet you outside." He flicked the red ribbon hanging precariously from her braid. It pulled loose and fluttered into the mud. He sauntered away.

She snatched up her precious ribbon and tucked it in her pocket.

In his dreams was she wasting any more time on him. Not when she and Klaus still had a night of walking ahead of them to get away from Askavol.

She rushed to the betting table to claim her winnings.

Ivan bounded to her. "In-cre-di-ble!" He patted her back. "This is one time I don't mind handing over coin to you."

She preened and shook his hand from her shoulder. "Ivan, next time, follow my lead with the betting. In fact, not just with betting.

With everything." No need to tell him there wouldn't be a next time. It pained her to leave Tarik's friends—her friends—to their fates, but what choice did she have?

Ivan shoved her shoulder. "Now you're getting ahead of yourself."

Goul gaped at her. "Stasha! That bloke is built like a mountain. How did you do it?"

Was Goul really too stupid to suspect that Averin had let her win? Poor delusional boy. She certainly wasn't going to clue him in. She winked at him. "Masterful planning combined with insufferable confidence."

Ivan tried to wrap his arm around her shoulders.

She sidestepped. "Ivan, to show how much you appreciate me taking all your money, how about donating your knapsack for me to carry my winnings home? I'll pay you a coin for your trouble."

"No trouble at all." Ivan sloughed his knapsack off his shoulders. Face an inch from hers, he leered. "I'll be around tomorrow to fetch it from you. Maybe we can go for a walk. I know someplace very private where we can explore some of those bulges you seem to like so much."

Idiot. "Would it be totally inappropriate to make a gagging sound?"

Ivan laughed. "Very funny." He opened the knapsack for her.

She tucked the silver coin into her pocket and scooped the rest of the winnings into Ivan's knapsack.

A heavy hand that smelled like wet sheep landed on her shoulder. "Keep that knapsack open, Stasha." Feral Fox beamed down at her. "Nice fight. It warms my heart to see you back with us. You've gone hungry more times than was necessary. Take this win and fatten yourself up a tad." He tipped her winnings into the knapsack and gave her a one-armed hug.

"Thank you. I will." She couldn't meet his eyes. He was one person she was truly sorry to part with. Before her face could betray her, she scampered out of the pits and into the shadowy forest.

Now for the mill and Klaus. She slung the knapsack across her shoulder and broke into a trot.

"Princess of the pits."

She skidded to a halt on the slippery pine needles.

Averin slouched against a tree. He lifted two fingers in greeting. The swelling on his nose had already subsided.

Every nerve pinged. She wasn't sure where to assign blame: the almost feline power he oozed, or her need to get away as quickly as possible. Either way, she was going to play this cool. Very, very cool. That began by striding on through the trees without another glance in his direction.

Her heart pounded when he peeled off the tree and followed her.

What did this man want with her? He'd obviously thrown the fight, and he'd said the coin was hers, so why continue to pursue her? Especially given the menace he radiated. Even walking at speed to catch up with her, his footfalls were silent on the pine needles and broken twigs. She wasn't exactly noisy, but her red boots still crunched over the foliage.

"How much did you bet on yourself?" he called.

She grinned in the dark. "*My* silver coin. I cleaned up at that table." He drew next to her, so she shot him a cocky smile. "Thanks to you."

Averin arched his eyebrows and snorted.

A shame she hadn't scarred those perfect brows. "Good fight, by the way." To cover up her and Klaus's plans, she added, "We should do it again sometime."

Averin's grimace suggested he didn't believe a word she'd said. "As much as I'd like that, I'm heading off in the morning."

Her nerves jangled. He wasn't going to Ruepa, was he? She kept her voice steady. "What a pity. Where're you headed?"

"North."

Ruepa was to the north.

"Where north?"

"Just north."

She huffed a sigh. "Well, if you're ever in the neighborhood again, come find me. I wouldn't want you making it out unscathed."

His broad shoulders shook with laughter. No evidence, it seemed, other than muddy clothes and the streak of dried blood on his cheek that he'd just been laid flat on his ass in a fight.

It was more than just a little annoying. Her shoulders were stiff and sore. It was too dark to tell if his tattooed hands were bruised. She flexed hers against the familiar post-fight ache.

Averin canted his head and looked at her with the same open interest. "You're proposing another meeting? In Ruepa, perhaps." A sly smile. "Would you like to borrow my horse? It responds well to carrots dangled in front of its nose."

She skidded to a stop. "How did you hear that?" No one had been behind them on the road to Drueya when she and Klaus had discussed riding horses. She shifted her weight, trying to bring some threat back into her posture.

"I have good hearing." Averin shrugged. "I wanted to see what you'd do, so I followed you."

Forget good, his hearing would have to be exceptional.

"You do realize that's creepy." And more than a little intimidating. If he knew their plans to escape—

Averin moved closer. So close, she could feel his breath on her face. "You must realize that stealing is just a wee bit illegal, right?"

Her eyes lowered to a vein throbbing in his neck. He should have been bruised where she'd chopped him, but he wasn't.

That was disconcerting.

Time to get her answers and leave. "What do you want with me?"

A casual shrug. "You do tend to harp on things, pit princess. Anyone told you that before?"

"Coming from you, that's rich. Now answer my question."

"Is it a crime to be intrigued by an attractive girl in a fighting pit? It's not every day you see that." His teeth sparkled in the silvery moonlight.

"What were you even doing there? It's our place. Not yours."

"I was passing by. Heard the noise and thought I'd see what was going on."

That made sense. She shrugged, ready to leave.

"You owe me a drink."

"I don't drink. And I owe you nothing." Her eyes settled first on his perfect nose and then on his full, bow-shaped lips. He really was breathtakingly beautiful.

Averin smiled wider, clearly amused by the hitch in her breath. "Lies as well as thievery? I saw you drinking at the pit. You really do fascinate me, pit princess." He glanced at her mouth.

She leaned in closer, her own breath brushing against his skin. He shivered, and she smiled. "I don't just lie and steal. I whipped your butt too." Darkness be damned before she'd admit he'd let her win.

"All the more reason to share a drink. I'm open to all the lies and thievery you can offer me."

She threw her head back and laughed like a pealing bell. "Really? You think stupid lines like that will get me drinking with you?"

She cut her laughter, pulled away from him, and started down the path again. The road to the village opened in front of her. Determined to shake him before she got to the mill, she stepped onto the cobbles and strode ahead.

Averin chuckled behind her. "Fair play. I'll accede. Your reaction is a bit unexpected. But, so far, that's all you've been since I found you —one big surprise."

In his way, he was as gag-worthy as Ivan. She glared over her shoulder at him. "So you're used to throwing out a few lines and smiles and having girls fall all over you?"

With quick, silent strides, he caught up to her. "Usually, yes."

She snorted. "Maybe I'd be more impressed if you didn't have such a high opinion of yourself."

"Pot meets the kettle, Stasha?"

She flashed a smile. "*I* have something to be proud of."

"Can't live without that insufferable confidence." Averin's voice bubbled with laughter.

She stopped and faced him again. "Do you make a habit of listening in on other people's conversations?"

Those fathomless blue eyes bored into her. "Only when it's worth my while."

"Your investment has just turned sour," she snapped. "I may have stolen your precious money, but I won it back tonight fair and square. So you can be on your merry way, pretty boy."

She stomped along the road. Just ahead, the lights of Askavol gleamed.

Averin sidled up to her. "I hear it's your birthday tomorrow. That's about now, you know."

A rumble tore through the ground, and the road tilted madly beneath her feet. She lost her balance and crashed to her knees on the buckling cobblestones. They rocked beneath her as if made of jelly. The pine trees on either side of the road screeched like wounded animals. Pine cones, branches, and pine needles pelted down on her.

Her hands flew up to protect her head. A pine tree tore out of the ground and fell towards her. She gasped, but before she could scramble away, an icy wind whipped up and grabbed hold of it. It thrust the enormous tree aside as if it weighed no more than a twig. It crashed harmlessly beside her, its roots grasping for the sky like claws.

"Stasha!" Averin was on the ground, a foot or so away from her. "Are you okay?"

Still on her knees on the writhing ground, she shook her head. More pines tumbled around her. A brief pause in the creak and snap of giant trees ... and she caught the unmistakable rumble of stone buildings collapsing. The earthquake had hit Askavol.

Klaus!

She had to get to him. Her knees wobbled, then buckled as she tried to stand.

Averin smacked the back of her calf.

She fell back down with a painful crunch. "Bastard! My friend's in danger. I have to help him."

"You have to help yourself," Averin replied, voice calm. "You do that by staying down until this is over."

"Move!" Hands and knees flailing, she scrambled away and tried again to stand.

Averin yanked her down and rolled on top of her. "Stasha, you can't get to the village with trees raining down on you."

Another tree thundered onto the road just a few yards away. Clumps of soil and stone pelted down on them. Most of the debris hit Averin, but her skin was also stung with flying stone chips. She wriggled to get away, but he held her tight. Her worn leather tunic ripped, and her amber pendant dropped out through the tear.

And then the world stilled.

Just as abruptly as the quake had started, it stopped.

Propped up on his arms above her, Averin didn't move. But instead of looking at her face, his eyes were locked on her necklace. But it wasn't his jubilant smile that almost stopped her heart.

It was his ears. Long, arched, and pointed.

Fae ears.

CHAPTER EIGHT

THE END OF THE WORLD

Stasha jerked out from under the creature looming over her. She scurried backward on her hands and toes until she bumped into a fallen tree. A broken branch ripped right through her new cloak and worn tunic to stab at her back.

"Stasha, it's okay." The fae rose slowly, hands outstretched, like *she* was the wild animal that might attack at any moment.

Tarik's sun-kissed face swam before her. Blood on his lips ... eyes dull ... neck snapped by a fae. Maybe even the monster standing before her with his arms spread, trying to reassure her. Calming his prey.

"Stay away from me." She clambered to her feet, but her knees shook so hard, she couldn't walk. Not even to escape the tall, powerful thing staring at her with those impossibly blue eyes—fae eyes.

Why hadn't she connected that before?

She locked both knees and looked around for an escape route. The shattered road was too open. Best to head back into the forest. Dodging fallen trees would cost time, but she *had* to get back to Askavol to find Klaus.

The fae's eyes also flickered to the forest. "Don't try to run. I'm—" He took a step forward.

"Stay back!" She pushed into the fallen tree. Although it was pointless, she flattened her hand into a fighting wedge and fixed him with her best raptorial glare.

The fae obeyed. "Just listen to me," he said, voice soft. "I'm trying to—"

She hurdled the log and landed in a heap of tangled limbs. Her cloak snagged as she scrambled to stand on the springy branches and fallen pinecones.

Not caring if it—or her skin—tore, she clambered through the pin-sharp pine needles and sprinted into the woods. Her cloak and knapsack full of money tore off her shoulders and fell into the dirt. She didn't even pause to consider picking them up.

The creature swore and leaped over the tree in chase. When would he use his fae powers against her? And what were they?

Cursing the dark chaos, she slammed from broken tree to broken tree to get away from him and to rescue Klaus. But for all the noise she made, the fae was silent.

Terrifyingly so.

She looked back over her shoulder. No trace of him.

Icy with sweat, she pushed on over broken branches, uprooted trees, and new gashes torn in the forest floor.

No doubt he stalked her, sniffing her out like a bloodhound, ready to shred—

She choked down a breath to stop her panic. For Klaus's sake, she had to keep a clear head.

Bruised, scraped, and bloody, she finally reached the first timber-and-stone buildings at the edge Askavol. They looked like a giant had crushed them under his thumb. In the wind-whipped dust, people stumbled aimlessly around the ruins.

She dodged past them into the square between the mill and the orphanage. Half the orphanage had collapsed. Her dorm was nothing but a mountain of rubble swathed in dust.

One foot in the air, she froze. Even her heart seemed to still.

Had any of the girls survived? Little Hathrine—was she...?

Numb with shock, Stasha shuffled forward, then stopped.

One the other side of the square, one half of the mill had gone. The other half teetered, held together on a breath. She'd instructed Klaus to hide there while he waited for her.

Tears stung. No. She hadn't lost him. He was alive—he had to be.

She ran to mill. "Klaus! Klaus!"

She was a handful of paces away when the walls rumbled, and the other half of the mill collapsed. Stone blocks burst from the walls and crashed onto the square. Some stopped just inches from her feet. In the screeching din, wooden beams groaned and snapped.

Dust swathed her, the square, everything. Breathing was agony. She covered her mouth and nose with her hand and held her breath. Tears streamed down her face, caused by grit and sorrow. This was Teagarta all over again. She could not lose Klaus the way she had Tarik.

Vaguely, she caught the sound of people screaming. It came from behind her.

In a daze, she spun. Although damaged, the boys' section of the orphanage had survived.

Chanting prayers, Martka led lines of sobbing boys out of the broken door and down the stairs into the square. Robes tattered and bloody, Acolyte Inna counted them off as they stumbled past her.

Would Klaus have left the mill and gone to the orphanage? She had to believe that. Anything else would be unbearable. She sucked in a dusty, hope-filled breath and sprinted to Inna to watch the boys shuffling out.

Klaus wasn't among them.

Stomach heaving, she made for the stairs. She'd search every inch of the building to find Klaus. A carriage, pulled by a pair of horses, one black and one white, cantered into the square in front of her.

The Kňazer had arrived.

She bashed her fists against the carriage window as she charged around it. The door flew open, and two Kňazer dismounted. They were dressed from head to toe in lavish silken robes, one man in white, and the other in black. Several of their acolytes—young men with shaved heads, scarified faces, and dressed in coarse brown robes —followed close behind.

"Dear children," the Kňazer in white cooed. He raised his hands above his head. "I bid you, be calm. Even in this devastation, the two-faced god smiles upon you."

Stasha spat a curse, then raced to Martka Gabika. The black-clad woman led another wave of boys from the crumbling ruins. Shouting Klaus's name, she pushed and shoved her way through the crowd.

And then she spotted him.

Klaus!

Pale and trembling, he seemed unhurt. He shouted her name and elbowed his way to her.

Sobbing, she wrapped her arms around his neck and buried her face in the cusp of his shoulder. His arms tightened around her. "You're okay." He pulled away, stuttering, "I thought you'd gone without me."

"Never!" She grabbed his hand and dragged him to the other side of a pile of rubble, away from the Martka and Kňazer. Before they'd even crouched down, she blurted, "He's fae. Blue Eyes from the fighting pits is fae."

Klaus went green.

She grabbed his shoulders to anchor them both. "I was with him when the quake came. After the quake ... I don't know what happened, but I could *see* him. See him as fae."

Eyes bulging, Klaus ripped out of her hands. He lifted a single, quaking finger and pointed at her.

Her breath hitched. "What?"

Klaus's mouth opened and closed wordlessly. It was almost as frightening as being grappled by a fae male.

"Darkness swallow us! Klaus, speak to me."

He pointed again. "Your ears."

"What's wrong with—" Her fingers grazed the rims of her ears. Where they had been rounded and human, they arched up and up into a ... fae point. She screamed and fell back into the rocks.

Klaus grabbed her forearms. His eyes burned with terrible fervor. "What did he do to you?"

Mute with shock, she stared at him.

He shook her. "What did he do to you?"

Her mouth gaped, then closed. She didn't know. A headshake was the only answer she could give.

"Please, Stasha." Klaus's voice cracked, and tears spilled. "Tell me what to do. Tell me how to fix this. Tell me how to help you."

Arms wrapped around her chest, she rocked. *I don't know. I don't know, I don't know.*

Someone on the other side of the rubble called out. "Who's there?" Footsteps ground on the gravel as the person drew near.

They couldn't see her like this. They couldn't—

Martka Gabika stomped into view. Pursed lips replaced her worried frown. "What did I say would happen if I found you two alone? Klaus, get over here. Now."

Klaus didn't move.

Martka Gabika's cold eyes fixed on her—and then the Martka's shout split the night. "Fae!"

The two Kňazer and their four acolytes came running. Eyes wide with shock and fear, they crashed into her.

She toppled over and smacked her head onto the broken cobbles. Fiery-pain ricocheted through her skull. Stars flashed before her eyes, and dust coated her tongue.

A fist crashed into her jaw.

Dazed, she hadn't seen it coming.

Two acolytes stomped on her ankles. It was as if scalding metal shards speared from them, along her shins to her thighs. Her breath was stolen from her for a moment. When it returned, it brought a chilling scream.

"Bind her!" an icy voice said.

Move! She had to move.

She'd barely started wriggling when someone flipped her over like a sausage in a pan. Manacles clamped on her wrists. Chains jerked and clanged as a second pair were shoved over her muddy red boots.

"Leave her alone!" Klaus yelled. He struggled to reach her in the crush of acolytes. "She's done nothing. It was him. The fae with the blue eyes. He did this to her."

An acolyte punched Klaus hard enough to send him shooting

across the square, arms pinwheeling in a desperate effort to stay upright.

Swearing, Stasha struggled against her manacles as Klaus was dragged away. "Leave him alone! He's done nothing wrong."

A Kňazer dropped down next to her newly pointed ear. "Fae, you will pay for what you did tonight." His hatred reeked like an open latrine. Foul and putrid.

She retched, and a gag slipped between her teeth. Yanked tight, it ripped her torn lips.

"We're going to stand you up and walk you to the Crekev." The Kňazer again. "I have a schorl knife. First hint that you plan to run, it goes straight through your filthy heart."

Schorl. A human's only defense against fae. It was supposed to weaken fae monsters. Was that what she had become?

Her body ached from her fight in the pits and her mad dash through the woods, and her head throbbed where it had hit the cobbles, so she couldn't tell if the schorl manacles were affecting her.

An acolyte dragged her up and pushed her forward. Her feet fought for grip. No one helped her balance. Blinking back grains of dirt, she looked for Klaus. He'd vanished.

If they hurt him....

The Kňazer pressed his knife to her back. The cold tip sliced through her tattered tunic. "Any trouble from you, and the cripple dies. Do you hear me?"

She nodded furiously. It didn't matter what they did to her as long as Klaus was safe.

A hard shove nearly sent her sprawling onto the rubble. All focus on her footing, she concentrated on walking along the broken road to the Crekev.

Shrieks rose from the crowds of children as she passed. The Martka encircled them like wolves with their pups. Prayers sprung from lips as more people joined in the wailing. Ivan and Goul were part of the mob. Their eyes widened as they gasped and pointed at her. They must have seen her very, *very* fae ears.

She reached the Crekev lichgate. The short walk to the ugly

stone-and-wood building had never taken so long. An acolyte opened the moss-covered wooden gate and shoved her through it. Apart from a broken statue of the two-faced god on the path to the front door, the Kňazer house of prayer seemed to have survived the earthquake without damage.

The Kňazer dressed in white opened the heavy door with a big key. The acolyte pushed her into the candle-lit gloom. She cried out, writhing as if a thousand invisible knives stabbed every inch of her body. It had to be the schorl in the Crekev. The dark stone paneled the inside walls like slick oil.

Did that prove she was fae?

An acolyte shoved her down a narrow set of stairs into the crypt. She slipped. No one helped her. If she hadn't tumbled into the acolyte ahead of her, she would have fallen flat on her face.

They reached a schorl door, engraved with the same patterns tattooed on the Martka's faces. The Kňazer dressed in obsidian-colored robes supplied the key. The glossy stone door screeched open on rusty hinges.

Dark, dank, and stifling, a tiny space gaped in front of her. She moaned before she could stop herself. More schorl.

The Kňazer hit her across the face. "Silence, fae! The two-faced god has delivered you to us. We will now convene to decide your fate." His heart was clearly as dark as his robes.

Someone kicked her from behind. She tumbled forward into the blackness and landed on the hard, cold stone floor.

The door slammed closed.

CHAPTER NINE

A SCHORL BOX

Shaking with cold, nausea, and pain, Stasha scrambled to her feet. She had to escape and find Klaus before they harmed him. He may not have been glamoured into looking—and feeling—like a fae, but he would be seen as a sympathizer.

She knew what they did to sympathizers.

There had to be a way out of the schorl crypt. Carefully, so she didn't fall over her manacles and chains, she shuffled along the frigid stone walls. Her arms brushed her terrible ears. Why had Averin done this to her? She screamed her rage. But even that was futile. The filthy gag on her blood-caked mouth muffled the sound.

After her fourth circuit of the tiny cell, she had to admit there was no escape. She slumped to the floor and rested her head on her knees. Her chains clinked together with the rhythm of her shivering.

Her eighteenth birthday had certainly gotten off to a rotten start.

If she and Klaus hadn't gone on that shopping spree, none of this would have happened. They would have been miles from Askavol by now.

But then Averin the fae would still be tailing them. There was no way she could have fought him off. There was no doubt now that he'd toyed with her at the pits. One punch, and he could have killed her.

But he hadn't. Why?

Maybe he'd been saving her for this moment. For the fun of watching her own people destroy her.

Stone screeched behind her. Unnaturally loud, it was like needles piercing her eardrums. She cringed and gazed into the dark to find the source. A narrow strip of light seared her eyes. She blinked and turned away.

"Stasha."

Klaus! He'd come for her. Of course he had.

A single tear slipped down her cheek. She scrambled to her knees and shuffled to the door.

Klaus's tawny eyes peered at her through the slit. The Kňazer with the knife was praying behind him. She wiped her eyes with her sleeve to clear her vision. Both Kňazer stood behind Klaus.

"They wouldn't let me come alone." Klaus's breath pushed out like smoke in the frozen air. "They said you'd start another earthquake."

The Kňazer prayed louder.

Klaus shoved his hand through the narrow space and pulled off her gag.

She swallowed to moisten her parched throat. "I didn't start any earthquake." Her throat and mouth hurt. But her lip, split in the fight with Averin and then again when the acolytes had attacked her, had healed.

So quickly?

More effects from that bastard Averin's spell.

"I didn't do anything," she said, loud enough for the Kňazer to hear.

"I know that." Klaus nodded, also blinking back tears. "It was him —" His voice cracked. "Blue Eyes."

At least Klaus believed her. She flicked a finger at the Kňazer. "Did you tell *them* that?"

"Over and over. They said you've taken my mind. That you'd put a glamour on us all to hide your fae form all these years."

"But I'm *not* fae!" Fresh tears burned her cheeks. "You've got to make them see that. And you've got to find a way to get me out."

"I'm trying." Klaus's fingers fumbled through the slit and brushed her manacles. They trailed down her wrists until they enveloped her hands. "I guess our escape plan is off."

Her chest tightened. He spoke of their plans so readily before the Kňazer? That couldn't bode well for either of them.

"Why did they send you down here?"

Klaus hesitated. Seconds ticked by.

Her heart sank even further. "Klaus. What's happening?"

"They think I can make you come quietly." Klaus spoke so softly, she had to lean in to hear him.

"Quietly where?" she snapped.

His bottom lip wobbled.

"Where?" she demanded.

"They're building a pyre. They're taking you there now."

*K*eening like a wild animal, Stasha backed away from Klaus. She bumped into the far wall and tried to push herself through the schorl.

Of course, there was no give, no escape, no mercy. Just burning pain where the stone touched her back.

In her world, fear was as normal as breathing. She'd been scared in the fighting pits. Scared of the dark as a child. Scared when Tarik hadn't come home that night. Scared in the forest when Averin had turned into a fae.

But there was no fear, no despair, no anger, no terror like knowing the people who'd raised her, who were her friends and housemates, were waiting outside to kill her.

The Kňazer in white threw open the door. "Stop that wailing, fae!"

Two acolytes pushed Klaus aside. He stumbled on his useless leg, knees crunching as he fell. The acolytes stepped over him as if he were dirt.

She snarled—a sound so inhuman, it shook her to the core.

Two acolytes blocked her view of Klaus. One was tall, the other short. In the pit, she could have wiped the floor with both of them.

But outnumbered, chained, and ill from the schorl, this was no pit.

Chains rattling, she lifted her manacled hands to stop them coming closer. "Please, you have to listen to me." Panic set her chest on fire. "I'm not fae—"

They grabbed her arms and tossed her out of the cell onto the stairs. She slammed against the wall. Something hard smacked into her back. She coughed a moan.

"Stop it." Klaus had thrown himself over her. "Leave her alone. She's done nothing wrong."

"We will not fall for trickery and lies." The Kňazer in black, by the sounds of it.

The tall acolyte grabbed Klaus by the collar. Klaus swung a fist at him. It caught the acolyte's jaw and sent him flying back. Eyes burning, Klaus stood between her and the rest of her tormentors. "She's innocent! You will not have her!"

The second acolyte lashed out his boot at Klaus's mangled leg. It connected with an agonizing snap. A gargled cry cracked Klaus's throat, and he dropped.

She lunged to catch him, only to be stopped by both acolytes.

Klaus collapsed to the flagstones in a writhing mess of pain.

Screaming curses, Stasha wriggled, kicked, and bit at the brutes. They didn't loosen their grip.

"You've fooled the dear Martka and orphans for long enough, creature," the Kňazer in white said.

A shuffle pinged her ears. Martka Gabika and Martka Alyona stood at the top of the stairs.

"Please, Martka, you know me. I didn't do this. I'm not fae."

Martka Gabika pursed her thin lips until she resembled a prune.

Martka Alyona's taut eyes flickered, something between fear and regret. She cleared her throat. "Perhaps we've acted hastily. Fae or not, if she and the boy"— she glowered at Klaus—"intend to leave, then why stand in their way?"

Hope kicked in Stasha's chest.

The old Martka clearly knew more about Stasha's history than she'd ever imagined. If only she could grill the old woman for more details.

First, she had to persuade the others to let her and Klaus go. "Yes, please. I promise we'll leave here and never come back."

Both Kňazer glared at Martka Alyona.

"Fae who venture into my town do not walk away alive," the

Kňazer in white said.

Stasha's heart dropped into her boots.

The Kňazer motioned to the acolytes.

They scooped her up and followed the sweep of Martka Alyona's dark robes up the stairs. Klaus's desperate pleading that they leave her—and him—alone echoed behind her.

Her insides writhed. She was supposed to take care of him. Her screams merged with his.

"Shut up!" The short acolyte punched her in the face.

She swore at him and then shouted to Klaus, "You're my world. Never forget it."

"Stasha, I'll love you forever." Klaus's voice was muffled.

What were they doing to him? She kicked out at the short acolyte. "Let me go!"

The acolytes' grip on her arms tightened. She slumped, making herself as heavy as possible. It made no difference. They dragged her into the Crekev.

Torchlight flickered through the open door. With quick steps, they carried her out into the broken square.

Gray dawn lit a crowd of at least two hundred people. None of them spoke, yet their shuffling feet and narrowed eyes leached hatred, fear, and confusion.

In the middle of the square, two ten-foot high stakes, ends embedded in blocks of dried lime, lay on a timber pyre.

Did they plan to burn Klaus, too?

"Klaus is innocent," she yelled, thrashing and kicking against her manacles as the acolytes dragged her to the nearest stake.

The short one dropped her onto the pole and fell onto her chest. The air flew out of her. He grabbed her arms while his companion hefted a hammer.

So much for hope.

"Beg for him, fae," the acolyte with the hammer spat.

"So you can refuse?" she snarled back.

The acolytes shot her twisted smiles. They were enjoying this. Just as she would have once enjoyed watching a fae burn. Now that hate chilled her to the marrow. They'd wait a long time to see her cry or to hear her plead again. It was enough that she and her chains shook uncontrollably.

A couple of sharp whacks, and the tall acolyte drove nails through the links on her manacles into the stake. Her feet were next.

She turned her head, looking for Klaus. Despite her defiant mask, she whimpered with relief when she didn't see him.

At least he wouldn't have to watch her die before they killed him too.

Biting wind gusted through the square. It carried a familiar scent: snow, and sun-kissed oranges stolen from the Křazer, mixed with spices swirling from a fresh cup of chai. It took her straight back to the woods just after the earthquake when—

Averin sauntered into the square. "Sorry your rescue was delayed, pit princess. Schorl is a real bitch. In future, do whatever it takes to avoid being tossed in a schorl box." His hands resting lazily in the pockets of his leather leggings and the casual sway of his hips belied the sharp focus in his blue eyes.

Two fae males flanked him. Long chestnut-colored hair snapped around the biggest fae's brutal, smirking face. The third was like a shadow, his presence so dark and quiet, he almost sucked up the light. It didn't help that his skin was blacker than schorl. Muscles rippled under their fine fighting leathers.

The immense power rolling off the three of them hit her harder than any wind or earthquake ever had. It sank deep into her bones. Every instinct pleaded with her to run from these predators. All she could do was squirm in her chains.

The acolytes and the crowd screamed. Both acolytes scrambled down the pyre to join the crowd elbowing and punching each other to escape the square.

The two Křazer emerged from the Crekev with Klaus in tow.

Cords bound Klaus's arms and feet, and a gag cut into his mouth. His mangled leg trembled against his restraints. His face was bleached white, probably from pain. A sob hitched in Stasha's throat.

The Křazer reeled away from the three fae. The Křazer in black hissed a curse and pulled his schorl knife free.

Averin rolled his eyes. The gesture did little to hide his glower. "Seems your human friends planned on burning your little companion too."

Averin stomped up the pyre and knelt next to her. His long-fingered hand picked up the acolyte's dropped hammer. Arm a blur, he struck the lock on her wrist manacle a glancing blow.

She yelped as the vibration rocked up her arm. But the schorl sheared, and her wrist was free. She gaped. "You're helping me? Why?"

"No time for all that, pit princess." He hit the other manacle, and it, too, split. "We're expecting company. And I didn't invite them." A smirk. "You did." His hammer went to work on her ankle restraints.

Poised for escape, she waited for him to free her feet. The severed manacles hadn't hit the wood, and she was already rolling toward Klaus.

Averin tsked. "Look at that. The rotten things scuffed your new boots."

She ignored him. "Klaus!"

The Kňazer had abandoned Klaus. Averin's companions had taken their place in the now-deserted square.

Klaus's bonds were gone. Bad leg dragging, he dodged the fae and clambered up the pyre. He grabbed her, squeezing so tight, she thought he might crack her ribs. "We'll never let them separate us again."

Although there was no chance of outrunning Averin and his friends, she whispered back, "Let's go. We can still make it out."

He nodded, so she pulled him onto her back. His fingernails dug into her shoulders as she slithered on the shifting wood.

The fae male with the chestnut-colored ponytail jumped in front of her. "Good plan, running," he said. His pine-green eyes swept over the cluster of trees behind the Crekev. "But we need to go together."

"We're not going anywhere with you!"

Thunder rumbled. She glanced up, but there were no clouds in the pink dawn sky.

Averin slid down the wood and stopped at her side. "You don't know what's coming, Stasha." Pointed focus had replaced his usual bored expression. He grabbed her hand.

A fiery shock blasted between them.

Averin gasped and dropped her like she'd scalded him. Even stranger, the stench of burnt flesh stung her ultrasensitive nose. Averin held up his hand to his friends, almost triumphantly. A red welt covered his palm.

Had she burned him?

Both fae males looked at her with caution, like she was an opponent in the pit who had to be handled with extra care.

She swallowed; Averin's hand was already healing.

Klaus's fingernails dug into her. "Come on, Stasha. Let's move."

Klaus was right. As usual.

She held onto him tightly as she clambered across the wood, away from the fae.

An eerie roar stopped her in her tracks.

Averin swore.

Breath snagging in her throat, she whipped around.

At least thirty fae males clothed in red fighting leathers with swords drawn ran down the buckled road toward the square. At their head, a fae male trailed tongues of golden flame from his fingers. A familiar sigil—two firebirds—was stamped to his leathers, above his heart.

Pyreack soldiers.

The same fae kingdom the monsters who'd killed Tarik had come from.

"We have to go." Averin reached for her arm, then hesitated. "Just come with us. Please."

How insane did he think she was? Averin was not only fae; he'd caused this. He'd done *something* to her that had led to this calamity.

"In your dreams, Blue Eyes."

Averin grabbed her arm. The world twisted and spun. Her vision blurred and bile surged into her throat.

"Stasha!"

Somewhere in the far-off distance, she heard Klaus call her name.

A surge of energy pushed through her body, rocketing up her spine to where Averin's hand clamped tightly around her arm. The scent of singed hair filled her nose. Orange light flickered to life around her. Sparks took flight like summer fireflies, rubbing against her skin in a gentle, loving caress.

She started. Why did they not burn her?

Averin yelped and let go. The world stopped spinning, lurching sideways. Stasha stumbled onto the pyre. Klaus tumbled from her back, and his leg hit the burning wood with a crack.

Averin was hunched over, beating at the bright flames licking his torso. Her stomach curdled, threatening to send vomit to her mouth.

His friends leapt to help him quell the fire.

A laugh echoed through the clearing.

The leader of the approaching army raised a hand. A ball of golden flame shot into the air. It exploded and rained fire over the remains of Askavol. The flames rushed like an asp for the pyre. It snarled and hissed at the flames surrounding Averin and his friends.

The wood beneath Stasha's boots burned.

She grabbed Klaus's hand and yanked him out of the blaze. His new trousers were burning. She frantically beat them with her hands. Astonishingly, she felt no pain or heat as the fire licked her palms. The flames quickly extinguished.

Klaus pulled away from her. "Go. Forget me. I'll just slow you down."

"Idiot." She scooped both hands under his armpits and dragged him to the edge of the pyre. She jumped to the flagstones, doing her best to support his bad leg. He flopped down next to her. "Now we run."

The Pyreack soldiers were just a block from the square.

Klaus lumbered to his feet and took her hand. "You'll have to carry me. Better to leave me."

"Shut up, or I'll hit you when this is over." Not caring about his stupid leg—it would recover when they were free—she broke into a run, dragging him behind her.

"Wait!" Averin had beaten off the flames and rolled down the pyre. The inferno surged ahead, blocking his path to her. "Stop! I can help you."

"Get lost! You did this. It's all your fault."

Something hard struck the back of her head.

A rock.

Head throbbing, she stumbled.

The Kňazer cloaked in white leaped in front of her. Where he'd come from in the deserted square, she didn't know. He clutched a schorl blade. The sharp scent of his fear and hate overwhelmed her. Despite the danger, she flinched from this new power to smell fear.

The Kňazer's lips pulled back. "No! You did this. You called them here!" He swung the dagger at her.

An axe flew past her face and embedded in the Kňazer's head.

She yelped and slammed a hand over her open mouth. As the hateful man crumpled to his knees and slumped into the dust, blood and brain oozed from his caved-in skull. She slammed her teeth together against the retching she couldn't contain. Klaus heaved and gagged, tugging on her to move, *move*.

The Pyreack soldiers spilled into the square.

Crackling fire snaked across the flagstones toward her. It forked into two tongues, quickly encircling her and Klaus in a scorching wall as broad as she was tall.

She swore, circling helplessly in her prison. The heat brushed against her skin like a lover's fingers, leaving no trace or burns. But Klaus....

Sweat ran down his forehead, evaporating into steam before it could reach his temples. He flinched against the searing heat.

Wind crashed into the flame, howling through the fire's laughter, trying to suck the air out of its reach.

Averin's power. Stasha yelped with relief. Was he really trying to help them?

Steel clashed where Averin had been, and the wind stilled. The army had reached him.

Through a small gap in the flame, she spotted a deserted side street that led to the forest.

"Now." Klaus must have seen it too.

They dove through the gap and stumbled across the square to the street at Klaus's fastest trot.

Golden flame seared the flagstones in front of them. They skidded to a stop. The flames circled them.

Trapped again.

Would another blast of wind rescue them? Or had Averin given up on her? The wind could only have come from him. A Zephyr soldier. He and his two friends were badly outnumbered here. The underdogs. Would Averin stand and fight, or would he flee? Not knowing why he—or any of the fae—were here made it impossible to tell.

The crackling fire parted, and the Pyreack leader stepped into the circle. The flames licked his flesh harmlessly as it closed behind him. He crossed his arms over his broad chest.

Stasha shoved Klaus behind her.

The fae's eyebrows tilted, and she saw her mistake. She'd shown weakness, told him she had something to lose. It took all of her self-control not to clutch at her clothing.

The fire reflected in his schorl-black eyes. They danced in delight. But at least they were fixed on her, not Klaus.

Good.

"Staa-sha-aa." The fae leader rolled her name off his tongue as if it were honey. "Is that your name?" A small, cruel smile twisted his lips. A monster waiting to devour her.

Trying to ignore the nervous sweat peppering her upper lip, she allowed her gaze to sweep from the black sword strapped to his belt, to his fae ears, to his merciless, immortal face. "What's it to you who I am?"

The fae's half smile didn't budge. "We've been looking for you for a very long time. Now I've found you." He stepped closer. "You're coming with us, and I'd suggest you do so without fuss."

Beyond the fire, steel crashed. Averin and his friends still fighting the Pyreack army?

What had gone so wrong in her world that Pyreack and Zephyr fae were both searching for her?

The fae raked his gaze up her skinny frame, smirking.

She wouldn't bet on herself in a fight against him. Still, she had to brazen her way through this. It was the only weapon she had.

"And if I don't?"

A cacophony of screams rose from beyond the wall of fire.

She flinched.

Carried on the smoke, the stench of burning flesh and hair reached her.

Had they rounded up all the inhabitants of Askavol? Were they burning Hathrine, Goul, and Ivan while she jabbered with this monster?

The fae's terrible smile darkened. "I see you've worked out what will happen if you argue, which we both know would be pointless anyway."

Sick bastards. She'd get him for this.

The encircling fire flared, as if it, too, was furious with the barbarous cruelty.

The fae snorted. "Enough! Come quietly, or I'll roast your little human friend you seem so determined to protect."

Her mouth went slack. Klaus choked on a cry behind her as the fire danced closer. His hands locked on her shoulders. She inched back into him, turning slightly to meet his eyes. They were drenched with fear.

She flicked her gaze back to the fae. "A deal. I'll go without a murmur, but you don't hurt him. You let him and everyone else in this village live. With no exceptions."

"No!" Klaus almost crushed her. "I'm not going anywhere without you."

She squeezed his thigh. In time, he would come to know that this was the only way—if he ever forgave her.

The fae flicked his fingers. The fire behind him thinned enough for her to see lines of terrified humans on their knees. Hathrine, Goul, and Ivan were there too. Pyreack fae circled them like wolves.

Four charred bodies smoldered at the head of line. She recognized Martka Alyona's shriveled face amid the mounds that had once been human. Any truth the old woman knew about Stasha had died with her.

She hissed out a breath, and her body slumped into itself. How carelessly these fae killed. Did they feel nothing for others? And she had just agreed to go with their leader.

"You have yourself a deal," the fae leader said, sealing her fate.

Gently, she pushed Klaus back. "Run. Be safe. I'll find you when this is over."

Klaus dug his fingers deeper into her shoulders. She met his tawny eyes, silently begging him to leave, to run, and to never look back. To have the incredible life they'd dreamed of.

Klaus's body melded into hers.

The fae leader motioned one of his companions forward.

Hard faced, the fae soldier tilted his sword at Klaus. Fire danced across its tip. "Back away, human. Unless you want to be lunch."

Stasha snarled, a horrible inhuman noise—a fae snarl—and lunged at the soldier.

The leader thrust his hand between them. "No one touches her little friend." But that same sick smile danced on his lips.

She nudged Klaus one last time and shot him a warning glance. *Please listen. Please understand.* She stepped away from him.

His bottom lip quivered, and his eyes dulled.

She wanted to yell that this wasn't over, that she would be back to find him. That he just had to believe in ... hope.

She didn't say a word. To do so would alert the bastards to her plans. It would tell the monsters that the deal she'd made wasn't worth a lick of spit. The moment their backs were turned, she'd vanish.

Just like smoke.

She'd come back here to find Klaus.

The fae leader grabbed her neck. Pain shot through her before everything went black.

CHAPTER ELEVEN

Through Stasha's foggy consciousness, she smelt something bad—a dark, bitter smell. Her nose twitched. Some sort of roasted meat.

Even the air seemed thicker than usual. Not thin and frosty as she'd always known it. It weighed heavily in her lungs, and her gasps were shallow.

She coughed and winced at a twang of pain in her chest. Her neck was stiff, like the muscle and bone had warped away from her spine, a sharp contrast to the softness pressed against her cheek.

Her eyes fluttered open. A low wooden roof hung above her. It was painted with bright orange, yellow, and gold swirls.

Fire.

Each plume was so finely detailed that she was sure it would flare down and scorch the skin from her bones. A shape emerged from the chaos: two firebirds with their wings flared around a crest. She had seen the terrible image before....

The Pyreack fae!

She bolted upright, smacking her head against the wood ceiling. Swearing, she rubbed her scalp.

What had happened?

The wooden floor beneath her jolted violently, nearly knocking her from the bench. She cursed loudly. A horse whinnied outside.

A carriage. A pretty little prison covered in deep-red cushions and swirls of paint. The armrests on the bench she crouched on were covered in intricate carvings and designs. The price of the carriage would have fed her entire village for decades.

Her empty stomach churned, and she wished she had something to throw up, if only for the relief.

She ran a hand along her ear, checking again to see if it was still pointed. Still fae. Her fingers probed the sharp tip, and she cursed.

That bastard Averin's glamour was still on her. How long could it hold? How long had it been?

The horse whinnied again, and this time, the carriage stopped.

Her fingers brushed the gold-trimmed curtain just as the door flew open. She yelped, jumping back against the hard bench as blinding white light flooded her.

"You're awake." The voice belonged to the same monster who'd threatened to fry Klaus. The Pyreack leader who had knocked her unconscious with a mere touch.

She squinted against the light, just making out his silhouette. His hand was extended. To help her out? Someone behind him sniggered. The sound battered her ears. If this was fae hearing, no wonder Averin had eavesdropped on her conversations without difficulty.

Only she wasn't fae, merely glamoured to look like one. To feel like one. Anything else was too abhorrent to believe.

More sounds assaulted her: fae sharpening weapons against whetstones, laughter, someone tossing out a bucket of water, fire crackling. As jarring as the sounds were, they gave her no real clues as to where she could be.

The Pyreack soldier flicked his outstretched hand. "Hurry up."

She glared at him, giving her eyes time to adjust while debating whether to spit on him.

"You can stay here if you like, but then you're not getting any food." His coal-dark eyes, now visible with the rest of him, danced, as if blackmailing her and then knocking her unconscious was vastly amusing. She wanted to rip both of them out of their sockets.

Without moving, she demanded, "What am I doing here? Where are we?"

He didn't drop his hand, but he didn't answer either.

"I'm not going anywhere with you until you tell me what's going on," she yelled.

His smile turned to a sneer. "I'm taking you to the Kingdom of Pyreack, where you belong. The king has need of you." His sharp face, the cold malice in his deep-set eyes, and the quiet menace in his voice told her he wasn't joking.

Her blood turned cold. "What for?" Is that why she'd burned Averin, because she "belonged" in the Kingdom of Pyreack? Is that what Martka Alyona had known? And was that why the old woman had allowed her to keep her amber pendant? She would never know the answer.

The fae's lips curled. "Get out of the carriage before I drag you out."

Her heart slammed against her ribs. Every muscle in her body screamed at her to run and find Klaus. Together they could figure out how they'd gotten into such a mess.

Her racing heart almost stopped. Had Klaus survived? And the rest of the villagers, who had tried to burn her to death? Or had this monster reneged on their deal the moment she'd blacked out?

She would never rest until she knew Klaus was safe.

Part of being reunited with him relied on information—information this fae held. It was time to cooperate. At least a bit. She batted his hand away and stepped out.

He scoffed but dropped his hand to rest on the carved pommel of the sword strapped to his belt. Beneath his grip, she couldn't make out the carving, but it glinted onyx in the fading light.

It had been dawn when she was taken. How far could they have gone in a day?

She looked around for a recognizable landmark—and gaped.

A sea of red-and-black tents flapped in the breeze. Flags flew from the peaked tips of the largest ones. Each was emblazoned with the flaming firebird crest.

At the farthest extreme, the lines of tents were flanked by a forest she didn't recognize. Instead of familiar pine, the trunks of these pale trees were ragged. The bark hung in long shreds like torn skin.

The pale trees, fluttering with brittle yellow leaves, all that was left at the tail end of autumn, *felt* wrong. Dirty. As if thousands of eyes peered at her through the thick, skeletal branches. Sizing her up. Tasting her scent on the frosty wind as if it were blood on a tongue.

She turned away from them, shivering. Wherever she was, it was a long way from home.

Smoke rose from a fire amongst the tents. It carried that foul aroma of roasting meat. The Martka claimed that fae ate naughty children. And the fae soldier in Askavol had also threatened to turn them into lunch. There had to be truth in the threat.

No! Stop it!

If she gave in to those thoughts, panic would overwhelm her.

"Finished gaping?" her captor demanded. Still that cruel smile twitched. He didn't wait for an answer before striding into the maze of tents. With nowhere to run and fae soldiers at her heels, she followed him.

Every fae she saw was male, and they all wore red fighting leathers with the Pyreack crest emblazoned on their chests. This had to be one of the camps the Pyreack fae had set up while invading....

Her eyes widened. What kingdom was she in? It couldn't be Zephyr. Pyreack hadn't established a foothold strong enough to house a camp of this size in the Kingdom of Zephyr yet.

Or had they?

If only she'd asked Klaus for more details from that newspaper. If she was somehow no longer in Atria.... If she'd been taken too far to get back and find Klaus—

She tripped over a guy rope. A firm hand grabbed her arm and steadied her. A fae soldier. Dark skinned with dark hair and intelligent brown eyes, he was surprisingly handsome, despite his pointed fae ears.

Not wanting to be touched by these creatures, she curled her lip back and hissed at him like a feral cat. He let go of her and gestured with his hand for her to keep up with the leader. She turned away and concentrated on her footing.

They stopped at a large black tent. Grander than any of the

others, it was trimmed with red tassels and golden braid. The familiar firebird crest was embroidered on the flaps, the roof, and on the flag waving above it.

She clenched her fists to keep from trembling.

Don't show fear. They could probably taste it in the air, and that was enough.

Two guards armed with crossbows and a baldric of daggers strapped across their chests stood at attention. One of them pulled open a tent flap. Warmth spilled from inside. It reeked of roasted meat.

Please let it not be human.

"In," the leader snapped.

Her face flushed hot, and her eyes burned. She pulled herself up and rolled her shoulders back.

Just another fighting pit. Just another fight.

Against a fae.

She stepped into the tent.

A table and four black velvet chairs stood in the middle of the space. Porcelain plates heaped with meat and overcooked vegetables steamed beside a jug of dark liquid. Blood? By all the darkness, no!

Tucked in the far corner of the tent was a bed laden with pillows and furs. Oil lamps lit the gloomy space.

Not a prison tent then.

"Lieutenant, keep two guards stationed at this flap at all times, and another two on each corner," the leader snapped to the dark-skinned, handsome fae.

"Yes, Captain Radomir."

Her stomach lurched. Were they trying to keep her in, or keep something else out? Both, she decided. Better to assume the worst. That's what Klaus would do. Her heart ached with longing for him.

The tent flaps folded closed behind the lieutenant. She was alone with the fae leader. Captain Radomir.

Radomir walked to the table in two easy strides and pulled out a chair. A chin jerk indicated she should sit.

She crossed her arms over her chest, rolling her weight onto one hip. This was just like the standoff with Averin outside the store where she'd bought her boots, when she'd worked so hard to look bored, intimidating, the underdog waiting to pounce.

Klaus would be so mad at her right now. She could practically hear him screaming in her ear, *What in all the darkness do you think you're doing? He's fae! Do you really think this is a good time to assert yourself?*

She pursed her lips, both at Klaus and Radomir, and raised one eyebrow. She let her gaze drag down Radomir's tall, powerful frame. He carried himself with such preternatural stillness. Did all fae look so ... so *animal*?

"Start talking," she commanded.

Radomir's smirk widened. He sauntered to a second chair on the opposite side of the table and sat. Grin in place, he loaded his plate with food. "Don't worry. It's only stag."

She swallowed hard but didn't sit. Had he read her thoughts? Was that even possible? Or had he heard the stories whispered among humans about fae?

Even though she was ravenous, she knew better than to eat food offered by an enemy. Especially food that smelled as bad as this did. What if it was magicked to poison her but not him? Poisoned food that tortured her for days was something she could easily imagine this monster enjoying.

Arms folded across her chest, she demanded, "Where are we?"

Radomir poured himself a glass of the red liquid. Thick and dark, it stank of stewed fruit mixed with his unique strawberries-and-honey smell. But at least it wasn't blood.

She shivered. Since when could she read smells the way Klaus read his newspapers? Worse, even as she stood there trying to bluff her way through the nightmare, her limbs seemed longer than she remembered. Too streamlined. It gave her no comfort that her muscles felt stronger, more powerful. The same animalistic quality Radomir possessed. This body was nothing at all like *her* body. Could a glamour run bone deep?

Radomir put his goblet down. "Ealvera War Camp."

She'd never heard the name before. What kingdom was it in? Or was it on another continent entirely? Her gnawing hunger evaporated.

"We're still in Atria." Radomir had at least spared her the indignity of asking. He straightened the spoon on his place setting. "At the edge of the Ealvera Forest."

Her eyes flicked to the place setting where Radomir had drawn her chair. She inched closer to the table on numb feet. Her fingers rasped on the carved backrest as she pulled the chair out farther. She sat. "Why am I here?"

"I told you," Radomir said around a mouthful of meat. "I'm taking you to King Darien Pyreaxos."

Her eyes narrowed. "There's nothing Darien Pyreaxos could possibly want from me. And I'd sooner die than serve a fae."

Radomir's fork slammed down on his plate. Gravy and onion sloshed on the white tablecloth. "*King* Darien to you." He hefted his knife and picked at a piece of meat lodged between his perfect white teeth. Sharp canines glinted. Had he done that on purpose? "Don't get ahead of yourself, little girl."

She tried to stop the chill that ran down her spine but failed.

Radomir's eyes dropped to her chest, narrowing on something there.

She clenched the table until she realized he wasn't staring at her breasts but rather at the chain attached to her amber pendant. It poked from beneath her filthy clothes.

Radomir pointed at it with his knife. The angle of his wrist told her he knew exactly where to stick that blade and when to twist. "That pendant has been working as a beacon. It's been sending out signals for a year now. All those earthquakes. Just waiting for someone to find you."

The earthquakes—

Deny. Deny. Deny.

"It's just a stone."

"Just a stone?" Radomir scoffed. "We suspect it tapped into your powers to create the glamour that kept you hidden for eighteen years.

Just another worthless human." He scoffed at the word *human* and went back to cutting his meat. "I guess Averin and his little sidekicks saw it. That broke the glamour, to reveal—" He waved his knife at her. "You. The fae you've always been."

She spat on his fancy carpet. "I am *not* fae. And I will never serve you."

His charcoal eyes twinkled. "Doesn't matter what you think, little girl. You're a weapon coveted by nations and kings, and with power enough that the entire continent felt it when you were born. We've been looking for you ever since." He leaned on his elbows and pointed his knife at her. "Then Teagarta was hit with that earthquake. We all knew it was you. It was a race to see who got there first." His cruel smile broadened. "I beat everyone to it. My men and I searched for you, but we couldn't find you." He sniggered and shook his head. "Funny, that, how you were less than an hour away."

Her world stilled. Bile rose in her throat. The fae who held her captive and intended to give her to his king had killed Tarik.

She snatched up her empty plate and—

Radomir leaped from his chair. And then she was flying.

She slammed into a thick, wooden tent pole. The plate shattered. Her fingers clawed around a broken shard of porcelain. "Bastard," she screeched.

Radomir gripped her hand holding the glass shard. She spat a glob of saliva at his cheek and angled the shard at his ribs. He dodged the spit and tore the glass from her with an effortless wrist flick. It *thunked* onto the carpet. He grabbed her by the collar and slammed her into the pole.

Head spinning, she jabbed her knee into his groin. Radomir blocked like he knew it was coming. He rammed his knee into her pelvis. She bit down to keep from screaming.

His forearm smashed into her throat, pinning her to the pole. Using all her strength, she landed a punch to his abdomen. He didn't flinch. His free arm wrapped around her wrist and twisted it back until her bones screamed in pain. One more twist, and her hand would crack.

"I was given instructions not to kill you." Radomir's hot breath scorched her ear. "But no one said anything about not hurting you."

She hissed, another inhuman, merciless sound.

A half smile tugged at his lips. "I made no such promises about you." His arm pressed harder into her neck, almost cutting off her windpipe.

She managed to croak, "I will kill you for what you did in Teagarta."

The pressure on her throat mounted.

Desperate for air, she clamped her hands around his arm and tugged. His leather-clad arm sizzled beneath her touch. Her hand burned through to his skin. If she could have breathed, she'd have retched at the stench of burning flesh.

Radomir barely seemed to notice. Face pressed right to hers—it would have been beautiful, she realized, if it weren't so void of soul— he whispered, "I suggest you behave, Stasha. My men haven't seen a female like you in many months. One wrong move, and there will be no one here to help you." He was close enough to kiss her. "And if you think my soldiers are bad, you have no idea what's lurking out there in the forest." His words dropped even lower. "Things that will make me seem as gentle as a lamb."

Her lungs ached, begging for air, for release. The edges of her vision blurred. She spat one last glob of phlegmy saliva at him.

He didn't dodge this time. His eyes turned feral. He released her throat to slap her face. Her head snapped back, and she folded to the floor.

It didn't matter. Regardless of what this bastard did to her, she would make him pay. For Tarik. For Lenka. For Hathrine's pain. For Klaus. For everything.

Stasha shifted on the large bed someone—Radomir, she guessed—had tossed her onto. Her cheek ached where he'd hit her. That meant she couldn't have been out for very long if she truly were fae, as he claimed. Otherwise, surely fae healing would have taken over?

"Cursed fae." After Radomir almost crushed her windpipe, the words were little more than a croak. "Curse every single one of them."

Someone cleared his throat.

She whipped around. The dark-skinned lieutenant with the pretty, pointed face stood at the tent flap. His baldric bristled with blades. As did his waist. He even had a sword slung across his back. He stood so unnaturally still that if he hadn't cleared his throat, she wouldn't have noticed him.

Her skin crawled.

He'd been watching her sleep.

A snarl ripped from her throat. "Creepy, or what?"

The lieutenant blinked.

Yes, fae. She may be the underdog here, but that didn't mean her bite wasn't just as bad as his. Especially in this horrible fae body.

"You're to wash and dress. Captain Radomir's orders." The lieutenant gestured a perfect hand to a copper bathtub that had replaced the table.

What a wonderful sight! Heated by a brazier of glowing coals, steam billowed from it.

"We have a long journey ahead of us," he added.

Oh, to lower her sweat-and-mud covered body into the bath, but the lieutenant made no move to leave. Was he here to ogle her? One of Radomir's soldiers she'd be thrown to if she didn't behave?

She glowered at him, then at the bathtub, and at him again.

He didn't even twitch.

Bath time would have to wait. She forced her features into something as close to pleasant as possible. She was sure it looked more like a grimace. "What happened to my friend? The boy with the brown hair and the lame leg at my village?"

"The one you bargained for?"

"Yes." She held her breath.

"The captain never breaks his word."

She wasn't sure if that was comforting, given the things Radomir threatened to do to her. "So he's safe?"

The lieutenant nodded at the bath. "I told you to bathe." He rolled a fireball between his palms.

"And I asked you a question. Is. He. Safe?"

A long pause. "He was when we left him."

She sighed with relief. "I have no other clothes."

He nodded at the foot of the bed. A dark blue woolen dress and a thick blue cloak were spread over the fur blanket. Her eyes almost popped out of their sockets. She'd never worn a dress in her life. They were for ornamental women who lived in cities and never lifted a finger to do anything other than summon servants. Or that's what Martka Gabika had always said. Faced with dressing in one, she agreed with the sour old woman.

But it did make her wonder how the Pyreack fae saw her. A weapon to be dressed up like a doll? Without answers to all these questions, she had no hope of winning here. Time to woo her guard.

Voice sugar sweet, she asked, "What's your name?"

A short hesitation, then a quiet, "Suren."

"Hello, Suren." She shot him a sultry smile, the kind she reserved for tricking idiot boys like Ivan. "I'm Stasha. But I guess you know that."

Suren's head bobbed, as if startled. His fireball snuffed out. "I know who you are. We all do."

"Right. I'm your new secret weapon." She placed a finger on her chin and fluttered her eyelashes at him. "Any idea of what I'm supposed to be able to do?"

Suren rolled an even bigger fireball. "The king knows. That's all that matters."

She huffed a breath. "So, the king.... Where exactly does he hang out?"

Suren frowned.

A warning to moderate her tone. "I mean no disrespect. I'm just trying to understand why he wants me."

"King Darien has his court in Phyrturq." Suren walked to the bath and swirled the water with a long, slender finger. "Temperature is perfect. Don't waste it. A good night's sleep is what you need now."

She ignored the hint. "And that's where we're going tomorrow?"

A snorted laugh. "We have to cross Ocea. But first we have to get to Logral. That should take about three days at the most. Maybe five if we're slow."

Logral, on the border with Ocea, was even further away than Reupa. So Radomir hadn't lied when he said they were still in her home kingdom. And neither had Klaus's newspaper when it had claimed that Pyreack was swallowing her land.

But if they were only three days from Logral, they had to have traveled at least four weeks to get here. She had *not* been unconscious for a month.

Suren seemed to notice her confusion. "You were spirited here. Or, at least, very close to here. We traveled the rest of the way on horseback."

Spirited. Like in the stories the Martka told about how fae disappeared with their prey amidst light and pain. The pain part they had right, the light, not so much.

"Not that the Kingdom of Ocea still exists. It's ours now." Suren said *ours* as if that included her. Her lip curled with distaste before she could stop it. "Even with your gray eyes, you're a Pyreack fae, Stasha. That makes you one of us."

Why did her eye color matter?

Suren glanced out the tent flap. "That's why I'm telling you this. It seems only right."

So he had a different view to his captain. Interesting.

"I'm still getting used to being a ... a fae, let alone a Pyreack fae."

"I saw the captain's arm." Suren's voice was barely a whisper. "You branded him with a perfect handprint. No doubt that you're Pyreack."

"I hope it hurt like seven lashes."

Suren grimaced. "Truth? Fire shouldn't affect any of us." He rolled another fireball to prove the point. "But with you...." He looked at her through hooded eyes. Like he was afraid of her. Was that why he was rolling fireballs? And why did she even have fire magic? And how could she use it to escape before they crossed into Ocea?

She pulled her feet up onto the bed. The sad state of her beautiful boots made her gasp. The red-stained leather was scarred, and the soft wool insides were rough with grit. She grunted as she unlaced them. These boots were supposed to be part of her quest for hope. Fat lot of good they'd done her.

At least she still had her red ribbon.

She ran her hands along her braid to find it. Filthy and hard as rope, her braid was caked with mud and not her precious finery.

Her heart stuttered. Then she let out a long sigh. All things considered, it was hardly surprising that she'd lost Tarik's gift. The last time she'd seen it was right after the fight with Averin, when she'd stuck it into ... her pocket!

Hands shaking, she dug for it. Her fingers brushed the smooth satin.

It had survived! Hope wasn't dead!

She was meant to escape to rescue Klaus, and to avenge Tarik by killing Radomir.

She froze. Never before had she wanted to kill a human. Not even when the Martka had tossed her in lockup for a week for stealing food to stop her and Klaus from starving to death. Or when the Kňazer had tried to burn her alive.

She tossed her shoulders back. Radomir wasn't human. He was fae, and he'd killed Tarik and had threatened to burn Klaus. That put him on par with rats. Such vermin didn't deserve to live. Not that killing Radomir would be easy. Any information she could glean would help.

"Why's the journey so long if you can spirit?"

A guttural growl rumbled from Suren. "Get. Into. That. Bath. You smell like a sewer."

The hair on her arms and the back of her neck rose. She was pushing her luck with this animal, and that risked raising his suspicions. But something was stopping them from traveling to Logral in a matter of seconds. Perhaps that could work in her favor.

"Your captain mentioned terrors in the forest. What lurks there?"

The sound of marching boots outside the tent reached her. Fae spoke and shuffled about. The guard changing?

Whatever it was, it wiped all expression off Suren's face. He pointed at her bathtub. "Enough talking. Last warning. Get cleaned up, or I'll scrub you myself." But instead of leaving her, he folded his arms and watched her.

Her eyebrows rose. "My bath time is your spectator sport?"

"Captain Radomir doesn't trust you. He said I was to stay here until you're done. And then I'm to put that on your ankle." Suren gestured to the floor next the bathtub. A schorl chain curled around a manacle lay on the carpet.

She choked on her own saliva. "You're chaining me like a dog?"

"Can't risk you trying to escape during the night."

"I thought you said I was one of you ... us?"

Suren shrugged. "Captain's orders."

"Tell your captain for me that he can bathe in his own piss before that happens." She lay back on the bed and closed her eyes as if she didn't have a care in the world. Meanwhile, her super-sharp ears monitored Suren's reaction.

He huffed. "Stasha, don't make things harder than they need to be."

Eye still closed, she said, "Harder for whom? Me or you?"

Suren's hesitation was all she needed. He would suffer if she didn't comply. That would hardly endear her to him. Right now, he was her only source of information, and she couldn't afford to alienate him. Teeth gritted, she sat up. "If I catch you looking at me, I swear I'll shoot every ounce of magic I have at you."

The blood rushed so fast from Suren's dark face, it left his cheeks ashen. He spun away from her. Could she really be that dangerous? "Not necessary. You have my word."

She mulled his reaction as she bathed. Whatever power lurked in her had to be impressive to warrant his fear *and* a schorl restraint. Pity she didn't know what it was. Before she escaped, she'd bleed Suren dry of everything he knew.

But first she had to survive the night wearing a cumbersome dress and a schorl manacle.

"It's day. Get up." Radomir's sickly sweet strawberry-and-honey smell assailed Stasha as she lay curled upon her bed. "We're leaving in ten minutes."

She kept her eyes closed, pretending to be asleep for no other reason than to irritate him. Not that it would have fooled him. Who could possibly sleep with a schorl manacle around their ankle?

At least if you were fae.

Given the fiery ache in her bones and the nausea bubbling in her stomach, she had to wonder at what she'd become.

Radomir slammed his fist onto her pillow. It puffed up to muffle her nose and mouth.

Her eyes shot open wide.

His mouth twisted with that faintly amused smile he wore like a weapon. How could anyone take such pleasure in torturing another?

Only a monster could.

No way would she let him know how much pain his schorl manacle had caused her in the hours she'd lain awake in this bed. "How am I supposed to move chained up like a dog?"

Radomir tossed back her bedcovers and grabbed her ankle before she could wrench away. In a blur, a key appeared in his gloved hand. It flashed, and her manacle rattled open.

By all that lived and breathed, he moved fast.

Still, everyone had weaknesses. She'd just have to watch Radomir closely to find his. And then think carefully about how to exploit them.

"Happy?" Radomir sneered as he yanked the manacle and chain

off her bed. "Keep me waiting and you'll wear schorl all day. Cooperate, and it'll be iron."

Iron she could cope with.

She rolled out of bed. Her sore, swollen ankle collapsed under her. She landed on the carpet in a heap of skirt and too-long limbs.

Radomir snorted a laugh. "I look at you and wonder...." His face hardened. "Now move."

Expecting him to watch her the way Suren had, she was surprised when he left her alone—until Suren strode into the tent. He carried a basin of hot water and a cloth, which he put on the table. From a bulging pocket in his leggings, he pulled out two apples. "I figured fruit would be the most palatable after a night of schorl." He put them on the table. "Get moving, Stasha. The captain is not joking about the schorl."

She didn't doubt it. She stumbled to the basin. Suren chuckled as she crashed into the table. Did all fae lose their grace and poise after exposure to schorl, or was that just her? Longing to deck him, she sloshed water onto her face and dried it on her skirt.

"Don't think I can eat," she said mournfully. Apples stolen from the Kňazer's pantry were a rare treat she'd always relished.

"You need to keep your energy up." The way Suren eyed her scrawny frame suggested he knew she was no stranger to an empty belly.

What he said about eating made sense. If she got the chance to escape, she didn't want to blow it because she didn't have the strength to run.

But could an apple be poisoned? Possibly. Then again, would Suren bring her poisoned food? That seemed more Radomir's style. Unless Radomir had commanded Suren to give it to her. But Radomir said that his king wanted her. So why would he....

You're being paranoid.

Possibly, but who knew what these creatures would or wouldn't do. Better paranoid than drugged—or worse.

She fixed Suren with a sharp eye. "How about we share? You eat one half, and I take the other."

Suren's nose scrunched in a frown. "You think I'd poison you? What would I gain from that? King Darien wants you alive. A dead weapon is of no use to anyone."

She sat back on the bed and shoved her feet into her boots. "Let's assess.... You and your captain attacked my village. You burned some of my friends to death, including the one woman who could have told me who I really am. You threatened to burn my best friend. You kidnapped me. You made me sleep in schorl. Seeing a pattern here?"

Suren pulled a knife out of his baldric and lopped one of the apples in half. "Pick."

She studied both halves. They seemed like very ordinary apples. She touched the one closest to him. "Mine."

Suren took the other, tossed it in his mouth, chewed, and swallowed. "As good an apple as I've ever eaten."

Stomach roaring with sudden hunger, she lunged for hers. He grabbed her wrist. "You're out of time. Your ten minutes is up. Come. Let's go."

She snarled as he dragged her away from the fruit and just managed to grab the second apple before she was through the tent flap. She rammed it into her dress pocket. Paranoia had done nothing for her. Better to just wing it, the way she always operated.

Radomir waited for her outside her tent flap. The iron chain and manacle he promised dangled from his fist. He grabbed her hand, and his fingers brushed against the thick scar on her palm.

How dare *he* touch the scar she'd gotten trying to free Tarik's body? She yanked her hand away from him. Pity she couldn't crush him the way he had Tarik.

The chain flew at her head.

Before she could duck, it crashed into her face with such force that blood splattered. She whimpered before she could stop herself. Fury roared like wild-fire through her.

"You hit me?" Her hand flew to her cheek. It was hot with blood against the chilly breeze ruffling the ribbon in her braid.

Radomir leaned in close and smiled. "It'll heal. Fight me, and I'll do more than hit you."

She locked eyes with him. "Fae monster."

A shrug, like her view didn't count.

It didn't.

Radomir slapped the manacle around her wrist and jerked the chain. When her arm pulled sharply in the socket, his dark eyes twinkled.

Spitting in them would be so easy....

Radomir handed the chain to Suren and picked a path through the tents. Suren followed. Led like a dog, she had no choice but to trot after them.

The camp was quieter than it had been the previous night. Instead of campfire chatter and laughter, the brutally beautiful fae who joined her guard detail were tight-lipped. Black steel glinted from the blades strapped across their chests, their thighs, their bulging biceps. They all carried swords shoved in sheaths attached to their backs, and axes in baldrics at the bases of their spines. Crossbows and quivers provided the final layer of armor. Wasn't fire enough of a weapon?

Radomir led them to a trampled clearing lit by torches. Golden flickers and black shadows danced across a dozen horses tied to posts. They whinnied and nipped at each other.

She gulped. They didn't expect her to ride, did they? With Radomir at the helm, this would be nothing like the joke she'd shared with Klaus about dangling carrots before horses' noses.

Tears pricked for Klaus. She lowered her watery eyes—they betrayed weakness she couldn't defend. She wiped the tears away with a flick of her sleeve. Better to pretend she had this all under control.

A heavy hand thumped her shoulder. She jumped. Radomir. "Do you ride?" He pointed to a fat brown horse with a white stripe that ran between its eyes down to its dangling bottom lip.

She tossed her head back. "That's what I did all day at the mill. Rode horses. While wearing dresses. And commanding my servants."

A few of the fae sniggered. She fought the grin twitching her lips.

Radomir threw up his hands. "Sort her out, Suren."

Suren offered her his hand. "Allow me to help you mount."

"Like you shared the apple with me?" She made a show of patting her butt. "Just as well I'm padded for when you dump me on the ground."

Suren grimaced. "Stasha—"

"Don't bother. I've got it." She grabbed the saddle, rattling her chains, and pulled herself up onto the horse. The stupid creature circled, and she almost slipped off. She gripped the saddle with bone-white fingers. It would be mortifying to tumble into the dirt in front of these fae. Especially Radomir.

Suren grabbed her boot and tugged it into the stirrup. "Bravery is one thing, Stasha," he murmured, "but blind stupidity another altogether. Take help when it's offered."

She crushed his fingers with her heel. He yelped and jumped back to glare at her. She raised her eyebrows innocently. "Sorry. Was your hand in the way? How careless of me."

"Don't push it." Suren snatched at her chain, attached a length of it to her saddle, and strode to his own horse. He clipped the other end of it to his tack and mounted in one fluid movement.

"Move out," Radomir called. His horse trotted toward a narrow path into the forest of ragged trees. They were even paler and more skeletal in the dawn light than that they'd been the night before.

Suren followed Radomir. The chain pulled taut, and her horse broke into a trot after him. She clutched her saddle with both hands and wrapped her legs around the horse's fat belly. Her skirt rode up her thighs.

A skirt but no sidesaddle? They obviously weren't used to having women around.

Not that a sidesaddle would have made any difference to her lack of riding skill. She still bounced on the horse's back like a tick on a dog. But over her dead body would she fall off the damn thing. She doubted the ten other horses with their fae riders coming behind her would stop if she did.

A canopy of ghostly-white branches closed above her. Their

cruelly twisted boughs blocked the glowing light. Bracken, brambles, and snakeweed curled at her horse's hooves.

Her ribbon fluttered into her face. Instead of dying off as she would have expected, the chill morning breeze picked up. But not even its mournful whistle could drown out the skittering and chewing of insects and critters she couldn't see in the undergrowth. Like a cat hunting a mouse, getting closer and closer until—

A bird fluttered past her. A raven, black as night and sleek as silk, swooped low over her head and then soared off to caw in a tree.

Her skin crawled with an unpleasant mix of presentiment and fear. Hadn't she had her fair share of ravens? She couldn't suppress the sickening feeling that Radomir had been true to his word. He and her other captors, born and bred to kill, were not the worst creatures in these woods. There was something here the heavily armed fae didn't like. Something that wiped away Radomir's smile as he searched the trees. Something that screamed at her human soul to run and never look back.

She reeled her chain in to get her horse level with Suren's. He stopped his vigilant scanning to eye her warily. She didn't want to break the silence, but she needed answers. "Why are we going through these woods?" she whispered. "Why don't we just spirit to Logral?"

Suren shook his head.

Perhaps stomping on his hand hadn't been such a bright idea.

She tried again. "I'm not stupid, Suren. I can *feel* that things aren't right here. Why is the captain doing this?"

More silence. But he did glance at Radomir. Focused on the track and the trees, Radomir didn't seem to notice her talking. But if his ears were anywhere near as sensitive as hers, he would have heard her.

Suren wasn't in a talkative mood. She sighed and let the chain go.

"Not all fae can spirit," Suren whispered before her horse dropped back. "This way, we all travel together."

That made no sense when they had spirited almost all the way to Ealvera War Camp from Askavol. "Why lie to me?" she hissed. "How does it help you? Other than make me want to stomp on your other hand."

Suren's lean body rocked with a small snort. "I'm not lying. You don't understand magic."

"Then educate me." Her chain rattled as she pulled it in to keep her horse at Suren's side.

Suren's big, brown eyes opened to their widest extent. "So you can stomp on my other hand? I'm not your enemy, Stasha, despite what you may believe."

"I'll take that under advisement. But if you really want to be my friend"—she made air quotes around the word *friend*— "then tell me the truth."

Suren was silent for so long that she snarled at him and let her horse drop back. He yanked on the chain, and her horse nickered but kept pace with him.

"The border of each kingdom is guarded by magic," Suren said softly. "No one can cross a border by spiriting if they don't belong to that kingdom. That's why we have to leave Atria and enter Ocea by foot."

Her eyebrows knitted together. "But Pyreack has taken over Ocea. Why do you—" Her eyes widened. Someone in Ocea who wasn't a Pyreack fae had to control spiriting magic. That meant Ocea wasn't quite as vanquished as Radomir and Suren claimed.

She shifted in her saddle, trying to get some blood flowing into her numbing backside as she considered the implications of Suren's admission—and how she could use it for her benefit. But without understanding the politics, and the fae who drove that politics, she made little headway. It was a pity that fighting for food had taxed all her strength while Klaus had become the scholar in their partnership.

Still, the Pyreack king wanted her. Did he hope that her unknown power would finally bring Ocea to its knees? If so, how would he tap into her power when *she* didn't even know what she could do? She flexed her fingers, hoping to make them spark.

Nothing happened.

She'd been angry or frightened every time fire had burst from her. Was that King Darien Pyreaxos's plan? To keep her in a constant state of fear so he could use her magic?

Yet another reason to escape so she could get back to Klaus. And when they were reunited, she wouldn't flee with him to Ruepa. They would leave this benighted continent far behind them. How they'd travel and where they'd go, she didn't—

Suren's hand curled around her chain. Her horse stopped.

The strange birdsong stilled, and the scuttling of life between the trees silenced. Nothing moved. Not even the wind. No one in the convoy made a sound. As if they were waiting for—

A child cried out.

Its weeping was more pitiful than anything she had ever heard. Radomir and two of his soldiers wheeled their horses around and tore off through the trees in the direction of the wailing. She rocked back, stunned that Radomir would care enough to help a child.

The tone and frequency of the child's wailing intensified until the thunder of hooves drowned it out. The hair on her neck bristled. If Radomir had harmed the little one....

She craned her neck to see through the trees.

The horses reappeared. Sword bared, Radomir rode behind the two fae. Between them, hanging from their hands, bumped a little boy no older than seven. He was dressed in a tattered tunic and ragged leggings. Her eyes shot to his ears. Rounded and ordinary, he was as human as she had been before Averin—

A hoof clipped the lad's leg. Her cry of dismay was lost in his screams. But he turned to look at her out of the strangest silver eyes.

So, not quite human. But definitely a child who did not need to be treated so brutally just because he wasn't fae. Worse, Suren's face relaxed at the sight of the suffering mite. He even loosened his grip on his sword.

The two fae tossed the child onto the brambles. He cried harder, pressing dirty palms into his eyes as he struggled to escape the barbs. His matted black hair fell into his grimy, tear-streaked face.

"You picked the wrong convoy, Tiyanak," Radomir snarled. He

swung his sword at the child's arm. The wicked blade slashed the boy's bicep. He howled, and his little fingers clamped down on the blood pouring from the wound. Radomir and the other fae—Suren included—laughed. The boy scrambled out of the brambles and stumbled to his feet. His silver eyes blazed with familiar fury.

"Bullies! Stop hurting him." Stasha slid off her horse and stumbled to the child, only to skid to a halt when her chain nearly ripped her arm from its socket. She glowered at Suren. "Let me go. He needs help."

"Suren! Control her!" Radomir barked.

Her chain jerked again—Suren reeling her in. She kicked and snarled but wasn't strong enough to stop him dragging her to his horse. He grabbed her under her armpits and hoisted her onto his saddle.

"Let me go, you piece of filth!" She rammed her elbow into his nose. Suren's head snapped back with a painful-sounding crack. He dropped her, and she landed on her backside. Needles of pain shot through her pelvis.

The little boy stopped weeping. Eyes fixed on her, his nostrils flared as if he were drinking in her scent.

Like a wolf would.

He took a deliberate step closer to her.

Her breath caught in her throat.

"It's not a child," Suren growled. He reached down with both arms and yanked her back onto his saddle. "It's a Tiyanak."

Radomir ran his sword straight through the little boy's stomach.

The lad's unsettling silver eyes bulged. Hatred and loathing poured like tears down his contorted face to his—

She blinked.

The tears glistened on thick, blackening lips, nothing like the mouth she'd seen before. Radomir withdrew the blade. Blood as bright and blue as a summer sky spurted from the gash. The air reeked of rotten meat, burning flesh, dead things, and pain.

She gagged, vomiting up nothing but bile.

The human-like flesh on the creature's face and arms melted. It oozed down its body, black and waxy, then across the frosty earth until all that remained of its body was tough, leathery hide, and matted hair. The hair hardened into two dark bones, which curled above his head into two half-moon-shaped horns.

The monster hidden beneath the mask.

Rattling bone and leather. That's what he was. Taller than any man she had ever seen, his brown, stick-like arms hung past his knobby knees. His bony hands, larger than the child he had been only a moment before, scraped against his ankles. Even his ribs and pelvis stuck out sharply beneath his dull, brown hide. His face, twisted in an open-mouthed scream, revealed black, spiky teeth.

A monster born of nightmares.

She'd have been utterly defenseless against him.

Radomir ran his sword through its girth for the second time. The creature toppled to the ground and didn't move.

Suren's hand brushed her shoulder. "I'm sorry. I couldn't let you near. It had already caught your scent."

She sucked in a sharp breath, only then noticing the cold tears on her chin shed for the beast. She wiped them away with her cloak as Radomir and his soldiers dragged the creature's body off the path. "What was that?"

"A Tiyanak," Suren repeated. He helped her off his horse and walked her back to her mount. "It uses glamour—the wailing child— to lure travelers to it. Then it eats them alive. Or, if they're lucky, it only forces them into bargains. These woods are full of them."

"So that was the threat you're all worried about?" That seemed unlikely. Radomir and his fae had dispatched the Tiyanak with no difficulty.

Suren shrugged. "Let me help you mount this time."

She was going to reject his offer but saw a trail of blood in the tiny crease beneath his nose. She'd done that, yet he'd saved her. She touched his arm. "Sorry for your face."

Suren grunted and wiped the blood away. "It's nothing. Healed already." He wrapped his arms around her and lifted her into the saddle.

Before he walked back to his horse, she grabbed his arm and asked again, "So that's what you were all worried about? The Tiyanak?"

Turmoil swirled in Suren's chocolate-brown eyes. "Stasha, your questions...."

So, she was right. The Tiyanak was not the real threat in the forest. If only she knew what the other dangers were, and if they were as terrifying—to her, at least—as the Tiyanak. "I need to know things, Suren. How else will I survive?"

"It's my job to make sure you survive. Orders from my captain. I'm to deliver you alive to my king. I can't do that if a Tiyanak gets you first. Even though we killed this one, it's no guarantee others weren't watching. They'll see you as easy meat."

Her blood chilled. "I wouldn't be stupid enough to fall for that trick again."

"And they would know that. They have other glamours to offer. They mold them to suit their prey." Suren tucked her boot into her stirrup. This time, she didn't crush his fingers. "But it doesn't matter. I won't let anything harm you."

Her gaze swept over the fae to settle on Radomir. Legs spread, he stood over the dead Tiyanak, wiping his bloody hands on a cloth. She whispered, "What's out there is equally as dangerous as what's right here."

Suren followed her gaze, and his lips tightened into a hard line. "There's only so much I can do, Stasha, but I won't stand by and let you be maimed. Or ... worse. Of that, you have my word."

"Thanks. But you wouldn't even let me eat an apple, so your word counts for squat." She smiled to rob the words of their sting. "I still need to know what the other threats are."

Stone-faced, Suren grunted. "I told you; when it counts, I won't fail you."

She grabbed a handful of his long, dark hair. It was surprisingly soft. "Tell me the dangers, or I swear, I'll punch you."

Suren pulled away, but a smile twitched. "Are you always such a pain in the ass?"

"You have no idea. And I'm only just getting started."

"Had that figured." Suren stared off into the trees. What he saw, she didn't know, but finally, he said, "Tiyanak don't always hunt for food. They also crave favors."

So, he was still deflecting. There definitely was something else in this forest the Pyreack fae feared. Could she use their enemy as her friend? Best not expose those thoughts. She feigned interest in the Tiyanak. "What kind of favors?"

"Usually ugly, terrible things they use to fuel the magic for their glamour."

How ugly and terrible did those favors have to be that Pyreack fae were wary of them? And if the Tiyanak liked to bargain, would it consider a deal offered by its "prey"? If anyone needed a favor, it was her. But time for this conversation was running out. Radomir and his soldiers were about to mount their horses.

Keeping her voice neutral, she asked, "How do they get favors?"

A long sigh from Suren. "Last question, Stasha. They threaten their prey with death if they don't agree to bind themselves." He walked back to his horse.

She stood up in the stirrups. "What happens if you break a bargain?"

Suren threw his hands in the air. "I said last question."

"But you didn't mean it. Not really. Because it'll make it easier for you to keep me alive if I know the threats."

Suren looked back at her with open exasperation. "You die, Stasha. That's what happens if you break a deal. If the Tiyanak doesn't kill you, the magic will."

She fingered her amber pendant as the convoy set off. The way back to Klaus lay in calculating risks and then acting on the best option. Her fate alone in the woods was surely little different to the plans the Pyreack fae had for her. So, no matter how pessimistic Suren may have been about her chances of survival in the forest, she would flee at the first chance she got.

CHAPTER FOURTEEN

THE VISITATION

Four more Tiyanak were slaughtered as the day stretched on. Some appeared as crying children, others as injured stag, but each time, their true nature was exposed through their silver eyes. Almost routinely, Radomir and his fae herded and killed them.

She wasn't foolish enough to think dispatching the Tiyanak was as easy as they made it look. Or that Suren was indeed sincere in his promise to protect her from Radomir. What sway did a mere lieutenant hold against his captain—a captain who watched her with icy eyes and lips twisted into a serpentine smile?

The sky above the tree canopy had finally begun to gray when Radomir pulled his black mount to a halt and ordered his fae to set up camp. And not a moment too soon. Her blistered hands, aching backside, and trembling legs could stand no more riding. She slumped gracelessly out of her saddle and almost wobbled into the mud. Suren grabbed her before she could fall. He looped her chain around his arm. "They'll set up your tent first." He pointed to where the tents were being pitched. "And then you can rest."

She almost sighed her gratitude, but she'd exposed enough weakness for one day to let on how exhausted she was. She cocked her eyebrow pertly. "So, being my guard dog gets you out of doing chores. You owe me. Big time."

Suren chuckled. "No doubt you'll find ample opportunities to make me pay." His laughter faded. "Maybe this time you'll eat when I bring you food."

Her stomach roared. "What's on the menu?" Apart from the

apple, she'd eaten nothing all day. Radomir hadn't stopped for a meal, with each fae munching on nuts and dried fruit to sustain their energy. She'd almost expected Suren to give her a handful of his stash, but he hadn't. Maybe it was his way of punishing her for doubting him over the apple. If it was, it seemed petty. Or maybe Radomir had forbidden it. That seemed more likely.

"Suren!" Radomir shouted across the clearing. Suren straightened. His face hardened, and his muscles tensed. Every bit the fae soldier. "Watch her. I'm taking out a hunting team."

Suren nodded once. "Yes, Captain."

She swallowed hard to bring some moisture to her dry mouth. "What are they hunting?"

"Stag. Real ones this time, not Tiyanak glamour." Suren's fingers brushed her elbow, directing her to the black tent quickly rising from the ground. This wasn't the palatial monstrosity they'd imprisoned her in the night before and was only big enough for a bedroll. By the time they reached it, it was ready.

Finally, an opportunity to escape.

Suren swept back the tent flap. Face pitiful, she held up her manacled wrist to him. The skin had rubbed raw. Unlike the cut on her cheek from Radomir's chain attack that had healed almost instantly, an open wound wept under the iron. "Please?"

Suren shook his head. "You know I can't."

She waved her arms around, clunking the chain. "And just where do you think I'll go? I've seen the Tiyanak. I'm not an idiot, and I don't have a death wish, no matter how much I'm hating all this."

Suren scratched the dark stubble on his jaw. "Stasha...."

She'd get nothing from him out here in the open with other fae watching, so she dove into the tent. Joined by the chain, he had no choice but to follow. He knelt on the bedroll next to her.

She turned pleading eyes on him. "C'mon, Suren. You keep telling me that we're friends. Friends don't chain other friends up."

Suren scrambled away, putting some distance between them. "I have orders."

Time to play on his obvious dislike for Radomir. She flashed her eyes at him. "Stupid, cruel ones. And how will it help if this becomes infected?" She took a guess. "We barely covered fifteen miles today. If I get sick, we'll be even slower."

Suren shook his head. "No. I'll bring you some salve. With your meal. Eat. Sleep. Tomorrow things will look better."

Suren stood to leave, so she tossed her pillow at him.

"Bastard."

Suren smiled—a good-natured one, unlike Radomir's smirks—and tossed the pillow back at her. "Just as well I have thick skin." He attached her chain to the tent pole and left her alone.

She propped the pillow up on her bedroll and slumped down on it, too tired to even think. Just a catnap before dinner. That was all she needed.

She jerked awake. Moonlight glowed through her tent flap. It had been dusk when she'd shut her eyes. How long had she slept? And where was the food Suren promised? Her eyes fell on a plate of congealed food next to her bedroll. Had Suren even tried to wake her? As much as she despised fae, Suren might have, but in her exhaustion, she'd thwarted his efforts. Even now, she was groggy and barely awake. So what had woken her?

Movement at the end of her bed. She shot upright.

Suren sat with his forehead resting on his arms.

"Still watching me sleep?" she snapped. "I thought we'd already decided that's just plain creepy."

Suren looked up at her, and she gasped. Suren's brown eyes glinted silver. A Tiyanak.

No weapons and no idea of how to fight a Tiyanak, she opened her mouth to scream.

The Tiyanak clamped a hand identical to Suren's over her lips. It shoved her back onto the bedroll and pressed all its weight on her. "Now, now." It may have looked like Suren, but its words rasped like a quill on parchment. "The little fae mustn't be getting upset."

Heart pounding wildly, she lifted her fist to punch its side, but her manacled hand refused to move. The Tiyanak must have pulled the chain taut.

By all the darkness! What now?

The creature chuckled. "She certainly has fire. Let's see if she can burn anything yet?" It grabbed her hand and squeezed so hard that fire burst through her palm and fingers. She caught the reek of burnt flesh. And death. The rotten smell exuded by the Tiyanak Radomir had killed.

But instead of releasing her hand, or flinching, the Tiyanak grinned. "Good, good. The little thing is powerful. Certainly. Very powerful. She is indeed the one we all seek."

She sucked in a breath. As disgusting as the creature was—even in Suren's handsome, lean frame—if it wanted her dead, it would have killed her already.

So what did it want? To bargain? In that case, she had a deal to offer. Better to speak first, before it tricked her into doing something she didn't like.

She shoved the hand covering her mouth and mumbled, "Get off me. I won't scream. We both want things tonight. And loosen my chain."

The silver eyes sparkled. "A wise little thing. Yes, very wise." The hand fell away. The Tiyanak clinked her chain and then settled back on its haunches. As it shifted, the glamour vanished, revealing the bony, horned, leathery monster beneath Suren's conjured skin. It took all of her self-control not to scream when it snapped its sharp, black teeth at her. "The little fae says we both want something. Oh yes. That we do. The little fae wants to escape, and I want to give her that favor." It brushed her face with a bony digit. "So much power. Giving the little fae a favor will bring so much power."

She sat up and pulled her knees to her chest. She was opening her mouth to speak when it hissed, "But the little fae must make haste. The fae named Suren will not be gone long."

Her heart stuttered. Outside her tent, she caught the distant sound of fae shouting and weapons clanging. Were they under attack?

"No time. No time," the creature snapped. "The little fae's escape already begins to unfold. Say in words what the little fae wants." It licked its black lips with an even blacker tongue. "And then the Tiyanak can borrow some of the little fae's power."

"Borrow my power?"

The Tiyanak tsked. "Just for a little glamour."

Was that good or bad? But then, what did it matter when she didn't even know what power she had? Her only goal was to escape back to Klaus. *And to kill Radomir,* a little voice in the back of her mind added. She gritted her teeth. Indeed.

The fighting in the forest had intensified, if the yelling and smoke carried on the breeze was anything to go by.

"Only for an hour," she said. "And why do I have to ask? You know what I want. Information and freedom."

The Tiyanak's silver eyes flashed, and it rattled its hands together. "The little fae asks two things! Oh my. How happy the little fae has made the Tiyanak!"

Her hand drifted to her pendant as she realized her mistake—this was no longer a simple trade, some of her power to glamour him in exchange for a favor. Now she had to offer a bargain—one that could kill her if she failed to deliver. But if she withdrew one of her demands, how would she know what she was escaping into? Especially with the pitched battle waging no more than half a mile away, if her ears didn't deceive her? And why hadn't Suren appeared to "protect" her? Was he also out fighting whatever had attacked the camp?

Eyes fixed on the amber, the Tiyanak dropped to its hands and knees and crawled forward. "What will the little fae give for the second thing?"

She held up her hand to stop his slow encroach. "W-what do you want?"

The Tiyanak clawed for her pendant. She quickly stuck it back under her dress. "Not that. Something else." Giving the pendant away would probably have been the easiest thing, but it had been part of her for as long as she'd been alive. And it was somehow connected with the mess she was in now. If she gave it up, she might never discover who or what she was.

The Tiyanak's skull wobbled on its bony shoulders. "The little fae is truly wise. She knows."

"I do," she said, lying through her teeth as the sounds of battle drew closer. "So what else do you want from me?" She hated being beholden, but what else could she do?

"The little fae's rescue draws ever closer. The Tiyanak will come another day to claim the second favor. Until then, the Tiyanak will borrow the power." It snatched at the red ribbon in her hair. She lunged her head aside to stop it touching her.

The creature hissed, and its eyes narrowed.

Her blood chilled. It wanted Tarik's ribbon? Tarik's hope?

Tarik was dead. His hope had done nothing to save him. But giving up the ribbon could save both Klaus and her. There was little doubt that the Kňazer were punishing him back in Askavol.

It was time to make her own hope.

She pulled the ribbon out of her braid and held it out. "It's yours. Take it."

Nose twitching, the Tiyanak sniffed the ribbon and her hand. Bright-blue saliva coated his lips and dripped on her palm. Its disgusting mouth was literally watering for her. "Black cherries and almonds. Like sweet, sweet wine." It breathed deeply again, drinking in her smell.

"Enough," she snarled, lips pulled back to expose *her* teeth. "Take it."

It lifted the finery from her hand with surprisingly delicate fingers.

She wiped her hand on the blanket. "Tell me what you know. And make sure it's worth that ribbon."

"The little fae is followed," the Tiyanak said, baring more teeth than she ever could in a rictus smile. "By a son of Zephyr. He and his companions are in these woods."

Averin. Her breath hitched in her dry throat. Was it him fighting Radomir and his soldiers? Her—and the Tiyanak's—gaze flicked in the direction of the noise. Horses whinnied and hooves clattered through the woods. Leather on crossbows strained and sprang.

The Tiyanak curled the ribbon around its thin wrist. "Son of Zephyr. Rebels. Pyreack fae. All here. All wanting the little fae." It swept its bony hand out, and she assumed it meant in the woods.

"Is that who the Pyreack fae are fighting? Rebels? And Averin?"

The Tiyanak's eyes gleamed.

She held up her hand. "No, wait. Don't answer. I don't need more bargains."

The creature chuckled, a nasty rasping sound. "Wise. Oh, so wise." Then it leaped off the bed. "Come."

"We're leaving now?" She tried clambering to her feet but was stopped by her chain.

The Tiyanak clicked its tongue. Its hand flicked out. A crack, and the chain snapped, leaving her with just the manacle encircling her wrist. It held a bony finger to its black lips and then crept to the back of her tent. She clambered over her bedroll after it. It extended a long, grimy claw and slit a long gash into the canvas. It parted the flaps and gestured for her to climb out.

"The guards?" she hissed.

Two silver eyes flashed at her, and the black claw pointed sharply at the slit.

So she was to have no understanding of the plan? She shrugged her dismay and, terrified, crept out.

No guards waited at this side of her tent. Where were they all?

The Tiyanak strode quickly toward the woods. As she trotted after it, her eyes widened. Four fae, Suren included, stood in a circle with their backs to her official tent flap. Weapons drawn, they focused on the fighting in the forest. Hopefully Suren wouldn't be punished when Radomir returned and found her gone.

The Tiyanak snapped its fingers. She almost tripped. Grimacing at her carelessness, she followed the Tiyanak into the forest farthest from the sounds of battle.

"The little fae must follow her nose," the Tiyanak whispered. "A horse awaits her. But the little fae must run. Run like the wind."

More riding? Argh! But she wasn't going to argue.

She mouthed a thank-you and bolted deeper into the woods.

"Until next time, little fae," the Tiyanak hissed after her. "Until next time. And then the Tiyanak will finally get what the Tiyanak wants."

CHAPTER FIFTEEN

OUT OF THE PAN AND INTO THE FIRE

ollow her nose, the Tiyanak had said. Easier said than done. Stasha's breath whistled painfully in her chest as she sprinted between the trees. Legs pumping, she jumped over a fallen log and stumbled into a gully. At least there was moonlight to see by. A fact both good and bad, given that, by now, Suren would probably have discovered she'd gone. He and his Pyreack fae would see her as easily as she saw the snagging brambles and snakeweed.

She sped up, not daring to stop to check the wind for a horsey smell. She just had to trust—hope—that the Tiyanak had pointed her in the right direction.

An island of brambles in a clearing made her swerve—right into the reek of horse sweat. Low branches choked with vines blocked her path. She scrambled through them into another clearing and skidded to a stop.

Tied to a low-hanging branch by its reins, a horse paced. The fire-bird crest on the saddle suggested it had been stolen from the Pyreack camp. Eyes frenzied, it bucked its head as she slunk up to it. Panting hard, she untied its reins and grabbed the saddle. It was much taller than her earlier mount. Her biceps flexed as she pulled herself up, swung a leg over, and slid her unsteady feet into the stirrups.

Without the chain tethering her to Suren, she had to ride and command the animal. She whispered, "Work with me. Please."

It didn't get the horse moving. Desperate, she kneed its sides; it whinnied and turned in a circle. She tugged on the reins to pull its head toward the west, away from the Pyreack camp.

Again, the horse circled.

Tears of frustration brimming, she kicked it with her heel. It darted off, almost tossing her from the saddle. She grabbed the pommel with one hand, the reins with the other. At least it was going in the direction she wanted.

But ears flat against its head, the horse broke into a gallop. Teeth chattering, body bouncing like corn in a skillet, she closed her eyes and begged it to slow. It ignored her. She clung on until her thigh muscles ached. The stupid nag's thundering hooves would likely wake every sleeping monster. Ivan's words, uttered so long ago in another world, came back to her: *A nice snack for traveling fae soldiers.*

A fae roar bellowed from the camp.

They knew she'd gone.

Something screamed through the air and whizzed past her head before embedding in a nearby tree. She only had a moment to look before her horse sped past.

An arrow.

They couldn't have tracked her that fast.

Heart galloping harder and faster than the horse's hooves, she risked a glance back and yelped.

An archer stood in the trees through which she'd just sped. A second arrow strained against a large bow clenched in the archer's fist.

Stasha tugged the horse's reins. He whinnied angrily but veered just as the arrow fired. They leaped over a log and through thick, thorny scrub that tore at her face.

A dark form plunged toward her, illuminated in the moonlight. Unbelievably, it ran along the tree line, keeping perfect pace with her horse.

Only a fae had that much speed.

"Go! Go faster," she pleaded to her horse.

A twang, and the beast stumbled. It shrieked, reared on its hind legs, and buckled over. She was thrown from the saddle. The horse's legs rolled over her. All air fled her lungs as the terrified creature kicked and whinnied. Fingers clawing the dirt, she groaned as she wriggled out from under it. A flailing hoof nicked the back of her calf. She cried out and stumbled before finding her balance.

"Try to run, and I'll put this arrow through you."

Not daring to breathe, she pivoted toward the archer.

Dressed in black fighting leathers with no insignia, it was impossible to determine where the fae female came from.

At least she wasn't Pyreack. That had to count for something.

Stasha opened her mouth to speak but stopped when the archer jerked the bow up to aim the arrow at her heart. Even in the dark, she recognized the tang of schorl.

Not a friend, then.

Her bleeding calf tingled with fae healing, but not fast enough if she were to run. Even if she could outrun an arrow shot from a fae bow.

A second fae archer appeared, then a third and fourth, all pointing schorl arrows at her.

She flushed hot and cold and lifted her hands to ward them off. A plume of wild, red flames shot from her fingers.

The fae who had spoken barked a warning at her companions and jumped back. The others swore. Someone fired, but the arrow went wide.

Stasha broke into a run, a river of fire trailing from her fingertips. It leaped from tree to tree and rushed along the ground, igniting the dry undergrowth between her and the archers.

Embers floated past as she sprinted faster than she'd ever thought possible. Ash coated her teeth, her tongue. She ignored the foul taste, running on tireless legs as her fire spread like a flood through the forest behind her.

Smoke blanketed everything, thick, gray, and cloying. Fiery sparks touched her skin but left no mark. No pain.

A lover's caress.

A gurgling brook finally stopped her. She slumped down on her hands and knees. Her fire snuffed on contact with the ground. Lungs rasping, she massaged a stitch in her side

"Well, well. Look who we have here," a familiar voice said from the shadows. "Having fun, pit princess?"

She jumped up, raising her hands to summon more fire as a warning. Not even a flicker responded. That left her nothing but her attitude with which to defend herself. She dropped her hands to her hips. "Averin."

"You don't sound repulsed by the sound of my name. I suppose that's progress." Averin pushed off a tree weeping into the brook. Hands tucked lazily in his pockets, he sauntered closer, then stopped. "You've sure been busy since I last saw you." His blue eyes gleamed in the moonlight.

How had she not noticed before how beautiful they were? Right, she had—until he'd turned into a fae. Worse, turned her into a fae too. If that was what he'd done.

But not all of her silence was driven by Blue Eyes' pretty orbs. She still wasn't entirely sure whose side he was on. Was he also seeking her as a weapon to manipulate and control?

It seemed likely.

During the attack on her village, Averin and his two companions had fought against the Pyreack fae. Clearly, he wanted her. Did he also have a king on whose errand he worked?

All the more reason to be cautious.

"Nothing to say for yourself, pit princess? That has to be a first."

She sought for a sharp comeback, but nothing popped out of her mouth.

Also, she didn't know how to move her suddenly awkward limbs. She settled for a canted head and a cocky smile.

Averin smiled back at her. "How's that underdog thing working for you?"

Now she knew what to say. "Shut up, you idiot."

Averin barked a laugh. But even as he teased her, his muscles were tense and his eyes watchful. Clearly not as carefree as he'd been just two days before. Having his "weapon" ripped from his hand by Pyreack fae must have ticked him off.

Something to remember.

Then again, Averin had tried to help her, both during the earth-quake and when he'd freed her from the pyre.

The question was whether she should trust him. But with no other options, and enemies all around, who else could she turn to? As long as she kept her wits about her, trusting him would be the safest route ... for now.

"We need to get out of here," she said urgently. "There're hunters in the woods. My fire would have delayed them, but—"

"They can't see us. I've put up a glamour." Averin took a step closer. His gaze swept over her. "Are you hurt?" The usual amused glint in his eyes was replaced by something darker.

She shook her head, but his worried darkness didn't lift. "How did you find me?"

Averin shrugged. "We've been tracking you since you left the village. Radomir is a predictable bastard." He spat the name. "It didn't take too many guesses before we found you."

Her eyebrows creased. "We?"

Averin extended his chin in a slight nod. A twig crunched loudly behind her, as if someone was trying to be heard.

She turned.

The two fae who'd helped her and Klaus off the pyre stepped around the bough of a thick tree. So much for keeping her wits about her—she hadn't even known they were there.

The heavily-built one with the long chestnut-colored ponytail moved with swagger, grinning like an idiot. The dark-skinned one was silent, his brutally sculpted face blank, his blue eyes icy. Pene-trating as a wolf's, they seemed to take in every detail with one measured sweep.

She had to look away.

"Stasha." Averin stepped closer and gestured to his companions. "My first, Trystaen."

The grinning one dipped his head. Classically handsome, his eyes, the color of pine needles, reminded her of home. Blades glinted on his baldric.

"And my second, Eliezar."

The silent one didn't move.

Neither did she. Instead, she gulped out the only question that really mattered. "Averin, is Klaus okay? Did you see him before you left Askavol?"

Averin's lips thinned, and his face locked up, all amusement and lightheartedness gone.

Her knees shook. She clutched her pendant. *No. Please, no.*

Averin took a step closer. "He's alive."

She could have cried with relief. But Averin's frown suggested he wasn't done yet. Bile rose in her throat.

"After Radomir spirited you away, more Pyreack soldiers showed up at the village. We were outnumbered, so we had to fall back." Averin's shoulders tightened, and he inched closer, as if he were scared she'd bolt or that her trembling knees would buckle. "They brought prison wagons and loaded everyone inside. Including Klaus."

Her entire world swayed. "Prison wagons? Going where?" She knew on some level that she was shouting. She didn't care.

Averin hesitated, glancing between her and his companions. "To Angharad. In the heart of the Pyreack kingdom. They call it a 'work camp.' The rest of us know it as a death camp."

Klaus was going to a death camp.

Every inch of her body crackled with fire, fire so hot it threatened to melt her bones and make her skin drip. Just like that Tiyanak's had when Radomir had killed it.

Trembling, she screamed, "What do you mean he's in a death camp?"

Averin's sapphire eyes filled with something like despair. Grief.

Tears spilled down her cheeks. They turned to steam before reaching her chin. She screamed even louder. "You stood by and did nothing while my people—my *friend*, the only person I have left— was carted off to a *death camp*." She launched herself at him.

Averin didn't budge as she slammed into his chest. Screaming at the top of her lungs, she swung both her fists at his face. Before she made contact, he grabbed her hands gently but firmly and twisted her around until her back pressed against the hard warmth of his chest. "I'm sorry," he whispered in a forced breath. "I'm sorry."

Sorry wasn't enough.

She roared, a primordial sound filled with pain and fury as she thrashed in his arms. Heat shimmered like rippling water above her skin. Tears burned off her cheeks in salty steam.

Still Averin held her, even though he, too, must have been on fire. She brought her foot up to slam into his shin, but it snagged on her stupid dress—a dress that didn't burn even though she was engulfed in flames.

Averin flinched but held her in a tight embrace. The stink of burning leather sank into her pores. But still his grip remained firm.

Trystaen's grin vanished. Both he and Eliezar had shifted forward, poised to pounce.

Averin didn't summon them. He just kept repeating, "I'm sorry. I'm sorry."

She hated him for it. And she hated herself even more for leaving Klaus. For leaving Tarik. For being the last one left.

She'd done this to them. The earthquakes had come from her, from the cursed beacon she wore around her neck and loved so much.

The fire of self-loathing roaring in her core would never burn out.

And she didn't know if she wanted it to.

A soft wind rustled through the clearing. It was so cold, her breath puffed and her steaming tears froze. A Zephyr fae trying to cool the terrible heat pouring off her skin?

And still Averin held her.

In the end, she wasn't sure how long she fought in his arms. It could have been minutes. Or hours. Maybe even days. She didn't care. Finally spent, she slumped forward against his biceps. Her chin dropped onto his hands.

Averin loosened his grip just enough to free her, but not enough to evict her. She pulled away, rubbing her aching hands over her stinging eyes. She faced him and gaped. Her fire had burned right through his leathers. His chest was blistered and raw.

Hating this power that turned her into a weapon, she looked down at her boots.

But there was no denying what had happened to Klaus and Averin. She looked up and locked eyes with him. Voice hoarse, she said, "I'm going to Angharad. Are you coming with me?"

*N*o one moved. Perhaps Averin and his friends were shocked at her radical announcement. "Well," she demanded. "Don't think I'm going anywhere with you until I rescue Klaus."

Averin ran a hand over his blistered chest. It was already beginning to heal. "Stasha, my glamour won't hold forever. The rebels are still out there. And by now, Radomir is on your trail." A wry smile. "You kind of led them here."

She thumped her hands on her hips. "I need an answer." She threw her head back. "No. Two answers. One—is Angharad near the Pyreack capital with the unpronounceable name?"

"Phyrturq? Nowhere near it," Averin said.

That ruled out going back to Radomir.

Averin frowned at her. "But, Stasha—"

"And two," she almost yelled over Averin's objection. "Are you coming, or do I make my own way to Angharad?"

Averin, Trystaen, and Eliezar exchanged a look that suggested she didn't know what she was talking about. She didn't, but that didn't matter. She would find her way to Angharad if she had to beg, steal, lie or kill to do it.

Averin inched closer but didn't try to touch her. "There's a fae inn nearby. It'll be easier to defend ourselves there. Let's head over and talk about it."

Eliezar dug into his knapsack and pulled out a tunic. He tossed it to Averin, who pulled it on.

"Fine. Lead the way. But don't for one second think that you'll dissuade me."

"I wouldn't debase your grief by trying."

But instead of leading, Averin walked beside her while the other two took point. He didn't say anything, but she caught his surreptitious glances. Trystaen and Eliezar talked quietly, navigating their way through the frost-covered trees.

It was cold. So very cold.

Even her thick dress couldn't keep her shudders at bay. Exhausted, thirsty, and hungry, her feet snagged on every loose root and branch on the dark forest floor. But none of that shifted the fire raging under her skin.

A death camp. They'd taken Klaus, and everyone else in her village, to a death camp. How much time did Klaus have? How long did *she* have to get him out? She needed answers.

"How much farther till we get to this inn?"

"We're not far now." Averin slowed and scanned the forest ahead. Trystaen and Eliezar had gone silent. "I'd suggest keeping quiet for just a few minutes."

"Why?"

"There're a lot of predators in these woods," Averin whispered. "We don't want to attract attention." At least he was more expansive than Suren had been, even if he veered from specifics.

She whispered, "But you're fae. You can handle something like the Tiyanak, right?"

"I'm not talking about the Tiyanak," Averin whispered back. "And, yes, we can handle most things, but not if we're severely outnumbered, as we were in Askavol. Manticore like to travel in packs." His hands inched closer to his weapons. "We'll be fine if we can make it through to the inn undetected."

She sidled closer to him, eyeing a curved dagger strapped to his belt. She hoped there would be no need to use it. "Manticore? Are they real?" She'd heard stories about the terrible manticore with their pincered tails but had never really believed them.

Averin's lips tightened, and he rested his hand on his dagger hilt. "As real as you and me. Just keep quiet for the next few minutes."

She nodded and focused on placing her feet more carefully as she walked. Twigs and leaves still cracked under her boots. Even her breathing sounded too loud. She hated these woods.

Through the mesh of tree trunks and shifting leaves, a dark form loomed. She slapped a hand on Averin's arm, eyes frozen on the threat ahead.

Averin's fingers wrapped around hers in a reassuring squeeze. He leaned in closer. "It's just a broken building. This used to be a fae town. It was ruined in the war. Nothing more. Now keep quiet until we've passed."

She slipped her hand from his and slowly picked her way through the undergrowth until the ruin came into view. The ramshackle building was one of many broken, blackened structures in the village. Stone walls leaned haphazardly, as if they would topple at any moment. On one of the walls, a firebird crest had been carved. Other buildings had crumbled into nothing but gray pebbles and dust. Ivy and vines swallowed others whole. Trees grew up through long-decayed roofs. Old roof tiles littered the forest floor. Any roads that once existed were choked by thistles, shrubs, and weeds.

This could have been Teagarta. Only a Teagarta inhabited by fae, not humans. Was nowhere safe? Was there no sanctuary on Zathryth that hadn't been polluted by Pyreack?

Her cheeks burned. Humans were not the only ones to suffer at the hands of Pyreack. How many fae—how many innocents—had dwelled in this town? How many bones hid among the weeds?

She glanced at Averin as if he had the answers. His lips were tight, and his star-filled eyes hard. The hand he rested on his dagger was clenched. Bone-white. His other hand twitched with magic. A sharp, icy breeze billowed around them, flooding her with the reek of ashes and decaying leaves. She guessed he did it to keep their scent from any hungry faeries squatting in the ruins. Like the manticore.

The fae who'd once lived here, who had kept her world free of monsters like the Tiyanak and manticore, had done nothing to harm her, Tarik, or Klaus. These creatures—these *people*—were innocent. Even Suren, a Pyreack fae, had been as kind as his circumstances had allowed. And now here was Averin, son of Zephyr, whatever that meant, allowing her to burn him while she cried in his arms.

Perhaps her hatred for fae wasn't as black and white as she'd believed.

Her fight was with King Darien. He commanded fae like Radomir and Suren. It was King Darien who'd hurt everyone, regardless of who and what they were. A reign of death and fire. No one and nothing escaped unharmed from King Darien's evil touch. And he wanted to use her as a weapon.

She would die before she let that happen.

A new scent hit her. Piss and blood.

Averin drew his sword and pulled a throwing knife from his baldric. More steel rasped as Trystaen and Eliezar pulled their swords free. The three fae males slowed their pace, closing in around her.

Averin's wind whistled to a stop, and the world fell unnervingly silent.

Her breath shallowed. Tired and shaking with hunger, she wished she had a weapon.

She had fire.

She flexed her fingers, feeling the familiar burn, and then frowned. Why had Averin stilled his breeze? Surely now was the time for him and Eliezar to be throwing gales around, not knives. With Trystaen's green eyes, she suspected he wasn't a Zephyr fae, but he had to have magic that would help in a battle.

Steel on stone shrieked behind them.

Her fae companions spun almost too fast for her to see. Averin shoved her behind him. A hiss seeped from his clenched teeth.

A *thing,* easily eight feet tall, perched on a boulder ahead of them. Beneath a hooked, bird-like beak, its humanoid mouth spread in a wolfish smile of jagged teeth. They looked powerful enough to crush bone. Feathers plumed down its hunched back. Monstrous wings, each easily the size of a horse, curled around its leathery chest. Even more horrific-looking than the Tiyanak, it rasped its steely claws against the stone. Like it was sharpening them. They left thick, deep gouges in the rock.

She gulped.

The creature purred and swished its long tail. At the tip, pincers, the length of Stasha's leg, snapped.

"Brothers," it rasped, scraping its claws on the stone for a third time. "We eat well tonight."

"Yes-s-s," something behind her hissed. "What luck we have."

She spun.

Another two monsters bounded across the undergrowth toward her, boxing her and the fae males in, herding them like sheep.

Averin moved. Silver flashed, and a throwing knife imbedded in one of the approaching creature's chest.

Before it had finished shrieking, he had another throwing knife in his hand. A flick of his wrist, and the knife sank into the creature's eye. The monster tumbled face-first into the shrubbery.

Eliezar swiped its head off with his sword.

Pincers snapping, the other one took flight, sending a rush of air beating at her. His brother on the rock flapped his wings and screamed a shrill, deafening cry.

She remembered her magic. Hands up, she pointed one at the creature on the rock and the other at the one bearing down on her. She willed shafts of fire to burn the foul things to a crisp.

Averin grabbed her arm and shoved her to the ground, into the dust. "They're shielded against magic. Only blades work," he snapped as yet another beast swooped down from a nearby tree. Its steel claws sailed just an inch above Averin's head before it landed. Trystaen's sword crashed onto its pincers.

She strained to sit up, but Averin shoved her down again. "Don't move!" He thrust a dagger into her hands. "Use it if you have to." He let fly another throwing knife at the creature closest to them.

The monster swatted the blade out of the way, snarling.

Averin lunged at it with his sword leading.

A shriek to her right pulled her attention away from Averin. The leader perched on the boulder had her in its sights.

Before it could land on her, she jumped up to lunge at it with her dagger. Its claws lashed out and nicked her arm. The force spun her to the ground. Pain shot through her spine, making her gasp. It morphed into a wail as the creature crashed on top of her. Its beak drilled down toward her neck.

She dodged and rammed her dagger straight into its stomach.

Leathery, hard, and unyielding, its skin fought the dagger tip.

She drew on her last reserves and shoved with all her strength. The dagger slid through its hide and sank hilt deep into the creature's belly. Sticky blood splattered her already filthy dress.

Head tossing, the bellowing creature dragged its claws through the dirt before swiping at her again.

A blade flashed.

She blinked. When she opened her eyes, the creature's head lay on the ground next to her. More blood pumped on her from its severed neck. She scrambled out from between the monster's legs just as its headless body hit the ground. She lay on her back, gasping.

Silhouetted against the moonlight, their bloody weapons glinting, Averin, Eliezar, and Trystaen encircled her. Severed heads and mangled bodies littered the ground at their feet. Tails twitched, pincers opened and closed erratically.

"Sorry to cut short your fun, pit princess." Averin held out his hand to help her up. "But the only way to kill a manticore is to chop its head off. Leave the bastards, and they heal and come back angrier."

She coughed, trying to force a steady breath as she took his hand. He hauled her to her feet. Concerned eyes trailed the length of her blood-stained dress. "Any of that yours?"

She shook her head. "No. Just a scratch on my arm." She looked at her bicep. The gouge was more than a scratch.

Averin touched her arm with gentle fingers. "Not even the best healer can fix a manticore cut. I'm afraid your body will have to do this without magical help. But it does need cleaning."

Wordlessly, Eliezar dug into his knapsack and pulled out a tincture bottle. Averin took it and unscrewed the cap. He steadied the bottle over her wound. "This may sting a little."

She ground her teeth together. "Just do it." She still wore the manacle that had rubbed her wrist raw. That ached along with the cut.

Averin's fingers brushed the manacle. "That we'll sort out at the inn." He studied her as he drizzled tincture, drop by drop, into the cut. She hissed in pain. Another couple of drops, and the pain lessened until it was no more than a tickle, and the wound ran clean. He inspected her arm and grunted his satisfaction. "It looks good. It'll heal cleanly." Next, Averin offered her his waterskin. She grabbed it and gulped down mouthful after mouthful. Water spilled down her chin, but she ignored it. Finally, she pulled the skin away and burped.

Averin's head bobbed, and his eyebrows rose around a half smile.

"We need to move." Eliezar, the one who never smiled, tossed her the dagger she'd thrust into the manticore's belly. Given how taciturn he was, she was grateful he'd cleaned it first. "The blood will attract other predators," he added. "And if Pyreack are nearby, they'll scent it too. We need to get to the inn and clean up."

Clean up? Really? She was the only one covered in blood. The other three seemed to have made their kills without even breaking a sweat, let alone ending up ragged and bloody. Only their boots were stained from the red-purple puddles spreading out around them. It was humbling, and she shivered at yet another confirmation that Averin had let her whip his butt in the fighting pit.

Averin shrugged his thick cloak from his shoulders and wrapped it around her. It was much too big, and the hem trailed in the blood, but his warmth still clung to it. She murmured a thank-you.

A distant howl made her shoulders sag. *Not another fight tonight, please.*

Averin's head snapped up. "Let's go." He took the lead this time. Trystaen and Eliezar fell behind with her in the middle. None of them had sheathed their weapons.

The animal howled again, closer this time. How many more monsters would come here tonight to feast?

She glanced at the ruined town one last time, trying to imagine what it had been like before darkness had swallowed the world.

There'd have been pointy-eared children playing games of magic and laughter in the streets. Adults selling sweet-smelling flowers or prettily made pastries. They'd be dressed in bright colors, not the drab, shapeless gray she'd grown up wearing.

Carriages—without the crest of the two-faced god, almost as bad as the Pyreack firebird—would have clattered down cobbled roads. Traveling musicians might have played jolly tunes on fiddles or flutes. There would have been color everywhere, coats of it decking the rows of townhouses and shops. Polished windows would have displayed beautiful boots for girls like her to admire and buy. Red ribbons would represent life—hope—and not objects to be burned. Just as no one would want to burn fae or humans. This could have been such a happy place.

But now ... now, it was only lost dreams, and weeds, and blood seeping into the stones from dead monsters. Was that all that was left of the world?

There had to be something more. Some hope for a better world for *everyone*, just as Tarik had believed. Somewhere out there, it had to exist. And she was going to find it.

CHAPTER SEVENTEEN

A ROYAL BARGAIN

Stasha and the three fae males only rented one room at the inn. Dark and dank, it couldn't have been worth more than a handful of irons, but Averin paid for it with another of his stupid silver coins. She guessed the difference was meant to buy the surly fae innkeeper's discretion.

A single oil lamp lit the blotched wooden walls, damp from years of wear and rain. A quick investigation revealed no bathing alcove, and the landlord didn't offer to supply a bucket of water for washing. She itched from clothes stiff with dried manticore blood.

Two small cots, dressed in worn, raisin-colored quilts and each with a single pillow with no casing, sagged in the center of the room. She sank onto one of them. The thin mattress groaned beneath her weight. How she missed her own pallet at the orphanage. It was likely still buried under rubble, if it hadn't been burned to nothing.

None of her companions moved to the second bed. Averin and Trystaen searched the room, while Eliezar crouched beside her. He held out a handful of the dried fruit and nuts all fae seemed to thrive on. As she took his offering, she remembered that he'd cut Klaus's bonds and saved him from the execution pyre.

"Thank you," she wheezed, before devouring a handful of food. A thousand flavors, all delicious, exploded in her mouth as she chewed. Almost instantly, energy surged through her. No wonder they all munched this stuff like it was the finest, lightest pastry.

Eliezar put the pouch of nuts and fruit on her lap. His gaze dropped to her wrist. He dug in his knapsack and pulled out a thin, needle-like tweezer. Delicately, he slipped it into the lock and twisted.

The lock clicked, and the manacle snapped open. He chucked it into his knapsack and picked up her wrist. His pale-blue eyes inspected the wound. "Not worth calling on a healer." He glanced up at Trystaen. "But you may have a little scarring from the wear."

Trystaen nodded. "You'll be fine."

She expected Eliezar to move away, but he remained crouched at her side.

"I'm sorry about your friend," he murmured. Her eyes met his. The brutally beautiful planes of his face softened, offsetting his quiet, wolfish gaze.

"We've all lost someone we love to Angharad. I wouldn't wish it on anyone." He stood, crossed the room, and leaned against the door.

Averin turned to her. "We can stay here for a few hours, but we need to be up before dawn if we're going to make it out undetected by Pyreack."

"And go where?" Even charged with fae-snack energy, her voice was hoarse and sore, and her eyes smarted from exhaustion.

Averin tucked one hand under his bicep and clasped his shoulder with the other. The movement seemed cautious. Careful. Like he'd been on the night of the earthquake. Was he scared he'd spook her?

"I'm not going to panic and run again," she snapped. "And honestly, what did you expect me to do after being cornered by a fae in the middle of the forest?" The word *fae* came out with more venom than she'd intended.

If it affected him, he didn't let it show.

He sat on the edge of the second bed. Trystaen stood sentry at the window, and Eliezar hadn't moved from the door. Did they really perceive a threat, or did they simply want to avoid intruding on this conversation? Or maybe they only sought to give her a little privacy in her grief.

"We'll go back to Zephyr," Averin finally said. "My family can protect you."

She sat up and scoffed. Did he really see that as a solution? And how would her cowering in Zephyr free Klaus? Still, she wanted to know who Averin was. "Who's your family?"

Averin's lips tightened briefly. Then he said, "My family rules the Kingdom of Zephyr. My older brother, Rican, is crown prince."

That made his parents king and queen of Zephyr. Enemies of Pyreack, where her supposed heritage lay. And the fae sitting before her ... a prince.

She grabbed the pillow and stuck it on her lap, chuckling edgily. "And you think the king and queen of Zephyr are going to *help* someone with fire magic?" Not to mention the extensive power she was supposed to have. If it were enough for the king of Pyreack to demand her as a weapon, what was to stop Averin's royal house from doing the same?

She laughed louder. There was no humor in the sound. "I'd likely be skinned alive. Or used as a weapon or bargaining chip and given over to Pyreack anyway. That's probably what you're already planning."

Averin shook his head. "Zephyr isn't like Pyreack."

All the stories the Kňazer and Martka had ever told about fae came flooding back. How they plundered and murdered. How they cared nothing for human lives, or any lives other than their own. How they enslaved, brutalized, and murdered for sport.

She'd seen firsthand what they'd done to her village and to Teagarta. To the ruined fae town in the woods. To Tarik and Klaus. Lenka and Martka Alyona, and countless other lives.

What Radomir had done to the Tiyanak told her most about how fae treated the faeries they deemed lesser than themselves. Whether those fairies were a threat or harmless innocents, she didn't believe it would make a difference.

Not a single shred of her believed that Zephyr would be any different than Pyreack. Therefore, Averin's only possible motive for helping her was to use her as a bargaining chip against Pyreack or a weapon for Zephyr to bring *their* war to a new level of destruction, thus ending more innocent lives—both human and fae, who had no way of defending themselves.

A weapon and a bargaining chip.

Two could play this game.

She tossed the pillow aside. "I'm not going to Zephyr with you." Her voice broke, but not with grief. With conviction. "I'm going to get Klaus."

Trystaen and Eliezar shifted. Both turned pitying eyes on her.

Averin's lips parted slightly, something like exasperation flashing across his perfect face. It was gone so quickly that she almost doubted she'd seen it. "Getting into Angharad prison is easy. Getting out, impossible." He spoke with equal conviction. His eyes dulled, perhaps at some memory she didn't care to enquire about. That was also gone in a blink.

She crossed her arms over her chest and lifted her chin. Defiant. Angry. Just another fighting pit. Even if he'd let her win last time. "I don't care what you say. I'm going to get him."

Averin leaned forward, bracing his elbows on his knees. "I understand. Honestly, I do." His hands danced for emphasis. "But no one has ever successfully broken out of Angharad. *Ever*. Everyone who has ever come close has been killed."

She ground her teeth together, glaring at him. "Seems like a pretty good way to die then."

Averin's hard face yielded nothing as he studied her. "Stasha—"

She slammed her hand down onto her knee. "I will *not* abandon Klaus to die in that camp. And I will not be going to Zephyr with you either."

Averin's lips thinned. "If Pyreack doesn't capture you first, the rebels will. And they weren't exactly keen to sit and chat with you earlier tonight, were they?"

The archer and the hunters. Rebels.

"Who are the rebels?" Her fingers tightened on the dirty, warn sheets. Would he answer? Or would he fob her off the way Suren had?

"Fighters," Averin said. "From Zephyr, Atria, and Ocea. They even have a few defectors from Pyreack. They patrol the borders of Atria and Ocea. They're good at picking off Pyreack soldiers one by one. But where one is killed, three more take his place. It's not a fight they can win. And going to Angharad is not a fight you can win either."

She stuck her nose in the air and ran her gaze from his head to his well-crafted fae boots, making sure to look singularly unimpressed. "It's as you said: I like an underdog."

Averin rocked back, sighing his frustration. "It's not possible, Stasha. My *entire* army couldn't breach those walls and get out to tell the tale. An entire army of the best fae soldiers in my kingdom. Males and females trained to fight over decades. Some for centuries. If we couldn't do it, what makes you think you can?"

She glared at Averin, heat rising in her throat. "Because I grew up human. I got no training other than what I taught myself in the fighting pits. But still it seems I've got more guts than you and your entire stupid fae army put together, because I will *not* roll over and let them take him." She glanced at Eliezar and Trystaen.

Their faces were guarded, backs straight.

"Eliezar, you told me that you've all lost people to that place. Yet despite all your training and armies, you let it continue to exist." She jumped up. "Over my rotting corpse will I give Klaus up simply because cowards before me failed and then never tried again."

Eliezar stared at her out of those unnerving pale eyes. When she'd given up on ever getting an answer, he said, "You'll never make it alone, Stasha." His voice was harsh, shielding an open wound she'd poked. Who had he lost to Angharad? It had to be someone very dear to him.

But if she didn't at least try and rescue Klaus, she'd also spend the rest of her life nursing a wound that would never heal.

Time for the biggest bet of her life.

"I can if I have to. But that part's up to you."

Eliezar's black eyebrows creased together in his dark face, twisting his annoyingly handsome features.

Trystaen shuffled closer to her. His hand rested on a beautiful, wickedly curved silver dagger strapped to his belt. He could kill her before she had the chance to blink. And he would, if she tried to hurt Averin.

She ignored him and fixed her eyes on Averin—the prince with the final say here. If Averin refused, neither Trystaen nor Eliezar would help her. Freeing Klaus was more important than anything. Killing Radomir and then defeating the king of Pyreack, whilst vital, paled to nothing compared to rescuing Klaus. Without him in her world, there would never be hope.

And she could not live without hope.

So, it was time to be wise. Like the Tiyanak insisted she was: a wise little fae. Perhaps she could employ some of its tricks.

In case Averin's skull was so thick that her objections hadn't penetrated, she said, "Averin, I'm not going with you to Zephyr while Klaus rots in a death camp." Before he could reply, she tossed her bet into this game of wills. "But I will make you a deal."

Exquisite eyes suddenly sharp and canny, Averin tilted his head. "What deal, pit princess?" He stood and paced. Like a wolf.

She took a deep breath, hoping he and his fae friends couldn't hear her racing heart. "Help me get Klaus out and somewhere safe, and I will help you with one thing. I will go to Zephyr with you."

None of them moved. None of them spoke.

"That's two things," Averin finally said.

"Take it or leave it."

Averin frowned, so she moderated her tone. "That's what you want, isn't it? It's why you bet a stupid amount of money on Vlad. To butter me up. And why you followed me. Cornered me outside the shop and challenged me to a fight and then followed me through the woods when the fight was over?"

Averin's face yielded nothing.

"You want your bargaining chip?" She tossed her hands out, and fire sparked on her fingertips. "Here I am. Outnumbered by three fae males all armed to the teeth. I've been around fae long enough now to know that eye color matters." She glanced first at Averin and then at Eliezar. "Blue eyes mean that you both have air magic." She glanced at Trystaen with his pine-green eyes. "Who knows what he is, but he wouldn't be with you if he wasn't powerful. So you'll have no trouble attacking me and taking me against my will." She flicked sparks across the room. They settled on the wooden floor and smoldered dangerously.

None of the fae moved.

She sauntered to the embers. "Just know that I *will* fight you every step of the way, and I *won't* hesitate to hurt you unless you help me rescue Klaus." She stomped on the fire, extinguishing it. "Help me get him and the rest of my village, Martka and Kňazer included, somewhere safe, and you can do whatever you want with me."

Klaus would kill her if he heard this.

Averin stared at her.

The blood pounding through her ears was deafening in the silence.

And still Averin stared at her.

Her mouth dried, but she refused to swallow. To do so would show weakness. Averin, son of Zephyr, would devour weakness.

"Trystaen—" Although Averin addressed his first, he didn't shift his piercing gaze from her. "Contact Princess Boadicea. Arrange a meeting. Don't tell her about Stasha. Just say Prince Averin requests an audience."

He wasn't buying her deal! Worse, he could be bringing more enemies to take her. She flitted her gaze from Averin to the closed window. It was too small for her to climb through, should she need to run. "Who is Princess Boadicea?" She struggled to keep her voice steady.

Trystaen nodded once at Averin and moved to the door. Fire twitched her fingers, a plea to burn Trystaen. Averin shifted between her and his first. Eliezar and Trystaen would kill her if she hurt Averin. She let the sparks die. Feet making no noise on the wooden floor, Trystaen left the room.

Averin raised both hands, almost placatingly. "Princess Boadicea is heir to the Kingdom of Ocea and the leader of the rebels. If we're really going after Angharad, we'll need help. Like all of us, she has a score to settle."

Relief made her knees weak. It was short-lived. "The rebels tried to kill me tonight. How do you think they're going to react when I come for help? I have fire magic, after all."

Averin nodded, forehead creased. "They might be more inclined to listen if they know your plans."

Plans? Her mouth opened and closed like a fish's.

A quiet chuckle from Averin. "As I thought. The pit princess is all fire and fury—until the fist needs to connect with the jaw."

She bristled. "That's not fair—"

Eliezar left his spot at the door. "Averin, do you want me to contact the Azura?" He towered like the shadow of death over her.

How old was this fae? How many years of training had he received to look so fierce? He didn't look a day over twenty-five. None of them did, but she knew her eyes deceived her. She glanced at the array of knives hanging around Eliezar's waist and was glad he was on her side—almost.

"They could all get here within five days," Eliezar continued. "The captains could spirit a few groups in tomorrow."

"No." Averin shook his head. "We can't risk this getting back to Rican."

"Our fae wouldn't talk."

"They also wouldn't refuse their crown prince if he asked." Averin's boot tapped on the floor. "We're not putting them in a position where they have to lie."

"Lie about what?" she demanded.

"We just need Princess Boa and the rebels on our side."

She bristled that Averin had ignored her question.

"Will that be enough?" Eliezar's dark eyes flicked to her for a moment before turning back to Averin.

"You can speak freely in front of her," Averin said. "She's not going anywhere."

She clenched her fists. "How many men are in your army? And what lie are you talking about?"

Averin pivoted slowly to look at her. "My armies are extensive. But that's not what we're talking about. I have a hundred fae I personally trained. We call them the Azura. They fight very specific battles for key objectives."

"And these are the fae you used when you tried to take Angharad?"

A shallow headshake, as if the question pained Averin. "No. I created the Azura after Angharad, in case we ever found ourselves in a similar situation."

"Then if this is such a situation, why aren't you using them?"

Averin's face shuttered. "I'd rather my family didn't know that we're risking so much on this venture."

Risking her? Is that what he wasn't saying? And if so, what exactly did the Zephyr royals want with her?

A worry for when Klaus was freed.

"How many rebels can the princess bring?"

Averin's lips tightened. "That depends on her, and what you have to say to convince her. You better pray to whatever gods you believe in that she agrees to help."

She crossed her arms. Over her dead body would she ever pray for anything.

Except maybe for Klaus.

CHAPTER EIGHTEEN

RAVEN REVEALED

Trystaen returned a few hours later, flushed with cold. Princess Boadicea had accepted their offer to meet, but on her terms. No spiriting in. All weapons seized upon arrival. And she chose the location. One day's walk from the pathetic excuse of an inn where they'd spent the night.

They left the inn before first light, having gotten no more than a couple hours of fitful sleep. A fluttering of snow had fallen in the night. It coated the ground and trees in a thin layer of crisp fluff. While her feet rasped through the frost, the others were as silent as ghosts.

Averin walked ahead with Eliezar. They talked in hushed tones. Trystaen followed at her side. She didn't need them to tell her that she was holding them up.

Despite her cold-numbed cheeks, she flushed at her clumsy *mortalness* compared to their otherworldly grace. Her limbs were more streamlined and agile than they'd been before, but she couldn't match fae who'd existed and trained for who knew how long. As always, her blush deepened as she recalled her "fight" with Averin. To add to her misery, she still stank of blood and mud. Averin had insisted that she wear his cloak. Grateful for its warmth, it was still heavy on her shoulders.

Thankfully, there was no sign of Pyreack soldiers or Tiyanak as they traipsed through the dark woods. She toyed with the idea of telling Averin about her Tiyanak and the deal she'd made. But Averin had his secrets. Why else would he risk his and his friends' lives by attacking Angharad?

No, better to keep that scrap of information to herself.

After two hours of trudging, the sun crested the horizon. It did little to thaw the snowy frost. Already winded and tired—it would take more than a pouch of nuts and dried fruit to repair years of malnutrition—her mouth was dry and her lips cracked. She rasped a breath, panting through the stitch that ripped her side. As usual, her fae companions had barely a hair out of place. They strolled like they were out on a morning jaunt through a tranquil forest.

She scowled at Averin's back and stuck out her tongue.

Trystaen chuckled roughly, the sound meeting his lovely pine-green eyes. He swept his ponytail over his shoulder. Like her braid, it was tied with a leather strap. How she missed her red ribbon.

"You'll get used to your new body," Trystaen said with certainty. "You just need to eat more." He gestured to the pouch of fae-snack hanging off her belt.

She shoved a handful of the sweet stuff into her mouth. She swallowed almost without chewing. "I'm still not entirely sure what anything is anymore. And those bastards from Pyreack weren't in the mood to explain. Or I wasn't in the mood to listen."

"Being one thing for so long and then being forced to survive as something else isn't easy."

"You say that like you know."

A sure nod. "I do know. Maybe not quite to the same extent, going from mortal to fae like you have, but I have my own story."

"Care to share?" Her foot snagged on Averin's cloak. The hem was soaked in a mixture of old blood and melting snow. She'd be glad to ditch the heavy thing as soon as she got a chance.

Trystaen smiled good-naturedly, as if he didn't mind chatting about himself. "Technically, I'm from Atria, not Zephyr—hence my eye color. It's where I was born, where I grew up. My family was one of the noble houses. Not one of the royals, but noble. Before your time."

Her stomach looped. How old was he?

"How much history do you know?" he asked.

She rolled her eyes and laughed. "Everything there is to know.

After all, I did spend *all* my time holed up in libraries reading books —when I wasn't fighting for survival in the pit."

Trystaen chuckled. "Dumb question then."

"No. You just asked the wrong person. Klaus is the one with book learning."

"I see." Trystaen cocked his head. "You interested in learning some?"

"Yes, please." It would help her make sense of things.

"Voltaic, the fifth kingdom on Zathryth, originally started the war. It didn't go well for them. Pyreack quickly wiped them out. King Darien got a taste for victory and conquest. Instead of withdrawing back to Pyreack, he went on the rampage. His forces almost destroyed every noble family in Ocea and Atria, mine included." He brushed back a low-hanging branch for her. "When King Darien attacks a kingdom in earnest, he always tries to eradicate any power standing between him and the monarch." He offered a hand to help her over a particularly large log.

She pretended not to notice, hitched up her ruined dress, and climbed over herself. Frosty air snaked up her bare leg, raising goose bumps. "I didn't even know there was a fifth kingdom on Zathryth."

Trystaen waited for her to start walking, then fell into step with her. "It's no wonder. Voltaic have been gone for a very long time. They occupied an island just off the coast of Pyreack, although it was still considered part of Zathryth."

"Voltaic." She rolled the word on her tongue. "What power did they have?"

Trystaen's eyes sparkled, as if he enjoyed teaching her. It was a change from Suren. And Radomir. "Lightning."

Her eyes widened. "Sounds powerful. How come they lost to Pyreack so quickly?"

Trystaen shrugged. "Ivarune, their king, fell. The rest were wiped out within ten years. No one survived."

"King Darien killed Ivarune?"

"No. Prince Cyran, his eldest son, poisoned him. At Ivarune's death, the keys passed to Cyran. He vanished just hours before King

Darien reached his palace. That stopped King Darien from stealing his magic." Trystaen laughed softly. "Darien has been in a foul mood ever since."

"That sounds rather cowardly."

"That depends on how you see things. Some would say it was wise. He stopped the keys to lightening falling into Darien's hands."

She hated to break Trystaen's jovial mood, but she had to know. "And your family?"

"They were destroyed in Pyreack's first attempt at invading Atria. I was the only survivor." He said it matter-of-factly, as if the massacre of his people had happened so long ago that he'd become resigned to it.

Still, her heart ached. He did know how she felt, perhaps more than he realized. Like her, he was the last one standing. Had he once hated himself for it too? Despite his apparent calm, did his heart fill with cold loathing whenever he thought of his dead family? His friends? Everything that had been stolen from him?

"Averin and Rican and...." Trystaen's voice trailed off. Before she could enquire, he cleared his throat and continued, "They were my friends, even then, when we were younglings. They and their father— King Seph—offered me sanctuary. And, eventually, a place in the Azura. And then as Averin's first." He offered her his waterskin as he spoke.

She accepted with a small smile. The icy water that spilled down her throat was so delicious, it could have been honey. She wiped her hand across her mouth and gave it back to him. "Pyreack ... have they ever attacked Zephyr?"

Trystaen took a swig, then capped the skin. "Many times. Never had much success, though." He glanced at her. "You know, of course, that Ocea fell sixty years ago? Darien captured most of King Appius's keys." He grimaced, shadows flickering in his pine-green eyes. "Atria isn't far behind."

She needed a good grasp of all this if she stood any hope of figuring out why the Zephyr royals wanted her. Was that why Trystaen took such pains to educate her?

"These keys ... are they actual keys that can open a lock?"

"Not exactly. It's more ethereal than that. Monarchs control all magic in their realms. We call that 'keys.' All it takes to steal the keys from a vanquished monarch is a simple spell."

Her nose crinkled; spells came straight out of the stories the Martka used to tell. "There are such things?"

"Oh yes. Very much so. Pyreack use a particularly nasty one when they marry. They bind the female's magic to the male, so it becomes his to use instead of hers."

Her stomach rolled with nausea.

Was that what King Darien had planned to do to her? She scowled. Why did the world think she could be farmed off in marriage like chattel? Just like she had tried to flee from Askavol, she would never agree to marry King Darien. But perhaps choice didn't even enter into the deal, if he found her.

Trystaen continued, seemingly oblivious of her need to launch the water and fae-snack she'd just consumed across the bracken. "When Pyreack soldiers conquer other kingdoms, Darien uses a similar spell to bind the monarch's magic to his. He uses his new stolen magic to control the kingdom. That's what he did to Ocea. He just didn't anticipate Boa getting in the way."

She absentmindedly stroked a chilled finger up her ear to the fae point. "Radomir said stuff happened when I was born. What do you know about that?"

Trystaen hesitated.

What could be worse than what he'd already told her?

A sigh, then Trystaen said, "The entire continent knew when you were born. Not because of some decree or declaration. The world literally shook with a new power." He looked at her with wonder. "Your power."

The blood chilled in her veins. "What did I do?"

"Earthquakes shattered northern Atria. Floods and drought hit Ocea. Tornados in Zephyr no one could control. Mountains rose and fell. Even the Blue Desert responded. It burned all night with wild-fire." Trystaen spoke so quietly and with such absolute *reverence* that her body pitted with goose bumps.

"And my parents? Does anyone know who they were?" She held her breath. Maybe he could explain her gray eyes.

Trystaen shook his head, then smiled sadly at her. "Sorry. I wish I had good news for you, but no one seems to know where you came from, or who you are, or why you have so much power."

"Could I be from Voltaic? Did they have gray eyes?" And how would Martka Alyona have met them?

"Theirs were gold. And you shoot fire, not lightning. And how could you have caused earthquakes and floods? That's not Voltaic's power."

She kicked out at a tuft of weeds. "How can nobody know anything after that ... display?"

Trystaen shrugged. "Everyone wanted answers, but the power disappeared right after your birth." His voice became wistful. "No one forgot that magic. An unstoppable wave of raw power that tore the world apart." He waved his arms in a flourish. "And voila! A year ago, we felt it again."

She hated asking but had to know. "As powerful as before?" That magic had led to Tarik's death. And Lenka's. How many others, both fae and human, had died?

"Just a rumble. But enough. More than enough to get Darien's soldiers hunting for you. Because your amber was sending out earthquakes, we all guessed you were somewhere in Atria." Trystaen's face hardened. "The rest of us could not allow Darien to get you." He glanced at Averin. "He's been looking for you for months."

She resisted the urge to clutch her pendant—betrayer that it was. She swallowed. "Why not just kill me outright if I'm so dangerous?"

Trystaen grinned almost boyishly at her. "Because Zephyr royals aren't Darien Pyreaxos." He waved a hand at her. "And you're of more use to the entire continent of Zathryth alive than dead."

She gnawed her lip. Whoever her parents were, they must have known the threat she posed, and the threats she would inevitably face. Yet, they'd left her defenseless in a human orphanage, where she could have starved to death.

Martka Alyona may have known more about her background than the old woman let on, but that hadn't resulted in better care or more food. Her parents must have had confidence in her innate ability to survive.

She blinked back the headache burning behind her eyes. She needed to think of something else. Anything else.

Klaus. Focus on Klaus. On getting him out. That was all that mattered now.

She stared ahead at Averin strolling with Eliezar. No doubt he'd listened to their entire conversation. Busybody. "What's his tie to Angharad?"

Trystaen's face locked up, an unwavering wall replacing the interest that had lit it just moments before.

"Rest break," Averin called out. "Let's eat."

Averin had indeed been eavesdropping. She scowled and sank onto a fallen log, breathing heavily.

Eliezar pulled a leather pouch from his knapsack. He held it out to her. Dried meat. She took a strip and sniffed. Very spicy. "What is this?" She grimaced. "Not human, I hope."

Averin and Trystaen burst into laughter. Even Eliezar cracked a smile.

"You're fae," Trystaen said through his laughter. "Would you eat one of your human friends?"

She blushed. "Of course not." She sat up taller and cracked a half smile to cover her embarrassment. "My enemies could be another matter."

"We'll bear that in mind." Averin grinned and bumped her shoulder. "Eat it. You're too thin to be healthy. You need to keep your strength up."

"Being an orphan will do that to a girl." She smirked, as if her scrawniness was a badge of honor.

Trystaen wagged a finger at her. "You aren't an orphan anymore. You're among friends now, not enemies. We care. Like family. So eat."

Her chest warmed with ... something. No one other than Klaus or Tarik had ever called her family. Feral Fox had come close.

They just want to use me.

She frowned the comforting sensation away.

But why not use them first to fatten herself up for the coming fight? She snatched a handful of the meat and tore into a strip with her teeth. It was surprisingly good.

Averin snorted, then turned to Trystaen. "I'm going to do a sweep of the woods. Don't move unless you have to. I'll keep track from the sky."

Trystaen gave a mock salute while taking another bite of meat.

Averin morphed into a flash of sparkling blue light so dark it was almost black.

She gawked.

When the light extinguished, Averin had vanished. In his place, a raven flapped inky-black wings. The same raven she'd seen at the shop with Klaus that fateful day. And the same raven that had flitted past her head when captured by Radomir.

Her jaw hung open. "That was *you* terrorizing me?"

The raven's caw was the only indication of Averin's laughter as he swept up through the trees and out of sight.

She glowered, heart, cheeks, and ears heating up.

Trystaen chuckled. "He's a shape-shifter. So's his brother, Rican. One of the powers bestowed upon a lucky few in Zephyr."

She grunted around a mouthful of meat. That must have been how Averin had heard all her conversations with Klaus. Was there any chance one of her "powers" would be flight? That would make all of this worthwhile.

Averin wasn't gone long before he soared back through the trees on effortless wings. One flash of blue-black magic, and he was fae again. No sign of the feathers and claws. He chuckled while she gaped at him. "You were so confident, bragging about your silver coins," he said, recalling the same memory she blushed at. "And then betting one of them on yourself. It was quite entertaining."

She snapped her sagging mouth closed. "You seem to forget that

I laid you flat on your ass," she said, trying to cover her shame. "At least for a short while." She tore into her meat, smirking. The pepper and spices made her mouth water. "Even if you did let me win."

Averin's sapphire eyes gleamed. "You've figured that out, huh?"

"I'm not stupid. You're a fae who's been training for, I don't know, a couple of billion years." Averin's eyebrows shot up, and Trystaen coughed a laugh. Even Eliezar's dark lips twitched.

Averin blinked, feigning offense. "I'm not *that* old."

"Could have fooled me," she said, not caring that her mouth was full of chewed-up meat. "Why did you let me win?"

Averin shrugged. "I didn't think you'd want to talk to me if you lost. As it was, you had a few"— a rakish smile—"issues. You still owe me a drink."

She glared at him. "I'm not a sore loser. And I pay my debts." She grabbed the waterskin from Trystaen and held it out to Averin. "Here. Drink."

Averin laughed and grabbed the skin from her. He took a long swig and wiped his mouth on the back of his long, slender hand. "Don't get me wrong; you're a decent fighter ... for a mortal. But you wouldn't last very long against a fae."

She tore off another piece of meat. "Well, I'm not mortal anymore." Pain lanced her as the words finally came out.

Not mortal. Not just Stasha. Fae. A weapon. And what else—who else—she had no idea anymore.

She swallowed the meat—it suddenly tasted like tar—and tucked the other strips into her fae-snack pouch.

Time for business.

"How long will it take for Klaus to arrive at Angharad? How long do we have?"

All amusement faded from Averin's eyes. "He'll be on a ship by now, crossing the Vocril Sea. The waterway was once under King Appius of Ocea's control. Now it belongs to Darien. They'll dock before the day is over, if pirates or rebels don't get them first. And then they'll be transported to the camp."

She clawed the log she sat on. "By that you mean, if someone doesn't sink it?"

Averin hesitated, then nodded. "Only half the ships make it. The rebels manage to liberate some, but not many. Pirates get the rest."

"It was never like that when Appius controlled things," Trystaen grumbled.

More lawlessness, thanks to King Darien Pyreaxos's greed for power.

Averin sat next to her on the log. "It's why Radomir chose to transport you by land. Even I wouldn't risk the crossing."

His body brushed her side.

Unexpected warmth rushed through her. The heat was way out of proportion to his touch. Surprised and unsure what to make of it, she shifted slightly to put some air between them. "When will we know if Klaus and everyone else from Askavol has landed?"

Averin stood and propped his boot on the log. "When we get to Boa. She has scouts and spies in every kingdom."

"And if his ship didn't make it?"

"We'll talk about that if it happens."

She scowled. "And once he docks?" She refused to consider the alternative. "How long do we have to get to him?"

The three friends shared a look that suggested history—a painful one.

Averin answered. "Once in Pyreack, they can spirit him wherever they want. Not all fae can spirit, especially over long distances, but they have captains and generals who can. It won't take more than a few hours for them to reach the camp. Darien is in constant need of labor to mine his gold. It pays for his war effort, so his fae won't dally."

Her gray eyes froze. She leaped up, almost knocking Averin over. "You're telling me he'll be in Angharad by morning?"

Averin quickly found his feet. But when he looked at her, unyielding sadness clouded his face. The shocking blueness, the sparkling stars in his eyes, was as dull as ditchwater.

Darkness swallow them all! What could have happened to make him look like that?

Guessing she'd get no answer, she asked, "And Princess Boadicea can get us there?"

"She's King Appius's heir," Trystaen answered. "Before his magic was taken and his capital sacked, he transferred the spiriting key to her."

"How does that help us?"

"Boa controls the border," Averin said. "No one can spirit into Ocea without her permission. It's the one card they have to play against Darien, the only foothold they have left in their own land."

So that was why Radomir and Suren couldn't spirit into Ocea. Radomir and his band could only cross over on foot. It explained why they had been so cautious, and why they wouldn't tell her the truth. It would have exposed weakness.

"So she can get us where, exactly?"

Averin answered. "Close enough to the Pyreack border to make it count. We'll have to walk the rest of the way. That's going to be the tricky bit."

So many rules. So many restrictions. So many obstacles blocking her path to Klaus.

"We should keep going," Averin said, closing his pack and swinging it over his shoulder.

No one said anything as they followed him through the woods.

She glanced south, as if she could see the ocean so many miles away. As if she could see the ship carrying the last person she had left to his death.

The time she had to save him was quickly running out. Everything depended on what she'd say to Princess Boadicea. She set her mind to creating arguments as to why the princess had to help her.

Pity nothing as impregnable as Angharad came to mind.

As always, she'd just have to wing it.

*E*xhaustion tugged at Stasha, begging her to stop and rest, to drink more water, to eat more food, to sleep for the next decade, but when Averin and then Trystaen offered to stop, she'd refused. Even Eliezar's pale-blue eyes watched her with concern.

Didn't they understand the urgency?

In just hours, Klaus would arrive in Angharad. With his crippled leg, not to mention his malnutrition, he would likely not survive long. Each moment she wasted on the trail was a moment stolen from him. There was no time to stop, no time to sit still and rest, and no room for error.

The sun set, plunging the already gloomy forest into darkness. Even though they lit no torches, she saw far more clearly in the dark than she had when mortal. A few minutes later, Averin finally stopped in the middle of a small clearing. This one looked exactly like every other clearing they'd traveled through—thick with dark papery trees. Wings fluttered as circling bats greeted the misty evening sky. Dead leaves and thorny brambles littered the ground.

"Is this the place?" she wheezed, resisting the urge to place her hands on her knees and pant.

Averin nodded. He wrapped his hand around the hilt of the sword strapped to his waist.

"There will be no need for that."

Stasha's blood stilled. She recognized that voice.

Five figures stepped from behind the trees. Four carried swords and daggers. The fifth had a bow and quivers strung across her back. The hunters and archer from the night before.

The rebels.

Averin released his sword, but the tension didn't shift from his shoulders. Who would win in a fight between them? "We requested a meeting with Princess Boa," he said. "We were told to meet here."

"Prince Averin," a tall, solid fae answered. His thick, dark hair was tied back with a cord. "We're here to lead you to Her Highness. And to relieve you of your weapons."

Averin's lips tightened, but he nodded once. Following his lead, Trystaen and Eliezar unbuckled blades and swords from their waists and baldrics, and then extracted more from hidden pockets on their thighs and in their tunics. Averin even pulled a blade out of his boot. Stasha handed over the dagger Averin had given her.

The burly fae hefted the weapons into a thick sack, which he hung over his shoulder. His fae companions patted them all down, searching for any concealed trickery.

Satisfied they were unarmed, the archer stalked to the line of trees where the fae had appeared from. "Right this way." A long, golden braid peeked from her hooded cloak.

The remaining hunters flanked them on all sides. She stepped closer to Averin, swallowing hard as they followed in tense silence.

Her heart burned. So much rode on this meeting. All she could hope was that Princess Boadicea would feel her passion and would respond in kind.

They hadn't walked more than five minutes before torchlight flickered through the labyrinth of trees. The rebel camp.

Unlike Radomir's, this was informal. Simple. And utterly intimidating. Perhaps even more so than Ealvera War Camp.

Torches staked along a path hacked through the forest illuminated every tent and flag that danced in the cold wind. A fish crest flew on some of them, on others, a great tree emblazoned with a woman's face. Some had both. Nowhere did she see the ugly firebird.

Good.

Still, how could the camp be so well lit, so ... open? How did it escape detection? And why hadn't they seen all these glowing lights from yards off?

The golden-haired archer led them silently down a row of torches. Her feet made no sound on the leaf-covered ground. Fae clad in fighting leathers stopped what they were doing to stare. Suspicious eyes narrowed on them, and steel rasped as weapons were drawn. So, being a prince of Zephyr didn't afford Averin any special treatment here? Would their lack of affection for him damage her chances of obtaining the princess's help?

Fists balled to hide her shaking hands, she stared straight ahead.

They reached the largest tent in the camp. The blue flaps were pulled back to reveal a makeshift dais, and the starkly beautiful woman seated on it. Her hands, as black as coal, lay folded in her lap. Hair the color of onyx hung in severe lines to her lower back. Gold seashell combs pushed it back from the high, sharp cheekbones any artist would drool to behold. No human woman could look like that—so predatory and feline in her brutal, elegant beauty.

Princess Boadicea. Heir of the Kingdom of Ocea. And her best chance at reaching Klaus before it was too late.

The fact that Princess Boadicea's throne was nothing more than an old wooden chair covered with a gray pelt did nothing to detract from her majesty.

The archer stopped before the dais and dropped into a low bow, the arrows in her quiver rattling. She straightened again, but her hands remained close to her weapons. "Your Highness, I present Prince Averin of the Kingdom of Zephyr."

Averin dipped his head. Respectful. Elegant. Diplomatic. A prince bowing to a princess. "Crown Princess Boa." A slight smile tugged his lips. "You are looking well."

Princess Boadicea didn't return the smile. Her startling mauve eyes were cold, unimpressed. Khol lines framed her lashes.

Sweat beaded Stasha's hands. She buried them in her cloak before the formidable princess could see her fear.

"It's been an age since I last had the privilege of your company," Averin continued, as if he hadn't noticed her disdain.

The princess's full lips pulled into a sneer. "Not long enough,

Averin. I'm curious to see what brings you here now." The princess's eyes flickered to Stasha and then back to Averin.

It took all her self-control not to back away.

Averin met the princess head on. Sapphire blue caressing that strange mauve rimmed with flecks of gold.

"I also wish to know who accompanies you." The princess threw out a hand. Stasha could have sworn she saw sky-blue lines snaking along the princess's arms. Some sort of tattoo. "I know the males. But the female I don't recognize."

Averin inclined his head to her, indicating she should step forward.

Her stomach churned as she met the princess's intimidating stare. "Princess Boadicea," she said, almost shocked that she could speak at all, let alone with such confidence. "My name is Stasha." She held her breath, waiting for any sign of recognition. None was obvious, at least to her. Undaunted, she pushed on. "I have come to seek your aid."

The princess didn't respond. Waiting. Watching. Unyielding.

She coiled her fists around her ruined cloak to keep them still. "I was captured by Pyreack a few days ago. I escaped. But they—"

"Why were you captured?" the princess interrupted. "What's so special about you that stopped them from just killing you?"

Stasha bit down on her lip. Despite deciding to wing it, every idea and thought had disappeared from her head. Cursing her trembling fingers, she reached into her dress and pulled out her amber pendant.

The princess's eyes fell on the stone. She gasped, the sound sharp in the silence. Something in her expression clicked into place. As if the necklace were enough to tell her what magic stood before her— the same magic that had shaken the world eighteen years before.

The archer and hunters standing on either side of the tent echoed their princess's sharp-eyed interest.

The princess's lips parted, her dark skin paling. "It's you—" She looked up at Averin. "You found her? Is she going to Zephyr, or—"

Negotiating for her already? Not happening!

Stasha raised her voice. "I had no idea who or what I was until a few days ago, but I have fire magic. Radomir claims that makes me part of Pyreack." She tucked the pendant back beneath her collar. "But I want no part in their war. They sacked my village and sent my people to Angharad."

Any blood left in the princess's face drained. Her now chalk-pale lips pulled together into a tight line.

Stasha didn't stop. She couldn't, or else she'd never say what she needed to. "I won't leave them there." Her voice broke. "I can't leave *him* there." She ground her teeth together to stop hated tears burning her eyes. It didn't help. Voice swollen with emotion, she finished, "So, I want your help getting them out."

The princess leaned forward. "Prove it," she hissed. "Prove to me that you are who you say you are and you didn't just steal that amber. And that you're not working with Pyreack." Rage poured from the woman. Icy, glittering rage. "And, believe me, girl, when I say that if you lie to me, I will *personally* spill your guts on the floor. And I'll enjoy doing it."

Every instinct in Stasha's body told her to run. That she wouldn't bet on herself in a fight against the fae princess.

But Klaus was just hours away from Angharad.

She took a deep breath as heat rose in her bones. She risked a glance at Averin.

He stood with his arms folded across his chest, leaving this to her. Just as he'd said he would.

So what could she show the princess to convince her? Fire would just prove that she was a Pyreack fae. That could make them think she was a spy.

Klaus would stumble and fall on his maimed leg. The fae would stomp on him, kick him. The bright wisdom in his very human tawny eyes would dull. He would—

"Show me your power, girl." The princess's fingernails dug into the arms of her chair.

Anger and fear. Fear and anger. Tarik and Klaus. Anger over her dead love, fear for the death of her only friend. The last person she had left.

What could she show?

Fire shot from her palms. It slammed against a shimmering barrier of water. Doused, the flames rebounded, crashing into the ground at her feet. Instead of extinguishing, they ran along the shield like a snake rearing its head, hissing to be let out.

The shield spluttered and steam crackled, but it stood firm.

This was her test. Breach the shield. Sweat broke on her lip. She had to pass.

She reached in, calling on the furnace in her core. Fire exploded from her feet, then from her ankles. The hem of her dress and cloak ignited, but still she pulled on the flames. They curled up her legs, yet she felt no pain. She tossed her head back, threw her hands out so the fire could flow, and turned in a full circle of exhilaration.

A living torch, she sprayed fire across the tent. Hastily tossed-up shields popped and spluttered as tongues of flame easily ten feet long and three feet broad raked them. On she reeled, head spinning with giddiness.

She had never felt so free. So alive.

Icy water doused her.

"Enough!"

Staggering to a stop, she peered at the princess through bleary, unfocused eyes.

Why did water pour from the princess's hands? It crashed down the dais to drench a sea of dancing flames. Pressed hard against the tent walls, everyone, Averin, Eliezar, and Trystaen included, cowered.

She dropped her arms to her sides, and the fire spilling from her fingers died. Steam hissed as more frosty water splashed her feet, soaking through her boots. Boots that had survived the furnace. Her eyes shot to her dress. Half sorrow and half relief filled her that the ugly thing had also survived. She guessed it beat standing in front of everyone naked. The very notion made her blush.

She forced a cocky smile and faced the princess. Had she done enough to pass?

The princess leaned back in her chair, and her steamy water evaporated into nothing. A thin line of sky-blue slithered around her fingers, then retracted as her hands folded in her lap. That strange, living tattoo.

Stasha let loose a shaky breath, trying to keep from gasping at the beautiful magic. She snapped her focus back to the results of the test —and the fae who held Klaus's destiny in her hands.

Black fingers rapped the rickety throne's armrest. "Impressive. Very. I defy that chamber pot swill who now calls himself king of Ocea to toss that much fire around."

Stasha's eyes drifted to Averin. He, Trystaen, and Eliezar had dropped their shields and straightened their backs. Averin watched her with his head canted. The speculation in his eyes instilled no comfort.

"Girl! Look at me."

Her head shot back to the princess. The golden-haired archer had sidled closer to Princess Boadicea. Bow in hand, the archer had a schorl arrow targeted at Stasha's heart.

Were they *that* scared of her?

Not that the princess needed such protection. No one seeing the waves of hate crashing in the princess's eyes at the mention of King Darien could doubt the power rolling beneath her skin.

What had King Darien done to her?

It wasn't just the invasion of her homeland. This was something else. Something far deeper. An invisible wound filled with schorl and salt, never healing, never dulling.

Much like Stasha's own.

"Convince me, Stasha," the princess said, "that you aren't working for that piss-and-pus King Darien who now rules my land. Convince me that I shouldn't kill you right now and send your head back to him in a schorl box."

Stasha looked at the floor. She vaguely recalled seeing a carpet there when they'd first come in. Now all that remained was sooty ground. She'd done that, but as she'd already guessed, displays of fire would never convince this woman.

Only one thing would do it. The one thing she never wanted to talk about. Ripping her own tongue out would be preferable to speaking about *this*, but if it helped Klaus—

She took a deep, calming breath and faced the princess.

"I grew up in an orphanage in Atria, and I had two friends—two people I love more than anything." She balled her tingling fists. More fire would not help her now. "One is Klaus. He's being dragged off to Angharad as we speak, where he will die. And the other ... the other. ..." Fire licked through her fingers and skirted her hands and wrists. She tucked them under her cloak. "Tarik."

She hated the silence. Hated that everyone watched her, listened to her baring her soul to strangers when she and Klaus could barely stand to talk of Tarik.

It had to be done.

She tossed her shoulders back. "A year ago, after the first earthquake, Pyreack soldiers came looking for me." Fire bloomed across her skin, covering her body in a cocoon of red and gold. Nothing she could do about it.

She spoke through the flames. "Radomir told me it was him." Her voice spiked. "Did I mention that I plan to kill him? Before this is over." She looked at the floor, knowing she was drifting off point. "I'd been with Tarik when the quake happened, but I left him to check on Klaus." Her body trembled, and her second skin of flame crackled. "I left Tarik there. Radomir came. And ... and his filthy fae. I didn't even say goodbye." She sucked in a sharp breath, trying to keep tears from falling. It didn't help. Steam spluttered on her cheeks. "They slaughtered everyone they found, including Tarik. Radomir boasted to me about it after he threatened to give me to his soldiers if I didn't behave." She raised her hands, making fiery air quotes around the word *behave*.

Even the chirping nighttime insects seemed to have stopped to listen. Hopefully to mourn. She rubbed the thick, jagged scar across her palm. It burned the way it had after she'd torn it open.

The princess's eyes followed the movement.

She dropped her hands to her sides and took a moment to collect herself before continuing. "I didn't know then who they were. Or who

I was to them. Only that they murdered one of the only people I have ever loved." She fixed the princess with her steeliest expression. "Now I do know what they are, and what they want. And now they have Klaus, the last person in the world I have left." She snarled, baring her teeth. "I will rip each and every one of them apart for touching him. And if he dies—" She didn't even try to stop the tongues of flame that blasted out of her.

Shields shot up around the tent. Behind them, fae raised their hands, poised to use magic. Perhaps they feared she'd burn the place down. She was angry enough, but it wouldn't help her. She tried reining her fire in, but the plumes barely obeyed. She tossed her head back, allowing them to burn. Let them know how serious she was.

Voice an icy contrast to her heat, she hissed, "If Klaus dies, I will stop at nothing to see King Darien's head on a spike." She risked a step closer to the dais. "And, Princess Boadicea, I want your help doing it. Help me free my friend from Angharad."

She'd said it. Now all she could do was wait while the princess studied her through pensive eyes.

It was the longest moment of her life.

And the quietest.

The only sound was the pounding of her heart. And she didn't care if they all heard it.

"I've waited an age for this," the princess mused. Did the even realize she was speaking aloud? Mauve eyes met Stasha's and ... smiled. "You want to sack Angharad Death Camp?"

Stasha jerked her chin in a nod. "I do. They must pay in blood for what they've taken."

"What will you give me if I help you?"

Must all these fae demand something? Can no one do anything just because it's right?

The princess leaned forward expectantly.

Stasha racked her brain. What, of her meager possessions, could she offer this fae? She blinked.

Hope.

Tarik's hope. It hadn't been futile or foolish. It had kept her alive, kept her fighting when she should have died from hunger, like so many others in the orphanage.

She splayed her hands. "Angharad is a gold mine. Resources Darien needs if he wants to keep fighting this war."

The princess nodded.

Relief flushed through her that she'd remembered that detail. She gripped her courage by the throat and declared, "If we can successfully sack Angharad and free his prisoners, we can cut off his funding for this war. We can slow him down long enough to buy you and your rebels time. You could still gain the upper hand." Knowing that Princess Boadicea would expect her to fight on the rebels' side— that's what everyone seemed to want—she added, "We might actually have a shot at winning this war."

Despite the arrow still trained on her, she risked another step forward. It closed the gap between her and the dais. "I offer you a better world, Princess Boadicea. One where fae and humans alike are no longer slaves to a tyrant king. I offer you hope."

The princess stood. Power flared in her mauve-and-gold-flecked eyes. "Then welcome to my army, Stasha."

*P*rincess Boadicea had ordered tents erected for them. One for Stasha, and another for Averin, Eliezar, and Trystaen to share. She'd also ordered their weapons returned, and fresh fighting leathers for Stasha, along with a bath filled with steaming water.

Stasha had been all too eager to shrug off her ragged clothing, bathe and then dress in the softest leggings and tunic she'd ever worn. They hugged her new fae body like a more comfortable skin. Black metal covered her chest and shoulders, blending with her dark fighting leathers. The breastplate was light and easy to move in, like the rest of the outfit. Best of all, it bore no crest of allegiance. A black velvet cloak clipped to her shoulders flared out behind her as she swirled in her tent. Her red boots, more and more scuffed each day, were a stark contrast against her light-sucking black attire. She had even been presented with a fancy sheath for the dagger Averin had given her.

Although Stasha was exhausted, the princess had insisted she, Averin, Trystaen, and Eliezar join her for dinner. She strapped her dagger to her waist and stepped outside into the freezing night.

Averin's canines flashed white in the darkness. "You did well, my pit princess." This was the first time she'd been alone with him since the meeting. He held out his arm to her. "Allow me to escort you to dinner."

She blinked, then blushed, and then blushed some more that she could have been so stupid to blush in the first place. Beautiful as he was, this was just Averin. And Averin was a prince. A prince who wanted her for reasons still unstated. A good fact to remember, especially when her pulse raced as his endlessly blue eyes embraced her.

Averin cocked his head. "Not going back to the days when my touch was an abomination, are we?"

She thumped her arm down on his. "Of course not."

"Good. Because that would be a shame." Averin tucked her hand under his arm and started walking.

Her pulse spiked when his skin grazed hers. How annoying.

Averin chuckled. "And if it came down to it, I'm not sure anymore that I'd fare very well in a fight with you—where magic was concerned."

She stumbled over her feet. "But—"

"No buts about it, pit princess. Your fire is ... noteworthy, if a tad uncontrolled. Eliezar will be speaking to you about that. I suggest you accept his help. No one trains warriors better than he does."

She barely heard his comments about Eliezar. Radomir had used fire to herd her and the other villagers in Askavol. That had seemed more impressive than what she'd done. She frowned as they strolled up a torch-lit path to another large tent. "I saw Radomir do more." She shivered as she recalled the scorched bodies he'd blackmailed her with.

"Radomir!" Averin scoffed. "I've had the misfortune to fight him before. Believe me, without an army at his back, his fire is nothing. And he knows it. He'll always take the first gap to spirit from a fight, if he can. Spiriting is all he does really well."

"Good to know." She tucked the knowledge away for future reference. "Is that how he got away from you?"

"It won't happen again."

They reached the tent flap. Before swinging it open, Averin stopped. "Boa and I have our differences, but under the circumstances, she is the best ally we could have in this venture of yours. Use the time at her table well."

She gnawed her lip. "No pressure?"

"No pressure." A half smile. "Remember, this was your idea."

Averin led her into the tent as if she were a queen, and not an orphan of unknown origin.

Princess Boadicea waited for them. Dressed in black leathers, she wore a silver breastplate with the fish crest of the Kingdom of Ocea etched in jade and a gold-flecked stone that Stasha didn't recognize. The burly fae who had met them in the forest and the golden-haired archer flanked the princess. Armed fae stood guard along the sides of the tent. From across the tent, the princess's strange eyes followed her and Averin as they walked toward her.

Trystaen and Eliezar had already arrived. Eliezar's hands hung in easy reach of the blades he'd strapped to his armored body. She'd seen how difficult it was to fight fae with just magic and understood the need for mundane weaponry.

Prompted by pressure from Averin's arm, she bobbed a curtsy. Averin merely dipped his head.

The princess waved right and left. "Lukas, my first. Frea, my general. They will be joining us for dinner." Lukas's smile was almost as broad as his shoulders. Frea's face didn't even twitch. "Come," the princess added. "Let's eat." She glided past a glowing firepit to a rough table hewn from the same pale wood that grew in the forest. None of the chairs matched. The princess sat at the head.

Averin pulled out a chair to the princess's left and gestured for Stasha to sit. Never more awkward, she shuffled into it. The legs scraped across the canvas ground sheet as she pulled it closer to the table. Of course, when Averin sat at the princess's right, his stupid chair made no noise at all. Neither did any of the other fae. Was she always to stand out as different?

Odd.

To cover her embarrassment, she studied the drool-invoking array of food spread across the table. Between lit candles, wooden platters overflowing with savory meat dressed in garlic and rosemary and drizzled with thick gravy fought for space with bowls of soft, sweetly spiced vegetables and a mountain of roast potatoes.

Her stomach growled so loudly, every rebel in the camp must have heard it. She grabbed a dishing-up spoon and scooped a pile of potatoes onto her plate. Next, she forked up half a dozen slices of meat. Hand shaking with hunger and anticipation, she slopped vegetables over the top and then drowned it all in gravy. She snatched up her slightly bent fork, stabbed a gravy-drenched potato, and popped it into her mouth. Her eyes fluttered closed as she chewed the very best food she'd ever eaten.

Averin clicked his tongue and, not too subtly, cleared his throat. She looked up from her enthusiastic chewing. Averin's face twisted into something that resembled a part grimace, part smile. Straining not to laugh? His starry eyes darted between her full mouth and her messy plate. She glanced around at the rest of the table; his expression was reflected in the other diners. Even Eliezar's lips turned up. Only Frea remained stone-faced. Also, none of them had yet dished up a morsel.

Her sharply pointed fae ears burned. She put her fork down and swallowed the mouthful. "I'm sorry, Princess Boadicea." Eyes glued to her plate, she shifted in her seat. Was there more gravy on her food, or on the table? Or on the front of her soft, new leathers? "I'm not really used to ... well, this." She waved a vague hand at her surroundings and peered up through her eyelashes.

The princess's perfect mouth quivered. "Call me Boa." She held out a clean cloth.

Stasha grabbed it and swabbed it over a splotch of gravy and meat on her tunic.

Boa took a sip of wine from a goblet at her elbow and then proceeded to fill her plate with an equally healthy pile of food. "I don't imagine there was much call for dramatic social graces where you come from."

Stasha frowned, unsure if it was a jab. She risked another glance at Averin. He still smiled at her, but this time with amusement and, astonishingly, care.

She relaxed. "No, there wasn't." She picked up her fork again and swirled a chunk of meat in the pool of gravy. "After you turn twelve at the orphanage, they only serve a free meal once a month at the Hiding of the Moon. The rest we had to pay for from our wages. I almost always showed up covered in mud and sweat. And they never served anything as good as this."

Boa cradled her wine goblet and leaned back in her seat. "Sounds like a carefree existence."

Stasha snorted softly. Right. Carefree. Watching people die of hunger because their wages weren't enough to pay for the meals. In memory of all those who had perished thanks to the loving kindness of the Kňazer and Martka, she tossed the meat into her mouth.

"When I met Stasha," Averin said, "she was betting in a fighting pit for coin to buy food. So, perhaps not as carefree as one would think."

What?

Stasha froze and gawked at Averin. Why did he have to say that here? His blue eyes stared back at her with—pride. She swallowed, not sure what to make of that. Was it all part of the show they were supposed to be putting on for Boa, or did he really feel that way about her?

Boa looked over Stasha's scrawny frame. "I suppose not. We each have our battles to fight. Most of them happen in the dark, where no one can see or understand. But we fight all the same." The line of blue tattoo snaked down Boa's wrist. It curled and twisted around her fingers before disappearing up her sleeve.

Stasha slowed her chewing. Boa was right in ways she had never acknowledged. That day in the fighting pits, when she'd stolen Averin's silver coins, she'd done it without remorse. She'd given no consideration to the hardship it may have caused him. She'd let herself believe that the blue-eyed stranger had no idea of adversity, or what it was to be desperate.

And now here she was, sitting across a table from him, trying to rekindle some hope in him that they could indeed destroy Angharad. No doubt he'd lost someone close to him in the death camp. His heartache and anguish might have been different from hers, but it existed nonetheless.

Everyone has a war to fight. Most battles rage in the lonely dark.

A lesson to remember.

To lift the mood, she responded with cockiness. "Don't despair for me. I didn't make life easy for the Kňazer and the Martka. They had no idea what to do with me half the time." She tossed in a smirk for Averin. "But then, I never make life easy for anyone."

Averin raised his goblet to her. "To that I can attest."

A goblet of red wine sat at Stasha's right hand. She lifted it, and he tapped his cup against hers.

Boa added her goblet to the toast. "I think we are all counting on that."

Boa and Averin—everyone at the table—took a sip of their wine. Stasha followed suit, almost gasping as warm, spiced silk caressed her tongue. Heady, it was nothing like the watered-down ale she and Ivan had passed around the pit while witty banter flew.

Another thing she'd never get back. Oh, how much she missed that.

She sighed through her nose and took another sip of wine. Were Ivan and Goul on their way to Angharad too?

Averin put his goblet down and dipped his fingers into an earthenware pot. He sprinkled salt on his food.

Her eyes widened. "I thought salt repelled fae?"

"Old wives' tale." Averin laughed. "Just like we eat humans. Don't believe everything you heard in the mortal world."

Boa ran her finger around the rim of her goblet. "Tell us a story, Stasha. Tell us about your mortal life."

Mortal life. She tried not to wince. Something else she'd never get back. Something she hadn't known was never hers at all.

So, what to share? What would ensure Boa came through with her promise of help? What would keep that glow of pride in Averin's eyes and make Eliezar's lips twitch? Trystaen had already proved he enjoyed anything she shared with him. And as for Lukas and Frea? She assumed they would be part of the heist, so she had to impress them too.

Perhaps inspired by the wine, a memory tugged at her. Like everything in her life, it was fraught with both pain and humor. As hard as it was to talk of Tarik, she decided to share it. "Tarik and I used to go to the fighting pits often. As Averin mentioned, that's how we earned money for food. But if we lost, we went hungry. That was a problem. Especially for Klaus. I hated it when he went hungry."

Boa's eyebrows rose. "Keeping him fed was your responsibility? How old is this friend of yours?"

Stasha's face flushed at the implied criticism. "He has a crippled leg."

Boa exchanged troubled looks with Averin. Stasha guessed what they were communicating: a boy with a damaged leg would have even less chance of survival in Angharad.

All the more reason to wow Boa with this story. She forced a smile into her voice. "The Kňazer's pantry in their private kitchen was always a last resort. They knew the contents were coveted like gold, so they had their toughest acolytes guard it. Getting into it took ingenuity and no small degree of courage." She took a quick mouthful of food and spoke around it. "One day, Tarik stole a set of acolyte robes." She grinned. "He was a sneaky thief. Much better than I ever was." She giggled at the memory despite her yearning for Tarik. "The fanatic acolyte he stole them from was stuck inside all day with no clothes."

Boa's smile mirrored hers. Happy but sorrowful.

Stasha's heart warmed, and she pushed more emotion into her voice. "We hid two knapsacks under the robes on the day Tarik wore them to take me to the Kňazer's home at the Crekev to be punished for my"—she made air quotes—"frivolity."

"Frivolity?" Trystaen leaned back in his chair. "That's punishable in the mortal world?"

She flashed him a smile. "Two days in lockup." His eyebrows rose, and she guessed he had no idea what lockup was, but she wasn't going to break the rhythm of her story to explain.

"The acolytes guarding the place didn't even stop us when we sauntered in."

"Just how many times had you been punished for frivolity?" Averin's eyes glinted with mirth.

"I thought I'd already mentioned that I never make life easy for anyone. Myself included."

Averin—and Boa—chortled. She had to stop herself from preening. Who knew that a boring story from her very mundane life would interest these majestic creatures. Some of the others chuckled, too, but the two royals were the ones whose opinions counted the most.

"The acolytes were watching us, the little busybodies, until we heard the crash from the Kňazer's parlor." She threw her head back and laughed. "Klaus had struck. Him and the goats. You want to know how to drive a Kňazer nuts? Let goats into his parlor."

More laughter.

She bobbed in her chair, smirking. "It was chaos. Goats crapping. Kňazer yelling. Acolytes running." She clapped her hands together, making sparks fly. "Before it was sorted out, Tarik and I had virtually cleaned out the pantry. We even stole an old bottle of wine." She didn't add that Klaus had ended up holding her hair back while she vomited after drinking too much of the sour stuff. "We ate well for days on that."

When the laughter subsided, Boa poured herself more wine. A bright teal stone set in a silver ring on her index finger caught in the light. Like everything about Boa, it was beautiful.

Averin leaned forward to put his elbows on the table. "Did they punish you?"

She grimaced. "Oh yes. Five lashes for me and Tarik. And three days in lockup."

"And Klaus?"

"Of course not," she snapped. As if she or Tarik would ever have allowed Klaus to be punished. "Tarik and I always took Klaus's punishments, even when he pleaded with us to let him take a stint in lockup. With his leg, we weren't risking the rest of his health."

"Now you need to explain lockup," Trystaen said softly.

She waved a dismissive hand. "A dark cell with no food and little water. You stay there until the Martka and Kňazer decide that the gods have forgiven you." She rolled her eyes, picked up her fork, and pushed a potato around her plate. "Not much different than regular life, really." The corners of her mouth pulled down. "Still, we all thought that was the worst thing that could possibly happen." She shifted in her seat, smile dissolving completely. "I guess we were wrong."

No one said anything, so she felt obliged to continue. She laced her fingers around the stem of her goblet so tight it might snap. "You probably think that Tarik and I babied Klaus. We didn't. He might be strong in mind, but his body is weak. And the weak don't survive in Askavol." She tipped her head back and chugged the rest of her wine. She thumped the empty glass back on the table.

Eliezar refilled her goblet. The protector of their little circle, he saw everything with those pale, wolfish eyes. She liked him.

Despite the wine, her throat was dry. She swallowed. "Averin." His stars were sparkling, but … mournfully. Pitiful. She wanted to hate him for that sympathy. That grief. But she couldn't. No matter how tough and cavalier Averin appeared, he was in bits and pieces too. Just like Boa. "How did you fail to destroy Angharad? What went wrong?"

Averin stiffened and glanced at Boa.

Face pale, Boa had frozen. Her extraordinary eyes locked on something Stasha couldn't see. That blue-lined tattoo slithered back over her fingers, wrapping around them like a noose.

Stasha's gaze shot between the Prince of Zephyr and the Princess of Ocea. "Were you two together?"

"Not at first." Averin sounded strained. "But it all started with the Battle of the Blue Desert, sixty years ago."

Blue Desert? Trystaen had mentioned the place. He told her it had caught fire when she was born. Other than that, she had no knowledge of it.

"My father thought we had Piss Swill on the run," Boa cut in, gaze still locked on something no one else could see. Perhaps something not in this world. "He persuaded King Seph, Averin's father, to send troops for an attack on Pyreack. Averin argued that it was a mistake. That Piss Swill was playing with us. Luring us into the Blue Desert to slaughter us."

"No one believed me." Averin's jaw clenched, and his face hardened into something vicious. "They all wanted to believe that if Ocea, Atria, and Zephyr united forces, we could defeat Pyreack. I knew our soldiers were marching to their deaths. In the Blue Desert, terrain is as much an enemy as Pyreack armies. I refused to commit as many troops as King Appius wanted."

Was that where the animosity between Boa and Averin came from? That Ocea had needed his help, but he had been unwilling to give it?

Boa sighed. "The battle lasted nine days. Nine days of constant slaughter. The ground was bathed in red and tears. Fae and mortal blood alike. Even at night, the sands didn't glow blue. Only red. They tell me nothing grows there now, even sixty years later."

Stasha shuddered. It would be easy to drown it all out with more wine, but she didn't want this story—this truth—hazed by alcohol.

"We knew there was no hope left." Boa's voice was a dull monotone. "Even before the main Pyreack army crested the dunes—the army they'd hidden from us."

The army Averin suggested awaited them? Unsaid, the words hung in the air.

"There were so few of us left, and their forces were...." Boa shook her head. Her gold seashell combs fell onto the table. Her hair tumbled across her face, exposing her pointy fae ears. "Their army stretched as far as the eye could see." She closed her eyes. "I still hear the beating drums. The horns and battle cries. They knew they'd already won, even before the first blade struck. And they reveled in it. The misery. The slaughter."

Averin stared at his wine goblet. But even though his eyes were dark, there was no triumph in them for having been right.

"They wielded flame and ash and smoke as though it were a blade. I could taste their victory in the air, like a spray of salt from the sea on my skin." Boa's voice was just as bitter as brine. "It was all I could smell for months after." Her gaze met Stasha's. "All Pyreack scum can wield orange-red fire, but you burn with blue-green flames. That's what we saw tonight while you played with fire. But we all *felt* the thrum of invisible flame—white heat—coming off you, straight through our shields. It took me straight back to the Blue Desert." Boa reached over and squeezed Stasha's hand so hard it hurt. "You need to understand how rare and dangerous you are. It takes bands of Pyreack soldiers working together to pool their magic to create white heat. You created it as easily as breathing. It explains why Piss Swill wants you so much."

Stasha resisted the urge to pull away. "What does white heat do?"

"The unimaginable," Boa whispered. "I've seen grizzled soldiers run into walls of orange or blue flame to escape white heat." Boa's hand fell away from Stasha's.

"If Boa hadn't doused you tonight, you would have melted us all." Averin's voice was somber. He gestured to Eliezar. "He has some tricks up his sleeve to help you control it."

"For control it you must," Boa said. "Or you will kill us all."

Stasha's stomach curdled. She pushed her plate away. "Tell me more of the battle."

A long silence before Boa spoke. "There was a legion of defectors from Ocea, Atria, and Zephyr fighting with the Pyreack armies, cowards who would rather fight as traitors than die as heroes. They turned on us, using our own magic against us." Her voice was thick. "We had one last gift to give. One last stand for our people. So we fought until our blades snapped, and then we fought with hand and foot ... until I realized that none of us had fallen in many hours." A bitter laugh. "I understood too late. They were herding us while they brought in their schorl wagons to take us to Angharad. And to capture my father."

Angharad. Stasha sat up straighter in her chair.

"My father was not a young fae, even then," Boa said. "Every day I sensed more of his power draining from him and into me as his living heir. He realized what they were doing at the same moment I did. He grabbed me—" Boa rubbed her temples. "The key he transferred dropped me to my knees. The last thing he could do to protect his people. I was writhing on the ground when he tried to kill himself with his broken blade." Pain twisted Boa's face. "White heat evaporated the sword in his hand. I had never heard my father scream before. Not in two hundred years. And I'll be glad to never hear it again." Boa gulped a mouthful of wine and wiped the drop that drizzled down her chin. "They spirited him to that son of a bitch, Darien. I knew the moment he arrived because the power that had been leaking into me for years ... just stopped. Darien had won. Not just the battle, but our entire kingdom."

"And you? And the rest of your soldiers?" Stasha asked.

"I had been so focused on my father that I barely noticed when they locked the first wagon door. Like you, Stasha, it carried the only person I had left in the world—my lover, Shyael." Boa's tattoos swirled across her hand. "I tried to stop them, of course, but Radomir spirited them away.

"I wanted to fight on, but my father had given me the key to spiriting into our kingdom, and I could not risk being captured. While I live, no one who isn't from Ocea can spirit into my kingdom." Boa turned haunted eyes on Stasha. "I abandoned Angharad and slunk out of the Blue Desert with Pyreack soldiers on my heels." She slammed her fist on the table. "But I swore I'd never slink again. I returned to Ocea to guard my borders and set up my rebel army." Her voice dropped to a mere whisper. "But I never forgot Angharad. Or Shyael." She waved at Averin. "I buried my fury over his betrayal and turned to him for help."

"As you can see, even in need, she doesn't forgive." Averin spoke lightly. He blew out a breath and rubbed a hand over his dark two-day stubble. All mirth gone, he added, "I lost fae to Angharad too." His eyes swallowed the candlelight. "I led an army to Angharad Death Camp. Even from five miles away, we could smell the bodies on the wind. The rot. The blistering heat in the Blue Desert didn't help. I flew over the camp only once—I think they let down their shields because they wanted me to see what they'd done to our soldiers. Many had been flayed and left to die and rot in the sun. The rest wore schorl manacles around their ankles and worked the mines."

Stasha's hands itched with fiery rage, mixed with fear for Klaus. "So what did you do?"

"Do?" Averin laughed hoarsely. "Rather ask what we didn't do. The walls are unscalable—guarded by magic. The two tunnel entrances are guarded and blocked by portcullises. Not that any of that really matters. Getting into Angharad is easy. It's getting out that's impossible."

"You lost fae trying?"

"More than I care to admit."

Trystaen nodded. Even Lukas and Frea added murmurs of agreement. Only Eliezar seemed untouched. Inscrutable.

Boa slammed her hand on the table. "Futile. Everything we did. Just futile."

"In the end, we tried starving them out," Averin said. "But after a year of failure, my father ordered the Azura back to Zephyr." He canted his head to appraise Stasha. "The low point of my very long life." A smile quirked, perhaps in memory of her accusation that he was two billion years old.

How she wished she could have a private moment with him to wipe that shame, pain, and despair away with a gentle hand.

Better, she needed to help him and Boa claw back a victory. Perhaps rescuing Klaus was no longer the only reason for going to Angharad.

"Ocea was forced to move out, too, soon after the Pyreack forces learned I was among them," Boa added, voice bleak. "Piss Swill wanted me for the key, and I was hunted daily. And by then, everyone they'd captured from the Battle of the Blue Desert was long dead."

Silence fell, thicker than blood or wine.

Stasha gnawed her lip. How was she going to get an army into Angharad when fae warriors so much better equipped and qualified than her had failed? And if it was so futile a venture, why had Boa agreed to help? Even Averin had been willing to try again.

What had changed?

Boa's goblet clicked as she placed it beside her empty plate. "We'll go over the maps tomorrow." Her mauve eyes glinted. "And perhaps our Pyreack...." She hesitated, then added, "Stasha can come up with a solution the rest of us have missed."

Was Boa going to say "weapon"? Or was Stasha's imagination running away with her? She allowed a grin to ghost her face. "I've always had a soft spot for an army of underdogs."

Boa scoffed a laugh. "What part of the story did you miss, Stasha? We have been underdogs for centuries."

Heat rolled in Stasha's bones. But not the heat that set forests and tents ablaze and needed Boa's water to put it out. This was different.

"You've never had a human-turned-fae working with you. Unlike you lot, I don't see failure when I think of Angharad." She saw a lad in the fighting pits who was beaten to a pulp and still outsmarted his opponent to win a hopeless fight. Her insides clenched as she remembered Hathrine, who kept getting up day after day when she had no one and nothing left to hold onto. And Klaus, who fought against the Martka and Kňazer to save her from execution.

She saw a bright-red ribbon.

CHAPTER TWENTY-ONE

A PACT

At first light, Stasha stood outside Averin's tent. She hit the flap. "It's day. Klaus will be in Angharad by now. We need to start planning this heist."

A low chuckle reached her. The tent flap parted, and Averin stepped out. She breathed in the mix of snow, sun-kissed oranges, and chai spices that was his unique smell. Despite his heady scent, dressed in black, and bristling with blades, he radiated his usual quiet menace. "Morning, pit princess. You'll be pleased to know that Trystaen and Eliezar have already been out this morning to meet with Boa. We are to grab some food and join them in the map tent."

She folded her arms across her chest. "I doubt Klaus is being offered breakfast. Food can wait."

"Which is exactly what I thought you'd say." Averin held out a chunk of cake stuffed with fruit and nuts. "I brought this for you."

She took it, smiling her thanks. They started walking. "You knew I'd come looking for you?"

Averin shrugged. "I like to keep a step ahead in my conquests."

She looked away to hide her blush. "Conquests? You're talking about rescuing Klaus, I assume."

Averin sniggered like she'd just told a dirty joke. "The maps are this way." He pointed down a path hacked through the forest. It was lined with small tents out of which rebels spilled, preparing for the day.

She took a bite of the cake—delicious and far better than talking about anything that could make her face betray her conflicted emotions about Averin. She swallowed her last bite. "How do they keep this camp hidden? All those lights last night. And this huge scar in the forest."

"Glamour. Unless invited in by Boa, anyone looking at it will just see a putrid swamp."

"If Piss Swill controls Ocea, how can Boa still wield so much power?"

"Because she has that much power. Darien rules the kingdom because he's the most powerful, having stolen from the true king. But other fae still use their magic uninhibited."

"Does he know when they use their magic?"

"No." Averin bumped her shoulder. "If he did, we'd have had an army descend on us last night after your performance."

A blue-eyed fae approached them. Averin's dark eyebrows rose, and his step faltered. The fae skipped, almost but not quite bowing, and then dipped her head, as if ashamed to meet his gaze. The two passed each other without a word.

"A defector?" Stasha couldn't resist asking.

Averin nodded. "We get them. All the kingdoms do. Hotheads who throw it in to fight with Boa. That fae was a captain in my regular army, not my Azura."

"I guess they've all lost someone."

Familiar darkness settled on Averin. "Losing someone isn't a good enough reason to be stupid. One still needs to be smart about how one wages this war."

"So joining Boa is stupid?"

"Boa's soldiers don't have a long life expectancy. That's wasteful."

Stasha bristled. "Perhaps they don't want a long life if they've lost the only thing that matters. But maybe you don't get that, Averin. I know you said you lost soldiers in the attack on Angharad, but it isn't really the same as losing someone close to you, is it?"

Averin stopped walking and bore down on her. "Not fair. You don't hold the world's corner on grief, Stasha." She recoiled and was about to defend herself when he snapped, "I lost my sister in Angharad. Nela was one of the hotheads who wouldn't listen when I said no to King Appius's request for a massive army to go against

Darien. Even Eliezar pleaded with her not to go." His voice hardened. "She rejected his counsel too."

Stasha had made assumptions about other fae's pain. Wrongfully. She rubbed the scar on her hand. Even though she guessed the answer, she had to know. "What happened to her?"

"She was one of the fae I saw flayed and left to die. I believe she was the reason they lowered their shields to let me see what they were doing." The hand Averin ran through his hair jerked his frustration. "I also wanted to go mad and send hurricanes against them." A bitter laugh. "In fact, I tried. For a year. With everything I had. But I couldn't destroy that mountain. Eliezar has never really recovered, but I have. And I no longer waste valuable resources on no-hope ventures." Back straight as an arrow, Averin started walking down the path.

She lengthened her stride to keep up with him. "Nela and Eliezar were lovers?"

"Sealed. Husband and wife."

She swallowed, gaining sudden insight into Eliezar's quiet watchfulness. His inscrutability when they had discussed the siege of Angharad the night before made sense. He was hurting, just as she was, just as so many were in this terrible war.

"Is that why you won't commit the Azura to our ... venture? Because you believe it hopeless?"

Averin tossed a cocky smile at her, the vortex of anger and pain gone from sight. "I'm a valuable resource, too, Stasha. If I believed it truly hopeless, I would not be going with you."

A large tent loomed at the end of the path. She guessed it was where Boa housed her maps. As anxious as she was to get the talking done and everyone moving to Angharad, she paused before having to face the rest of the team. Averin slowed too.

She grabbed his hand so he would focus on her. "Klaus is everything to me, but I'm not stupid. I have a plan. A good one, but it's risky. I need your support in there to make it happen."

Averin cradled her hand in both of his and swirled her up into the stars that were his eyes. "You are not a resource I can risk."

She tsked. "I'm a weapon. Radomir said so. And Suren. You've implied it." She pulled her hand away from his and swept her arms in an arc. "Everyone here thinks it. Let me do what I was designed to do."

Averin canted his head, and she knew a speculative gaze would follow. She wasn't disappointed; she was beginning to read his shifting moods. A moment later, he shook his head as if he'd made a decision. "You're not an object, or a means to an end. I want you alive and happy." His voice dried. "And just a tad fatter, so I know that a stiff breeze won't blow you over." He tucked her hand under his arm. "Now, come. Let's get this done so we can get you home. And by that, I mean Zephyr, where we both belong. There's a bed waiting for you in the palace in Ilyseryph."

So Averin was going to be difficult? She scowled as she walked with him between the tent flaps. In that case, she'd have to find another ally to help her do what Averin wouldn't.

Her gaze settled on Boa.

Dressed in black leathers, the rebel leader stood at a trestle table covered with rolled-out maps, held open with stones. The edges of the parchments were frayed and the maps worn, like they'd been pored over a hundred times by fae trying to discover their secrets. Trystaen, Eliezar, Lukas, and Frea were also gathered around the table.

"Averin. Stasha," Boa said. "I was just saying that I've received a report about a ship loaded with human slaves. It docked in Kyhox during the night."

The name of the port that fed Angharad? Stasha grabbed the table to stop herself from swaying.

Averin stepped right behind her. He stood so close, she sensed him brushing her through her clothes. His breath even tickled the back of her neck. It surprised her how much it centered her, having him there. She managed to keep her voice steady enough to ask, "Where are they now?"

"Some of them were taken to Angharad in wagons, but the majority were spirited into the camp." Lukas ran thick fingers over the black words on the map. They swam before her, finally decoding to read: Angharad Death Camp.

Averin slipped his arms past her sides and placed his hands on the map. "We need to brief Stasha on the layout of Angharad."

Both Trystaen and Eliezar looked up at Averin. Trystaen's mouth parted, perhaps in surprise at Averin's weird protectiveness. But it was Eliezar's thoughts that interested her the most. As usual, the wolfish fae gave nothing away, but she thought for the briefest moment that something had flickered in his eyes. Whatever it was vanished too quickly for her to interpret. But it was enough to make her push back against Averin.

He stepped away instantly and moved next to her at the table. Without missing a beat, he pointed at a sharp-peaked mountain drawn in tight lines on the map. It had a crater in its heart. He tapped one side of the mountain with a long finger. "Entrance here, guarded by a schorl portcullis. Leads to a tunnel." Then he tapped the mountain slope inside the crater. "And here."

Two schorl portcullises. That meant she couldn't just melt the gates and walk right into the camp. "What else do we know?"

"Nothing." Averin shrugged. "Wish I could tell you more, but no one Boa and I sent in ever came out to share details."

Boa flicked the map. "Averin and I always assumed they keep the fae and humans separate. At least to quarter them when they aren't working."

"Why? Surely they won't care that fae would terrify the humans witless."

"Schorl." Stasha glanced up at Eliezar, who manacled his wrist with his fingers. "They would want to keep the fae from using magic. They would do that with schorl-clad walls and manacles. Humans don't need that."

That made sense. "Just how much schorl is there in the world?"

"Supplies aren't limitless," Averin said. "So it makes sense that they would use it judiciously. But before we even think about where they stash everyone, we have to get in."

"We have a plan." Boa glanced at Lukas and the surly Frea. "We stayed up most of the night talking about this heist."

Apart from bleak faces, none of them looked sleep deprived. A fae thing, no doubt.

"We'll use the hijacked-prison-wagon routine again," Boa said.

Averin, Trystaen, and Eliezar all frowned. Averin even huffed. "Boa, not that old chestnut." He turned to Stasha. "We used that a few times. We always got people in. They just never came out."

"Have you any other ideas to get warriors into an impenetrable camp?" Boa's voice was icy.

Averin ran a hand over his eyes. "No. And you know that."

"Then stop arguing." Boa turned her back on Averin. "Stasha, Averin and I are experts at this. We will get you through the portcullis. But the rest will be up to you."

At least that was something.

Averin opened his mouth, but Stasha cut him off. "I have some questions before we get into details." She poked the crater in the center of the mine. It had to be where they had staked Nela, Averin's sister and Eliezar's wife. "What's this used for?"

Averin folded his arms. "Barracks. Guard houses. The tower from where they control the portcullises. I had a good look at it when I flew over." Another shrug. "Things might have changed in the last sixty years, but that's what it was back then."

Stasha bit her lip, embarrassed about what she was about to ask. She tossed her head back. They all knew she was an ignorant orphan who had never traveled more than twenty miles from her home before this. "Where are we now in relation to Angharad? I'm somewhat confused."

Frea snorted low in her throat, but loud enough for everyone to hear. Stasha bit her tongue to stop a sharp retort. Infighting wasn't going to get Klaus rescued. Given the heavy silence, everyone else must have agreed with Frea, but that didn't stop Averin from glaring at her.

Lukas pulled another length of parchment across the table and tossed it on top of the Angharad map. One of the corners curled, so he held it down with a slab of jade carved with the fish crest.

Even Stasha recognized it as a map of Zathryth.

"We're here. In Atria." Lukas pointed to a blank spot on the map not far from the border between Atria and Ocea.

Boa waved at the fae in the tent. "I can spirit us across the border into Ocea. I'll make it as far as Laughing Pools. From there, Averin will have to take over. But even he'll need to rest up overnight. We can't have us both weakened by spiriting."

"Spiriting weakens fae?" Stasha asked. "That doesn't make sense when you all seem to do everything so effortlessly."

"Magical strength and physical strength aren't the same thing," Lukas said. "And it takes magic to spirit."

"Physical strength comes from bone and muscle and endurance," Eliezar added in his usual quiet way. "Spiriting is a very specific talent that only some fae possess. Not many could spirit seven people over huge distances."

Radomir had been strong enough to spirit an entire schorl wagon.

She'd always been taught that the fae were all-powerful, capable of doing anything imaginable with no limitations. She'd been foolish for believing it. "I guess I've got a lot to learn."

"You'll get there. It may just take some time," Eliezar said.

Boa prodded the map. "Once we cross the Laughing Pools, Averin and I can work together to spirit us across Ocea to the border with Pyreack." She turned to Averin. "You'll have to get the Azura to meet us at the border."

Averin's face hardened. "The Azura won't be joining us on this mission."

"What?" Boa's mauve eyes swirled with currents of disbelief.

"You heard." Averin's jaw remained hard. "I'm not involving the Azura. We handle this on our own or not at all."

"Not again, Averin!" Mist sprayed from Boa's fingers. "The Azura are the best fighting force on Zathryth. This time, with them *and* Stasha, we can't lose."

"Thanks for the compliment." The hard lines of Averin's face showed no signs of appreciation. "I've worked hard during the last sixty years to hone them, and they are good, but not for this mission."

More mist billowed around Boa. She clenched her hands together. "This is what they were designed for! You told me that yourself after our failure. We lay under the stars together, and you told me you planned to create the ultimate fighting force to take on the Pyreack. So use them, or we might as well not bother going!"

Not go? Over her dead body.

"Enough! Even underdog orphans know that you don't turn against each other!" Stasha slammed her hands on the table. Sparks flew and ignited the edges of the map. She slapped them, but the fire spread.

Eliezar pulled her away. He leaned in. "First chance we get," he whispered, "you and I are doing some training."

By the time she'd struggled out of his arms, the fire had been extinguished. Boa, Averin—everyone—glared at her.

"You have to stop doing that," Frea snapped, speaking for the very first time since Stasha had arrived at the camp.

Utterly remorseless, Stasha shot back, "Then stop annoying me. All of you. And while I would love to know the reason why Averin is mollycoddling his soldiers, I'm not letting that get in the way of me rescuing Klaus." She spun to Boa. "You said you can get me through the portcullis. Do that." She rounded on Averin. "And you won't bring in your precious Azura, so you have to cope with me waging this war on my own."

Averin paled and threw up his hands. "No, Stasha—"

"Shut up! You don't get to have it all your own way, Averin. I'm the last thing the Pyreack will expect to drop into Angharad." Heat burned through her skin, and with it a shimmer of blue-green fire. "And trust me: when I'm done, I *will* be the last thing that *ever* drops into that place."

Averin closed his eyes and pinched the bridge of his nose. "I can't let you do this."

"Then bring in the Azura." Boa punched Averin's arm. "Make up for how you failed me sixty years ago."

Wind whipped Averin's hair, and he levitated a foot off the floor.

Trystaen jumped between him and Boa. He grabbed Averin's tunic and yanked him back to the ground. "Boa," Trystaen said. "The Azura will not be coming. One word to the Zephyr royals about this adventure, and King Seph will command Averin to return to Ilyseryph." He jerked a thumb at Stasha. "With her. And you know Averin. He would rather beg for forgiveness than ask for permission."

Boa lunged at Trystaen. "You don't leave here without my permission. And if you think I'd let Stasha go, then you're insane."

Trystaen tossed his hands in the air. The ground shuddered so hard, a map slid off the table onto the floor. Stasha's heart almost stilled as she struggled to balance. Moments later, the earth settled.

"Now that I have your attention," Trystaen said, as if he'd done nothing shocking. "Stasha is bound by promise to Averin. Just as he is bound to her."

Boa's eyes weren't the only ones to flash.

Stasha blinked like an idiot.

But Boa spoke first. "What promise?"

"Averin agreed to help her free Klaus if she agreed to go to Ilyseryph with him. Stop either of them, and you know what happens."

Boa's shoulders slumped. She looked at Stasha. "Is this true?"

While she'd made a promise to Averin, she didn't know what Trystaen was talking about. But if he kept the rescue on track with whatever game he played, then she agreed with it. She folded her arms. "Yes, it's true. But rock the earth again, Trystaen, and I will set your hair on fire."

Trystaen chortled. "I don't doubt that." Despite sporting with her, he watched Boa.

The rebel leader faced Lukas and Frea. They shared a look filled with exasperation and something more—regret.

"It seems we have no choice but to accept Averin's terms," Lukas said.

Frea looked at Averin with such loathing, it even made Stasha cringe.

Boa rubbed her hands together, her fingers chasing the tattoos that swirled through her skin. After what seemed an eternity, she touched Stasha's face with a gentle finger. "I will not risk your life by requiring you to break your promise to Averin, even if he"—she scowled at Averin—"would be so low as to require such a bond from you."

Like a dark cloud, Averin stood dead still. Stasha guessed he'd been maligned in this whole deal but had chosen to say nothing. That he'd let Trystaen's assertions stand reconfirmed how valuable she was to him and the other Zephyr royals. Even though she had no idea what he wanted her for, she could not bear for Boa, Lukas, and the awful Frea to think badly of him. She moved next to him. "Now that we're all friends again, let's plan the mission that really matters."

"Good idea." Trystaen slapped Lukas on the back. "Where do you want to hijack this prison wagon?"

Lukas grinned like an idiot. "Come, let's get the map out, and I'll show you."

As Trystaen and Lukas busied themselves with maps, Averin leaned in to Stasha and whispered, "You might have won this round, pit princess, but just know that I hate your plan."

She smiled at the tickle of his sweet breath on her ear. "How can you when you haven't even heard it?"

Averin squeezed both her shoulders. "The Pyreack don't care to guard their prison wagons. That tells me they have something inside the camp to expose imposters. I believe that's how our people always got caught."

"Something that destroys glamour?"

"Possibly. If I knew the answer, the fae I sent in to attack the place would have been successful."

"Then I have to plan for that."

"You aren't listening to me. Get yourself killed, and I will never forgive you."

"Then join me. In the mines." The notion of taking on the Pyreack with Averin at her side made her heart skip. "And we go in fighting, so it doesn't matter what magic they use to expose imposters."

Averin's eyes gleamed. They sobered when he glanced at Trystaen and Eliezar, poring over maps with Lukas and Boa. "I won't risk them. Not without knowing what's waiting for us inside the camp."

"But you'll risk yourself?"

Averin shrugged. "I'm hardly going to let you go alone, pit princess. Where's the gallantry in that?"

She grinned, loving his spirit of adventure—or maybe he just wanted to be on hand to protect his weapon. No matter his reason, she was glad to have him on her side. "Good. Gives me a chance to keep an eye on you. I would hate you getting your butt kicked. Again."

Averin smirked. "My gallantry prevents me from reminding you what happened *after* you thought you'd kicked my butt."

She chortled. "True." All mirth faded. "First thing we do is find Klaus."

"It would be better to go for the gates. Get our team inside."

There was logic in that, but she couldn't bear being in the mines without knowing Klaus was safe. "The gates will be heavily guarded. If we can release the prisoners, they can act as a diversion. While the guards are busy with them, we open the gate to Boa and everyone else."

"You aren't going to listen to reason, are you?"

"You handle the fae. I'll look after the humans."

"If you didn't have white heat, I'd definitely be arguing with you." Averin offered her his hand.

She took it. Shoulder to shoulder, they faced the rest of the team. "So, Averin will be riding with me in the hijacked wagon. Who will be waiting outside the gate for us to let you in?"

*T*he talking was finally done. Every detail had been dissected, argued over, rehashed, and finally settled. Stasha and Averin's knapsack of clothing, provided by Boa for their mission, was packed and ready. Her dagger was strapped to her waist. Now, she, Averin, Eliezar, and Trystaen stood under a tree with Lukas while they waited for Boa to appear and spirit them to the Laughing Pools in Ocea. Frea and her bow and arrow hovered a little distance away.

Compared to everyone else, Stasha carried the least weaponry. But then, even Averin had finally admitted that her primary weapon was her magic, and the extraordinary way—apparently—she wielded it. It was her magic they would use to free Klaus and the other slaves from Angharad.

Frea glowered at her.

Mystified, Stasha nudged Averin. When he looked at her, she nodded for him to follow. Together, they stepped away from the tree. Even though she guessed with fae hearing that Frea would have no problem listening in, she said pointedly, "What have I done to tick her off?"

Averin scratched his stubble. "Exist? Or maybe she just has a problem with fire magic. She gets tense every time you burn."

"Which is all the time when she's around." She sighed. "She brings out the worst in me."

Averin brushed a wisp of hair off her face. "Don't let her. It could jeopardize everything. It's bad enough that Boa has issues with me. You said it yourself—we can't afford to fight and distrust each other."

"I don't distrust *me*," she said. "It's her who gives me the creeps."

Averin studied Frea and her bow. "She doesn't send the wind through my hair, either, but Boa and Lukas trust her. That should be good enough for us."

Stasha was marshaling her arguments against Frea when Boa strode up the path to join them. Armor coated Boa's body like fish scales. "I have a gift for you," she called to Stasha.

"For me?" Stasha bobbed and flashed her eyes at Averin. "Take notes. That's how to persuade me that you're my friend."

Averin snorted. "So easily bought." But he smiled as she hopped over to meet Boa.

"I will happily accept whatever you offer me." She stopped a few feet away.

Boa's grin was so kind, so much in contrast to her usually stern mien, that Stasha almost gasped in surprise. To cover up, she looked at Boa's hands for her gift. Boa carried a leather sheath as long and wide as Stasha's forearm. It rattled with leather straps and brass buckles.

Stasha frowned, not sure what she was supposed to do with an arm muff.

"Ah!" Hands in his pockets, Averin sauntered to her and Boa. "Very good choice, Boa, for a pit princess who likes chopping people with her hands."

Boa nodded curtly at Averin. "For once, it seems we agree. Even with Stasha's magic, she needs a backup weapon." Boa made a scoffing sound at the dagger hanging from Stasha's waist. "That thing won't help her in a battle if she can't use magic."

Before Stasha could stop herself, she said, "I did slow down a manticore with it." She smiled at Averin. "It's a very good blade."

"Keep the dagger." Averin dipped his head. "My gift to you. But in truth, Boa's hidden blade is the better weapon for you."

So that's what this was—a hidden blade. She'd heard of them but had never seen one.

Boa fiddled with the sheath. A blade the length of Stasha's forearm but far, far deadlier shot out of one end. The black steel glistened in the light dancing along the honed edge. "Allow me." Dexterous fingers strapped the sheath to Stasha's arm as she gawked. "There's a trigger here." Boa flicked a small steel knob, no bigger than a pea, on the inside of the weapon. Steel hissed as the blade retracted into the safety of the sheath. "Trigger it when you want to use it, and the blade shoots out. Press the same button when you want it gone. And mind your fingers."

Stasha blinked, eyes wide as she triggered the switch. Steel shot out over her tightened fist, wicked and lovely. Perfect for ... for killing. She swallowed. Passion and hatred had driven her claims that she would kill Radomir and everyone else who had harmed Klaus, but as she studied this weapon—so tangible—she wondered what it would do to her soul to take someone else's life. Human or fae, it didn't seem too different anymore. The distinction between the two was no longer as stark as it had been only a few days ago. She curled her finger against the trigger. The blade shot back in. "Thank you."

Boa didn't seem to hear her. Shoulders back, head high, Boa faced their inner circle, the ones who would lead the offensive. Boa already had spies and a platoon of rebels waging a low-key war of attrition against Pyreack in the Blue Desert. Messages had been sent through her spy network to call some of them in for the attack. Boa tightened a strap across her chest, pulling taut two long swords lashed across her back. "Tonight, we'll camp at the Laughing Pools, so I can get my strength back. Tomorrow, on the way to the border, we're stopping at the temple to call down a blessing on our mission from Jahena, goddess of rivers." Boa bunched her fingertips and raised them to her mouth.

Stasha huffed to herself. She fully understood the need for Averin and Boa to rest. They were key warriors in their team and needed to be at their fighting best, but the temple trip seemed like a pointless waste of time. The idea of communing with gods who either didn't exist or didn't care was criminal when Klaus was in mortal danger. She opened her mouth to question the decision, but Averin nudged her in the ribs. She met his frown with one of her own.

"Boa does nothing without first petitioning the gods," Averin whispered. "Respect that."

She muttered, "It's a waste of time."

Averin shrugged. "Not all fae share your views, and you have no choice but to humor her."

How did Averin feel about the gods the fae believed in? Somehow, she didn't think he set much store by them either.

Boa held out her arms. "So, if we're all ready, the next stop is the Laughing Pools in Ocea."

While the others shuffled around Boa, Stasha stood uncertainly on the periphery.

Averin grabbed her hand. As her callused fingers scraped against his, a traitorous blush heated her face. He huffed a laugh, and she scowled. "You've spirited, haven't you, pit princess?"

"I was unconscious." Her pulse raced as he tugged her into his chest and wrapped an arm around her. Part of her was scared to spirit, but another part loved his exotic smell, so different than Radomir's sickly sweet strawberries and honey.

"You'll be wide awake this time." Averin's breath fluttered her hair. "It'll be the ride of your life." He grabbed Boa's hand.

The earth turned upside down and spun like a top. Her hastily eaten breakfast rose, and then spun with it. And then her feet hit the ground—the right way up. She fell forward against Averin's arm, spitting profanities and vomit onto vibrant green stones rimming a stream of tinkling water.

Averin leaned over so she hung in his arms. "That happened to me, too, the first time my father spirited with me," he whispered in her ear. She heard the smile in his voice. He'd made no move to release her.

"How old were you?" she gritted out.

"About three. One of my earlier memories."

"And that's supposed to make me feel better?"

Trystaen pulled out a waterskin and handed it to her, also laughing. She wriggled away from Averin and snatched it from him. She washed her mouth out. Averin's hand twitched. A gentle breeze wafted the stench away. She plunked down on a low wall next to the stream to catch her breath and wait for her stomach to forgive her.

As far as the eye could see, an intricate maze of streams stretched out like rippling mirrors. Her jaw slackened at the never-ending labyrinth of green, silver, and blue. Large jade boulders formed small islands—stepping stones—between them. Willows draped long, sad leaves into the constantly moving water. Lilies in shades of pink and white bobbed their heads in the current. In the shallows near her, silver fish skittered, while thumbnail-sized red-and-pink crabs scuttled along the white sandy bottom. The air tasted of salt and sand.

The Kingdom of Ocea.

"Let's get moving." Frea interrupted Stasha's gawking. She blinked in surprise to hear the sour fae speak. Frea's bow was no longer strung across her back, but in her hand. A schorl-tipped arrow was nocked into place. "We need to reach the end of the Laughing Pools by nightfall."

"She's right," Boa said. "It's not safe here. And don't be fooled by how pretty the water looks. Don't touch it, or we'll have Pyreack soldiers on us in a flash."

Stasha jumped up off the wall. The last thing she wanted was a showdown with more soldiers who could alert their leaders that she and her band were on the move. It was a stretch to think they'd link her movements with Klaus in Angharad, but she couldn't risk it. "How will they know?"

"Piss Swill charmed the water to betray anyone who wasn't in Ocea at the time of his coronation." Boa glared down at the stream. Stasha could imagine Boa's frustration that the element from which she drew her power would consider her an enemy.

Frea hopped up onto the wall. She looked from one stepping stone to another, finally picking out the driest. She jumped across to it. Boa followed her. Lukas waved to Stasha to go next. Never more aware of her balance, she jumped the chosen path. Averin, Trystaen, and Eliezar came next, with Lukas bringing up the rear.

"Want Eliezar and me to dry off the stones?" Averin called to Boa. "We can whip up some wind to do it."

"That would be helpful," Boa said. "Should have thought about it before we started."

Averin and Eliezar shuffled passed Stasha and the others to take point.

Sandwiched between Trystaen and Lukas, Stasha trailed at the back of the party.

A bell-like laugh spluttered from the rippling surface, echoing on everything and nothing. Stasha's head jerked up, and her foot almost slid off her stone. She waved her arms frantically, and it was only Trystaen's steady hand that stopped her sliding into the stream.

She cursed at her carelessness.

"It was just the water. That's why it's called the Laughing Pools," Trystaen said, hopping from one flat jade stone to another.

Stasha scowled at her ignorance, eyeing the laughing water with mistrust as she leaped onto the next boulder.

A fish splashed, and she had to fight to stop herself from jumping.

"It's right to be cautious," Trystaen added. "As you've already seen, Darien cares little for the faeries and magical creatures that don't benefit him. Regardless of the threat they pose to travelers, he lets them run wild. Like the Tiyanak and the manticore."

She shivered and gulped down a salty breath. She hadn't mentioned her bargain with the Tiyanak yet.

Aware that she was strung too tightly, she said quietly to Trystaen, "Tell me about fae sealing." Almost unbidden, her eyes flitted to Averin. Lithe and deadly, he jumped from rock to rock, following the breeze streaking from his fingertips. Another stupid blush followed by a grimace. How was it possible she could be dreaming of him when she'd sworn after Tarik she'd never want anyone in *that* way again?

Trystaen eyed her sharply. "What makes you ask that?"

She avoided his gaze as they hopped onto adjacent rocks. "Averin told me about Eliezar and Nela. He said they were sealed. It piqued my curiosity."

The tight lines around Trystaen's eyes and mouth relaxed. "They were. Fae who choose each other say they're sealed. It's like marriage." He grunted. "Or rather, it is for fae outside of Pyreack."

"How does sealing work?"

Trystaen shrugged. "How does any love work? Chemistry and compatibility. Get it in the right proportions, and the two life forces connect. Those fae become sealed on a level that nothing can break." He waited for her to jump onto a rock ahead of him. "There are no second fae marriages after they've been sealed."

Her eyes were drawn to Eliezar and Boa, both of whom had lost partners. "So they won't marry again?"

"Eliezar won't. He couldn't, even if he wanted to, which would never happen. The sealing continues after death."

"And Boa?"

"She and Shyael weren't sealed. In time, she will have to open her heart to fresh possibilities. A male to help her secure her succession."

"I'm glad you're that confident she'll get her throne back."

Trystaen smiled. "It might have something to do with finding you."

That. Again. Not willing to let him change the subject, she asked, "So what happens to the magic when fae get sealed?"

Trystaen blinked, and then his face cleared. "Right. You're thinking about how things work in Pyreack. It's nothing like that in Zephyr. If fae seal, they share the magic." He gestured at the water around them. "I guess you can say it's pooled, and they can both draw on it."

"That sounds far more civilized."

"I thought you might—"

A shout cut him short. Stasha stood on her toes to see the front of the line.

Frea's foot had slipped off her rock, and ripples scurried across the pond.

Water rumbled behind Stasha. She snapped her head around and gasped. Bubbles and dead fish rose to the surface. Angry water sloshed onto her rock. Steam billowed up at her feet like a hissing snake.

"Run!" Trystaen yelled.

"Here! Get to me," Averin shouted above the boiling water. "I'll spirit us out." He threw his hand out toward Stasha, his sapphire eyes beseeching her to hurry.

She yelped. Behind him, a wave of water and dead fish crested.

Joining him would be deadly.

The pond behind her roared. Spray, hot as boiling kettle water, hit the back of her head. She stumbled forward, just managing to keep her balance. If she toppled headfirst into the pond, she'd be boiled alive, if she didn't drown first.

Trystaen grabbed her hand and jerked her off her feet. The world spun, and then she and Trystaen landed clumsily on Averin's rock. Still clinging to her, Trystaen staggered for balance. Averin grabbed her and pulled her close while Eliezar clutched Trystaen.

Frea and Lukas teetered on the green slab. She guessed Lukas had spirited, just as she and Trystaen had.

"Hold my arms," Averin shouted above the tumultuous water.

The wave crashed over them as Stasha's hand landed on his arm. Scalding liquid washed across her face and hands and soaked through her leathers. She screamed.

And then she was flying again.

CHAPTER TWENTY-FOUR

THE HIJACKING

Stasha landed on one foot in a long trail of scree tossed down from the brooding white cliff above her. She stumbled to balance on trembling legs, failed, and collapsed to her knees next to Averin. The only difference was that he'd landed on both feet.

"Sorry, everyone," Averin called. "I tried to get us into the temple, but—" A grimace. He dropped to his knees in front of her. "You okay?" His face was enflamed and swollen from the boiling water. He huffed a breath. "Your skin is blistered."

That explained the sharp burning in her cheeks. He grabbed her hands, and she winced. Those were blistered too. In fact, her whole body, drenched in the boiling wave, ached. "I'm okay." Her voice sounded hollow. She cleared her throat. "Really, I am. No worse than you. Nothing that fae healing won't solve." She gritted her teeth against unbearable stinging that ran up her body like a colony of biting ants. It was made worse by the icy wet leather clinging to her. "Burns to my back, stomach, and legs." Her toes throbbed, as if to say, *What about us?*

Averin canted his head, dripping water into his eyes from his hair. His face had already begun to heal. "Only fire resistant, not heat resistant. Interesting."

Not wanting to delve into her weird fae abilities, she glanced around. "Anyone else scalded?"

"As you say, nothing that won't heal." Boa had landed with the rest of the group, a few feet from her and Averin. Boa and Averin must have known to let go while landing, while she had clung to Averin as if her life depended on it.

Would she ever get used to spiriting? Everyone other than her and Averin started to gather together, clearly readying to leave.

"What happened back there?" she asked, anything to delay moving before her body was ready to cooperate.

"Frea's foot slipped off her stone," Boa said curtly. "She wasn't in Ocea when the water was charmed, so it attacked her. And the rest of us. By now, the pools will be swarming with soldiers."

Bow in hand, face pointed to the cliff, Frea showed no emotion at almost killing them.

"Can they track us here?" Stasha asked, dreading the answer.

"Depends on whether they have spiriting readers with them," Averin said. At her raised eyebrow, he added, "Fae who can sense a spiriting path." He pulled out his sword. "Boa and I won't be much help if we need to throw magic around, but I can whip their asses with my blades."

"We've got this," Eliezar said with his usual quiet certainty. He flexed his hand, and a sharp breeze whipped up the stones around them. They would make deadly projectiles in a fight.

"Whatever happens," Boa added, "defend Stasha. We cannot have her captured."

"They'll struggle to take me." The fire sparking from her fingers matched her indignation.

"Trystaen, Lukas, and I won't let them get close enough to try." Eliezar glanced at Frea. "And I'm sure you'll lend us the support of your water magic."

"We need to get moving if we're to reach the temple by nightfall," Frea replied. "Inside the temple will be easier to defend than out here."

The deep shadows confirmed the sun would not be long in setting. Already it was icy. Hypothermia would stalk on a night like this. She wasn't human anymore, so hopefully hypothermia might not be such an issue, but she wasn't keen to test that theory.

Averin held out his hand to her. When she took it, he whispered, "If you need help, ask. If you don't want me helping you, Trystaen or Eliezar will do it with pleasure."

"I'm fine. I don't need special treatment." She let him yank her to her feet. "Is there a path?"

"You're standing on it." Boa's eyes flashed angrily as she looked around the barren scree. It was lined with stunted, burnt-out trees. "This used to be known as the Thousand Stairs. The first part of the pilgrim's sacrifice to be worthy of meeting the gods. Piss Swill's fae destroyed them when they sacked the temple. A double sacrilege given that this temple wasn't only sacred to Ocea. Fae came from everywhere to worship here."

Stasha studied the shale and cliff face more carefully. Scars on the mountainside suggested that once stairs could have been carved into it, stairs now lying in shattered ruins at the foot of its forbidding slope.

She swallowed. Scrambling up the cliff wasn't going to be a picnic, especially with an enemy trailing them. Her scrawny frame took longer to heal than the others. Apart from wet clothes, they were already showing no signs of their injuries. Add her general physical weakness to that, and she would be the tail end of this climb, holding everyone back, as usual. She almost wished she could ask Averin to spirit her to the top to save everyone time, but if he'd had the magical strength left to do that, he would have offered. As it was, by his targeted spiriting, he had cut a day off their trip. She would be ever thankful to him for that.

Everyone waited for her.

She smiled pertly. "Race you to the top."

"You're on." Averin's bright eyes looked first at her and then at the rocky trail. "If you win, I'll make you something to eat. If you win—" He chortled. "I'll settle for a few handfuls of dried meat and nuts."

She punched his arm, hating to admit he was wise in his assessment of her cooking skills.

"I'll take that challenge, too." Boa grunted. "I'd love to see the great Prince Averin don an apron and do some cooking."

"Omelets for everyone." Averin rolled his eyes as they all started walking. "Right. No eggs. You all lucked out."

Only Frea showed no reaction to the banter. The surly fae set off at a brutal pace.

Stasha brushed her hair back from her face and tested her itching legs. The first step was tentative, but when the skin didn't slough off her body, she increased her pace.

Instead of racing ahead, sword in hand, Averin and Boa flanked her. The threat of pursuit meant they walked faster than she, Averin, Trystaen, and Eliezar had before meeting up with the rebels. She dug deep into her energy wells to keep up with them.

Although Averin was watchful, true to his word, he didn't offer to help her scramble over the rocks and boulders strewn in their path that he and the other fae sailed over as easily as breathing. It endeared him to her even more, for she would have hated to be singled out. Although she spent much of the hike looking over her shoulder, there was no sign of the Pyreack fae.

The higher they climbed over loose rocks and shifting soil, the thinner the air became, until she was wheezing. It was also punishingly cold. No birds nested here. No life existed among the treacherous slopes and crumbling rock faces. Not even insects chirped to greet the night closing in around them.

She considered coating her skin in a film of fire to warm her but decided against it. If they were being followed, it would draw unnecessary attention. Also, she didn't know what wells of magical power she had. Spiriting had taxed Boa, Averin, and Trystaen, and they were more powerful than she could imagine. Until she understood more about her magic, she didn't want to waste an ounce of it before Klaus was safely out of Angharad.

She took her mind off her misery by practicing with her hidden blade. The first few times she triggered it, she almost cut her fingers off, but after an hour of climbing and flicking, the blade became less treacherous.

They reached a gap in the mountain. Like an axe, an earthquake must have cleaved the rock apart, making a clean cut straight through the glowing white marble and deep-gray stone. Through the cleft, the

Sword constellation flecked the swiftly blackening sky with silver. A trail of purple and blue twinkled between the silver hilt and blade, like a river of gems. She had always loved that constellation. Now she had a sudden urge to fly up to the Sword, where it was quiet and peaceful, and no one was dead or dying. And no one hunted them.

"Almost there." Boa's step lightened, and she sped up.

Stasha pulled her attention from the sky to the mountain. Black and white faces, carved from marble the size of wagon wheels, ran the length of the cliff's edge. Waterfalls poured from their gaping mouths and fell endlessly into the valley below. Stasha grimaced. "Fae worship the two-faced god?"

"He is one of our many deities." Boa jumped over a gully. She landed perfectly on both feet. Her fae limbs were feline in their grace. "I've heard fae claim that the gods forsook us when the temple was sacked, but I've never believed it." Boa smiled. "And now we have you. That's a sure sign that the gods are listening."

Stasha resisted the urge to roll her eyes. How could Boa even suggest the gods cared after all that had happened to them? Hope was one thing, but this—

She burst out before she could stop herself. "I was almost burned at the stake to satisfy the Kňazer who worship the two-faced god. Trust me; the gods did nothing to rescue me. They don't care if we live or die. If we're slaves or kings. Human or fae."

Boa's eyes widened with something akin to shock. Before Boa could comment, Averin said, "Yet I arrived with Eliezar and Trystaen. We cut both you and Klaus free."

Averin believed in the gods?

She couldn't resist adding, "Yes. Just moments before Radomir arrived. We all know how well that turned out."

Boa gripped her hand. "You talk of bringing us hope. Perhaps it's time you believed in miracles."

Stasha's mouth opened and closed as she sought a comeback that didn't utterly offend her allies.

"I think your Kňazer may have been in for a bit of a surprise if they'd tried to set you alight." Averin bumped her shoulder. "I've visited this temple before, and I'm sure you'll find it interesting." He took her hand and broke into a trot, pulling her along with him. She tried not to pant like a dog on a hot day as they left Boa and the rest of the group behind.

A small slit appeared in the lattice of stone and darkness. Averin pulled her through it into a narrow tunnel. Her fae eyes adjusted to the thick blackness, and her nose scrunched at the reek of mildew and stale water. The stench deepened the farther they pushed into the darkness. No scent of human or fae mingled with the smell.

A bat swooped overhead, chattering as it rushed out into the night.

"Was holding my hand and dragging me in here your way of ensuring neither of us have to cook?" she whispered to Averin. "If so, I approve." Her voice bounced and echoed through the tunnel.

Another bat squawked, flapping its leathery wings as it took flight past her ear. If anyone was hiding in the temple, they would have heard her for sure. She dropped her voice lower. "Is it safe here?"

"Keep your weapon handy," Averin whispered. "And yes, it was a ploy to get us out of cooking."

She stumbled over a rough patch of ground.

"Want to shed some light on the subject, pit princess? You know, use all that fire for something useful."

Could she light up the tunnel? She guessed she could, so she lifted her hand and let it glow. Dust motes floated in the stale air around her. They rounded a bend only to have their path blocked by an old wrought-iron gate. Averin creaked it open just far enough for them to pass through in single file.

Golden light spilled out to greet them.

She extinguished her fire as she and Averin stepped into a wide stone cavern.

In a pool of bright magic towered a shining tree. She gasped. Not just at the living tree giving light in total darkness, but at the wave upon wave of fire magic pouring off it. Yet, when she searched for flames, there were none. Mouth gaping in wonder, she took a step closer.

Bearded with moss and ivy, its branches scraped against a mural on the domed ceiling. Roots burrowed beneath the marble floor, cracking and bowing it in places.

The tree had a vast girth. Even with their arms extended, their party could not have encircled its trunk—a trunk scarred with axe blows and scorch marks, which had nothing to do with the fire magic spilling from the majestic tree.

Deep-red amber clung to the wounds or ran like tears down the crevices and gnarls. Beneath her feet, crumbled jewels glittered. She gaped up at the dome. Soot and scorch marks blackened the gold-painted rock, rock pitted with holes, where the gems might once have gleamed. Now only a few glinted in the reflected light from the ancient tree.

"Wait here," Averin hissed, "while I check that we don't have company."

She nodded lamely, transfixed by the tree.

Boa's boots clipped across the dusty stone floor. "Lukas, Frea," she called softly. "Secure the place while I watch Stasha."

"I don't need watching."

"Not taking chances." Stasha was about to flounce off after Averin when Boa added, "Piss Swill's savages tried to destroy the tree, but the magic resisted them. Can you feel the fire calling to you?"

"Yes." Something unfamiliar but powerful and insistent prickled her skin. She shivered. "But there's something else. Something I don't recognize."

Boa rested her hand reverently on the bark. "Not surprising. You feel fire. I sense water. I bet Averin and Eliezar would tell you they feel air."

"Earth for me." Blades drawn, Trystaen joined them. "It's indeed a sad thing that we have to come in here armed and expecting trouble. This temple used to be a sanctuary for us all."

The strange, uncomfortable prickle faded. Stasha opened her

arms, letting the fire magic embrace her. She closed her eyes and bowed her head in awe. To an outsider, she must have looked like the Martka kneeling at the feet of the two-faced god. "Where does the magic come from?" she whispered, not wanting to break the reverent stillness.

"No one knows. But this tree has grown here for a long time."

Averin, Eliezar, Lukas, and Frea rejoined them.

"All clear. No one has been here for months," Eliezar said.

Averin bumped her shoulder. "I told you it would be worth seeing." He offered her his hand. "Care for a tour?"

Eliezar stiffened. Even Trystaen frowned. Perhaps they'd seen her attraction to Averin and didn't approve of him encouraging it. That made sense, given that he was a prince and she—

Well, who knew what she was?

Or maybe it was simpler, and fae kept to their own magical type, and they didn't want her getting ideas of mixing fire and air. Clearly, they didn't understand that her heart—or at least most of it—still belonged to Tarik.

Averin wriggled his fingers. "Today. Because this is a one-time offer."

She took his hand. "How can I resist such backhanded gallantry?"

Head held high as a snub to Eliezar and Trystaen, she let Averin lead her like a queen out of the tree's glow and into the shadows on the far side of the cavern. He stopped at an unlit torch in a wall holder. "How about you fire that up for us, pit princess?"

She cupped a handful of fire and was about to touch the cloth woven around the tip of the dried wood when the gentlest wind cooled her fingers. Mirroring her pulse, the flames leaped out of her hand and caught on the fabric. Heads almost touching, she and Averin watched the flames curl until the torch blazed.

"That's how it starts, Stasha," Averin whispered. "A small spark and a tiny breeze. Next, we have a blazing fire not even a hurricane can quell."

Had he listened in to her conversation with Trystaen about sealing? Knowing busybody Averin, he had. Goose bumps burst over her skin. "What do you mean?"

"I think you know." Averin's mouth hovered so close, she could almost sense his skin on hers.

He closed the distance.

Warm, firm lips brushed hers. She gasped, and her lips parted. He smiled, opening his mouth to her. She clutched his tunic with both hands and pulled her body into his as his lips and tongue caressed hers with gentle strokes. Her eyelids fluttered closed, and her knees shook. It took all her self-control not to burn with pleasure.

Tarik's laughing face flashed before her.

Disgusted with herself, she started to tug away, but Averin pushed her first. His hand shot to his mouth. "Sorry, Stasha. I shouldn't have done that. I don't know what I was thinking."

Legs trembling, she stepped back. "No. No. It was me. I shouldn't have—" How dare she betray Tarik with a fae? She gnawed her lip— it still tingled with delight at Averin's touch, his taste, his smell, his.... What had Trystaen said about falling in love? Chemistry and compatibility in the right proportions.

How could she even be *thinking* about liking Averin in that way? Betrayer.

Never more conflicted, she yanked the torch from the holder and stomped away. "You were going to show me this place."

Averin grabbed her arm and spun her to him. "This ... thing." Cool air wafted between them as his fingers flicked from him to her. "No matter what...." Face haunted, he swallowed and sucked in a breath. "We can't let it get in the way of our plans."

"As if I ever would. Rescuing Klaus is everything to me." But even as she spoke, she knew she would hate it if things between her and Averin changed. Especially since the only reason he could have rejected her was because she was a nobody weapon while he was a prince.

Familiar darkness settled over Averin. Eyes hooded, he said, "And taking you back to Zephyr is everything to me."

Averin in pain. Averin suffering from wounds she could only guess at. Wounds she longed to heal but didn't know how to even start fixing.

She tossed her shoulders back in the hope that a firm posture would steady her voice. "Then we both know what to do ... and what not to do." She forced a sassy smile to cover up her sorrow at what she was losing. At the chasm dividing her and this beautiful, tortured creature.

Averin tossed a cocky smile her way, one that tumbled her straight back to the Averin she'd met outside the shop when he'd confronted her about his stolen coin. "Now that we understand each other, care to continue the tour?"

"Of course."

Why did it hurt when he didn't offer her his arm? And when had she become so needy as to want it?

Numbly, she followed him along a length of stone wall, carved with alcoves. In the torchlight, life-sized statues flickered in them. Here the marauders had been more successful in their destruction. Cracked and broken, some of the effigies wore the black and white robes she was so familiar with. The carved robes clung to their frames, spilling like frozen waterfalls to forever pool at their bare feet.

The two-faced god.

The only difference between these statues and the ones in the orphanage, or at the Crekev, were the delicate, pointed fae ears that had survived on some of them.

She flinched, tucking a hand under the bicep of her torch-holding arm. Her nails dug in so hard, she thought the skin might split.

She forced herself to keep walking.

"We see the two-faced god differently than humans do," Averin said, still keeping his distance. "To us, he represents power—the font of *all* magical power. Him and the tree." He looked around and sighed. "Or they once did." His boot nudged a broken arm. "Before all this."

"So he doesn't punish and burn at the stake?"

"No. For that, you need to look to the other gods." Averin ambled to the opposite wall. Its alcoves were stuffed with statues of gods she'd never seen before. Some bowed cracked heads over broken hilts of great swords. Others were emblazoned with strange words in a language she didn't recognize. Stone owls or ravens perched on the shoulders and outstretched arms of others. Perhaps once beautiful, now they were chipped and deformed by war.

She sighed, tired of yet more signs of senseless conflict.

She was about to turn away to find Boa and the others when Averin reached for her hand. He hesitated, as if remembering their pact to stay clear of each other, and then wiped his palm on his leggings. "There's more to see."

Not wanting to part with him, she waited.

"Why do you hate the gods so much?" Averin's voice was a mere whisper, as if the stone statues towering over them might smite him down for suggesting such a thing.

She palmed her pendant in a dust-covered hand. It dug painfully into her scar. "I prayed once," she said, so low she didn't know if he'd heard. "I prayed the day Tarik died." After kissing Averin, Tarik's name sat awkwardly on her tongue, as if she didn't deserve to say it.

Averin stiffened beside her.

She ground her teeth together so hard, her jaw ached. "I begged the two-faced god to save him. I *pleaded*." She opened her palm and stared down at the ugly, thick scar. "And he did nothing. He let all those people die." She blinked back tears. "And I will never pray for anything again. Either the gods don't exist, or they don't care." She dropped her hand. "I have no interest and no time to waste on them."

Averin's fingers brushed against hers. A reassuring, gentle touch, like she would share with Klaus, reminding her to breathe. "You're not afraid?"

She tilted her lips up in a coy, rueful smile. "Of damnation? The day the two-faced god stands accountable for what he's done, I will too." She stood a little taller. "What about you? Are you afraid of them?"

Averin shrugged but didn't answer. His sapphire eyes hid his thoughts well.

"May I ask you a question?"

His perfect eyebrows arched, and he waved a hand for her to go ahead. His sleeves were pulled up, revealing just a hint of tattooed skin.

"What are those?"

Averin blinked, then smiled sadly. "They're a promise. A promise I made to Nela the last time I saw her in Angharad. I had them tattooed so I'd never forget. That's why I'm going back tomorrow with you to rescue your friend. I owe my sister that much."

Her heart broke for him. For all he had lost. But all she could do was hope that no more broken prayers or promises would be borne in Angharad.

Averin tipped his chin at another wall. A web of cracks and carved symbols traced the dark stone. A few gems still gleamed in the intricate murals, but most were gone. "Come. Let's finish this tour so we can eat. I'm starving, and I'm sure you are too."

Stasha's eyebrows knitted together. The stone was flaking, like blackened bark, or ... parchment. She walked with him for a better look. "Are those messages stuffed in the cracks?"

"Prayers. Fae would write their heart's desire and leave them here for the gods to answer."

"And did they?"

"Enough believed they did for this temple to stand for generations."

"How did they answer?" she asked, doubting every word.

"Notes shoved in the crevice with the original prayer." Averin pulled out a curl of scorched parchment. It was the only one in the nook. A cloud of ash and dust made them both sneeze. He unfurled it and traced the faded blue lettering with a long finger. The swirling calligraphy was grand. He read, "I love a female who loves another male. I pray for his pain. I pray for his death. I pray for her heart. D.R."

Stasha gagged audibly. What a vile prayer. She grabbed the parchment and stuffed it back into the wall.

But now she wanted to know more.

She grabbed another. This curl was so delicate, it threatened to crumble to dust and be lost forever. She mouthed the letters, taking far longer than Averin to stumble through the greenish ink, faded into almost nothing. *She loves a human. I let her go. I pray for my own traitorous heart. E.A.*

Were the gods sporting with her? Or were these real prayers of desperate fae, so fervently written? She pulled out another. The yellowing paper was thicker and sturdier than the others but folded badly. Hurriedly. Carelessly stuffed into the cracks. A date had been scrawled on the top right corner. Thirty years ago. *Remember us. Deliver us. Fulfill your promises. They're coming. They're here. And now we burn.* Ink smudged the parchment, as if the writer had begun to sign his name and had been forced to stop.

"That must have been the day the Pyreack soldiers came." Averin was reading over her shoulder. His warm breath sent so many shivers through her, she nearly dropped the hopeless prayer. Her mouth dried. She placed the parchment gently back where she found it. "I'm done. Let's join the others."

"As you wish."

But as she turned away, her gaze snagged on another folded sheet. Instead of being stuffed into a crevice, this prayer fit into a tear-drop-shaped hole from where a gemstone had been prized. Unlike the rest of the prayers, the cream-colored parchment wasn't charred. That dated it to after the attack. Intrigued, she pulled it out. The stiff, newish paper crackled as she unfolded it. Undated, the scrawled lettering was still clear, still perfect. *I pray for the child who carries the world. I pray that the child will know us. I pray that the child will serve us. I pray that the child will recognize the key. I pray that the child will use it to free us from our bonds of stone and wood. C.L.E.*

Her lungs tightened, and she just managed to wheeze, "Who was C.L.E.?"

Averin took the sheet from her and turned it over to see the other side. Nothing had been written there. He tapped it against his finger-nail. "I don't know."

With no answers, she snatched the prayer from him and shoved it back into the wall. Hatred for the gods and all these unanswered pleas sent sparks flying off her body.

Averin skittered out of range. "You really need time with Eliezar. He must help you control your fiery emotions."

She glared at him. "So you all keep telling me. But not tonight. And not tomorrow, because I want my emotions running wild and free in Angharad. I want nothing to stop me burning."

"Perhaps so, Stasha. But we need you to come out of Angharad as the same fae who went in." She almost jumped out of her skin when Eliezar stepped out of the shadows.

How long had he been there?

She glanced at Averin. His expression suggested he wasn't surprised by the visitation. Still, he glowered at his second. "I've got this, El. You don't need to panic."

Eliezar panic? That was almost worthy of laughter if she hadn't been so irritated that the wolf-eyed fae had stalked them. She plunked her hands on her hips.

But before she could reprimand him, Eliezar said, "Stasha, places like Angharad change us. They have to. If they don't, then we need to question our values—our very right to existence. Be careful of what you allow to be wrought in you tomorrow. None of us want to see you changed by hate and fury."

Her hands slid off her hips. Eliezar had lost his wife in Angharad, yet he could speak so calmly of guarding against hate? Her irritation dissipated, dissolving as quickly as honey doused by water. "You're a better person than I if you can lose without hate."

"Fae live a long time, Stasha, when our lives are not cut short. Although I fight daily against the Pyreack—and will until I die—I choose to live in peace with myself. I want that for you too." Eliezar's eyes softened. "Let's call that my first lesson. Go to Angharad and burn, but do not let what you see there ignite your soul. Because if it does—" His gaze drifted to Averin. "Not even a hurricane will extinguish it."

Indestructible as he seemed, Eliezar feared the power of her destruction?

She dipped her head to him. "I give you my word. If Klaus is alive, you have nothing to fear from me. But if he's dead, I make you no promise. I will burn until every Pyreack fae is dead."

King Darien Pyreaxos had no idea of the force he'd unleashed.

*M*ore spiriting. This time, Stasha landed up to her ankles in ochre-colored sand. Her stomach rolled, but she didn't vomit. That would have been progress if the harsh sunlight hadn't made her flinch.

Ahead of her, towering dunes stretched to the horizon. Dust drifted above their sculpted slopes, caught in a moaning wind that did nothing to cool the scorching heat. The contrast to the icy cold of the last few days almost made her lightheaded. Above her, the sky was impossibly blue and almost painful to look at. Nothing like her crisp, cold sky in Atria, now so very far away. She shook her head in wonder. If anyone had told her that she, a waif from Askavol, would live to see a desert, she'd have laughed in their face.

But here she was at the border of Pyreack and the start of the Blue Desert. Three of Boa's healers and a half a dozen rebel soldiers awaited them. The healers would be responsible for protecting and caring for the prisoners Stasha and her team were about to release. The soldiers—all defectors from Pyreack who now fought alongside Boa—would ride with her in the wagon. Dressed as Pyreack soldiers, Averin and Lucas would sit up front with the horses.

Clad in rough, grimy clothes befitting prisoners, the soldiers and Lukas would free the fae, part of the distraction she and Averin needed to buy time while they opened the prison gates. Back in the map tent at Boa's camp, they'd debated bringing a bigger force, but neither Boa nor Averin had been willing to risk more foot soldiers when they'd already lost so many trying to take Angharad.

Stasha nodded her greetings and tugged her feet out of the mire to walk over to them, only to sink even deeper with each step. Sweat beaded her forehead and trickled down her back. Slogging through these dunes would be exhausting. Fighting in them—well, she had some appreciation for Averin's claim that the terrain was as much of an enemy as the Pyreack who lived and thrived in this hellhole.

"Are the Pyreack colorblind?" she asked no one in particular. "There's nothing blue about this desert."

"It shines blue at night. I once thought it magnificent." The blades in Averin's baldric, and the ones attached to his arms, legs, and back, glinted in the sunlight. Those were the visible ones. No doubt he had more stashed in his secret pockets and boots. He handed her a waterskin. "Make sure you stay hydrated. We can't have you weak once the heist begins."

She drank greedily.

"Enough chitchat." Boa tossed a cloak at Stasha, who caught it with one hand. "Everyone get ready. That includes setting up the bivouac for the prisoners. Behind those rocks will do." Boa pointed to a jumble of golden boulders on the side of the track. "As soon as the wagon is hemmed in between the dunes and the rocks, we hit it."

Stasha quickly detached her black velvet cloak from her shoulders. A cloud of dust stirred upward as it fell. The cloak Boa had given her was tattered and worn—pale gray, like she'd worn every day of her mortal life. Holes peppered the fabric. Even though they suspected all glamour would be swept away when she passed through the camp's portcullis, she was still going to try to present herself as human.

She grunted. Pity her nose was undoubtedly fae, given the reek of mildew and filth that wafted over her as she slung the ragged garment around her shoulders. Horrible as the grimy thing was, it would hide her dagger and allow her hidden blade to remain truly hidden in its folds. And keep her hands concealed should they start to spark—a fact no one had mentioned but had to be utmost on everyone's minds. No matter what happened, she had to control herself, only revealing her fire once Klaus had been found and the slaves freed.

Or at least that was the plan.

Averin tossed a Pyreack-foot-soldier's cloak around his shoulders.

While she was sure that she appeared like nothing more than a peasant from nowhere in particular, he still looked every inch a prince, despite the ugly firebird crest on his back.

Eliezar tsked. "Averin, I wish you'd let me and Trys come with you and Stasha."

Averin wrapped an arm around Eliezar's shoulder. "We've been through this a dozen times, El. I won't risk you. If things go badly, and Stasha and I don't make it, I need you and Trys to explain it to my parents and Rican." Averin stepped away and added sharply, "And I need you to take over the Azura and the regulars. We can't risk everyone and everything on this heist."

Eliezar sighed. "I hope the glamour lasts long enough to get you through the portcullis."

"A risk we have to take," Averin said firmly. "Now cast it."

Eliezar lifted his hand, then hesitated. "Averin, I know I can't stop you, but at least tell me that you've fully recovered from yesterday's spiriting."

Averin punched Eliezar lightly on the shoulder. "Being at the tree was highly restorative. And I slept well after my watch."

Stasha blushed. She'd woken this morning with her head on Averin's chest. His arm had been tight around her. How she'd gotten there, she didn't know, other than to say that despite wanting to avoid each other, after circling the cavern when their watch ended, they'd gravitated to the same shadowy corner to sleep. She hadn't been the only one to stutter and huff with embarrassment when they awoke. They had parted instantly without saying a word, neither questioning who had closed the distance in their sleep. She hoped no one had seen them, although with Eliezar, that was unlikely.

Eliezar fixed her with a penetrating stare, confirming her suspicions that he knew in whose arms she'd spent the night. "In that case, I'll cast the glamour," he said tersely and waved his hand.

Stasha gulped when Averin looked at her through very ordinary, very brown Pyreack eyes. His pointed fae face changed from achingly beautiful to merely handsome. "Your turn," he said.

She raised her hand to stop Eliezar before he could glamour her. "Is that enough? You still look like Averin. At least to me."

"Like you, no one is expecting Prince Averin Trysael of Zephyr to drop into Angharad. All it has to do is get us through the portcullis."

"Ready?" Eliezar asked her. Even though he clearly didn't approve of her relationship with Averin, he spoke softly. Kindly.

She nodded. Eliezar flitted his hand across her face. Magic trilled through her. Her fingers shot to her ears. Round. Ordinary. Human. Boring. The perfect match to her eyes.

Next, Eliezar changed Lukas's mauve water-magic eyes to Pyreack brown.

"Dirty up." Lukas passed her a tincture bottle. A firebird crest adorned the back of his soiled, stolen cloak. "It'll help hide your scent, if nothing else."

She pulled out the cork and gagged. It stank of rotting leaves and pig manure. "What, in all the darkness, is this stuff?"

Averin grinned. "In circumstances like these, I find it best not to ask."

She wrinkled her nose. "Fine for you. You don't have to use it." Only she had to cover her fae smell. She slapped a blob on her face and rubbed it in. Next, she did her hands and clothing.

Everyone except Averin shifted upwind from her.

Boa rounded on them. "Frea, Trystaen, Eliezar, positions." Like shadows, the three fae slipped behind the boulders. "The rest of you, out of the way until called."

Averin grabbed Stasha's sleeve. "I think you smell awful enough." He dragged her behind the boulders. "Don't forget. No fire. Save it for the guards operating the gates. Just use that hidden blade until we free Klaus and the rest of the prisoners."

She wanted to snap that she wasn't a child and that she knew the plan as well as he did, but she stopped herself. They all knew how unreliable her fire control was. Boa joined them and crouched low with a crossbow in her hand.

Lukas took off through the boulders until he reached the narrow road. He opened a can and poured pig's blood over the sand. He tossed the can over the boulders and dropped onto the blood, lying there as if he'd been clubbed.

Stasha hunched in the limited shade cast by the boulders. Sweat trickled uncomfortably down her temples, her spine, and between her breasts. She wiped her brow with the foul-smelling cloak and tried to slow her rapid breathing before she hyperventilated. The heat was going to kill her before she even reached the portcullis. Where was that damn prison wagon?

Finally, the rattle and squeal of wheels in desperate need of oiling reached her.

Her head shot up.

"This is it," Boa whispered. "You all know what to do."

Stasha held her breath as the prison wagon rounded the track and entered the passage between the dunes and rocks.

It was huge. The box behind the horses was far bigger than even the Kňazer's fancy carriage. As expected, the door was bolted shut. A crisscross of schorl bars revealed little of the dark interior, but from the pressure in her head and the nausea rising in her stomach, she guessed it wasn't the only schorl in the box.

The driver jerked on the reins and pulled the wagon to a stop; he must have seen Lukas lying in the middle of the track. The four black horses pulling the wagon bucked their heads and nickered impatiently. One nipped its companion's neck. The horse kicked out, snorting angrily.

"Aye!" The driver brought a thin whip down on their rumps. The pair danced in their shafts but didn't bolt. He spoke to the fae sitting next to him on the bench. "There's a body in the way. Go move it."

The soldier stood and peered at Lukas. "He's wearing a Pyreack cloak. Bloody rebels. Do you think they got the last wagon?" He unsheathed his sword.

"Must have done." The driver's eyes darted around nervously. "Hurry up and shift him. This could be another ambush."

Childlike weeping spilled from the box at the back of the wagon.

Stasha flicked the trigger on her hidden blade, and it shot free, as if it also wanted to punish these monsters for imprisoning children.

Face taut, the soldier stood and pulled out his sword. He jumped to the sand and looked around before loping to Lukas. His boot shot out and caught Lukas in the side. Lukas lay as still as any corpse.

"Go. Now." Averin shoved her forward.

With feline stealth, she and her companions crept through the stone, keeping low until they were mere yards from the wagon.

Averin's hand flicked. A throwing knife whistled through the air and embedded into the heart of the soldier standing over Lukas. Soundlessly, the fae crumpled to the sand.

The driver yelled and raised his hands to flick the reins, but before the horses reacted to the command, an arrow wedged in his chest. Frea.

The driver grunted and tumbled off his bench. Startled, the four horses bucked. Boa and Trystaen grabbed their reins and steadied them.

Just as Averin and Boa had said, no more guards appeared to take up the defense. Robbed of all opportunity to use her blade by the warrior fae, she ran to the door at the back of the wagon. The box thrummed with what she assumed were prisoners' beating fists. Children wailed. She rattled the lock and was about to yell to Averin to find the key when he skidded around with it in his hand.

Boa trailed him. She shouted, "Frea, Lukas. Wash the blood off the bench."

Averin shoved the key into the lock. Worn with use, it turned easily. He flung the door wide.

Bright light flooded the crowded darkness. At least fifty brown-eyed fae, both male and female of all ages, were manacled together in the box—a box made repellent not just by the schorl panels cladding one wall. Urine, feces, and blood sloshed on the floor. She gagged, eyes watering stench.

In the doorway, three children—two girls and a boy—hunched next to each other. They were joined by manacles at the wrist. The source of the weeping, they looked like siblings. Stasha's practiced eyes recognized what they were—orphans. Little fae ears peeked through hair matted with dried blood. Their little bodies bore bloody streak marks—whippings already healed. How many more could they endure before they succumbed to the abuse? How long would they have suffered in Angharad?

Boa stumbled back, all color draining from her face. She clasped her throat. "Doesn't matter how many times I see this, I never get used to it."

Stasha tried to clear the horror from her face with a smile and bent down until she was eye level with the children. "Hey there," she cooed. "You're all right now. We've come to get you out."

A few hisses from the adults. They fidgeted, disbelieving hope stirring slumped postures. Some of them stepped forward, even though it would pull all of them out of the wagon.

Stasha held up an imperious hand. "Children first," she snapped. "Especially if they've just lost their family, as I'm sure is the case with these three."

Perhaps it was the presence of the armed fae behind her, but they drew back to let her coax the children out.

The little boy wrapped his free arm tighter around the girls.

She addressed him. "My name is Stasha," she said softly, extending her hand. "Can you and your sisters climb down, or should I help you?"

Bottom lip wobbling, the little boy looked at her hand warily.

Stasha pointed to Boa. "That's Princess Boa. She leads the rebels." Another hiss and more shuffling from the adults. She ignored it and continued crooning to the children. "We need this wagon for something very important. Something that will punish the fae who have harmed you."

The child's cracked lips parted. "Where are you taking us?"

Boa pointed to the three healers who waited just beyond their circle. "They're here to clean your injuries and give you food. And I have rebel soldiers who will protect you. They'll take you to one of my camps in Ocea." Boa smiled at the boy. "No one will hurt you again."

The little boy fixed huge brown eyes on Stasha. "You promise?"

Her heart stuttered. "I promise." She extended her hand again, and the boy took it. She helped him and his sisters down and led them to the healers.

One of them—a female from Atria—had already found the key to the manacles. She tried to unlock the bands around the little boy's wrist, but he pulled away and nudged Stasha.

Time was racing, and Klaus was into his second day in Angharad, but she quelled her impatience and unlocked both his and his sisters' restraints. She turned earnestly to the healers. "This little family is very important to me. I'm entrusting them to you because I know you'll take care of them until I get back."

The green-eyed fae nodded just as earnestly. "I take that responsibility very seriously."

Stasha gave the boy a quick hug. "Until later, my friend."

He hugged her back and then took each of his sisters by the hand, and they clustered around the healer.

Averin leaned in to whisper to her. "Now that you've sorted out your charges, we need to go."

She walked with him to the wagon, empty now except for the stench and filth. And the hated schorl. She eyed it sourly. "I seem to recall you telling me never to allow myself to be tossed into a schorl box."

Averin canted his head. "Ironic, isn't it?" A wide grin. "But let's not forget who came up with the plan for raiding Angharad."

"True. Hope I don't live to regret it." She waited by his side while the six rebels climbed in, clambered deeper into the wagon, and slumped down against the wall.

"You know I'd have you on the bench next to me if the Pyreack weren't so chauvinistic about women soldiers," Averin whispered, all mirth gone.

"I know. The plan is good, and we must work it." She held out her hands for him to manacle.

The iron was cold around her bare wrist and tight about the wrist sheathed with her hidden blade. He slipped the key into her pocket, within reach of her fingers. The pressure of his hand so close to her skin sent a shiver through her. "Take care, my pit princess," he said, eyes dark as a moonless night. "Remember, I don't want to go home without you."

Her chest tightened. She gripped the door with her manacled hands. "You, too, Blue Eyes. Life without your pretty face just wouldn't be the same." She brushed his perfect eyebrows. "And don't let anyone mess those up. That's my job." She yanked the door closed. Averin had to jump out of the way before it slammed on him, but that was better than letting him see the sorrow brought on by the thought of losing him.

The door closed with a deafening click. Averin turned the key.

She and the six other fae were plunged into near darkness. And then they were moving. To Angharad.

CHAPTER TWENTY-FIVE

ANGHARAD DEATH CAMP

S tasha and the six fae males were tossed about the wagon as its wheels lurched and dove into every pothole and rut in the seemingly endless track. Although it could not have been more than two hours since they'd stolen the wagon, she felt as if they'd been traveling all day. She guessed Averin and Lukas were doing their best to pick the smoothest path, but she'd still be black and blue with bruises by the time they arrived at the prison camp.

It added authenticity to her claim of being a prisoner.

Sweat streamed down her body. Strands of hair had slipped free of her braid and stuck to her neck. She missed the comfort and usefulness of Tarik's red ribbon.

Still, by the time they arrived at the camp, Boa, Eliezar, Trystaen, and Frea would have rendezvoused with Boa's rebel soldiers. Once she, Averin, and Lukas opened the prison gates, Boa and her army would march into Angharad to help with the fighting. That was the plan, at least.

The wagon slowed and then stopped. She clambered to her feet and peered through the schorl bars. The back of the wagon faced the way they'd come, the unending sand dunes telling her nothing.

Her nose twitched, and she gagged.

Carrion. Nothing else smelled as bad.

Metal shrieked and groaned endlessly. A portcullis opening?

Footsteps crunched outside. "You're late."

When would the door fly open and reveal her? She wished she could extend her blade, but that would alert the guard that she wasn't the helpless human she needed him to think she was.

"Rebels," Lukas answered. "Blocked the road. Had to move rocks."

"Did they attack you?"

"Took most of our prisoners. We just managed to get away."

The soldier slapped the side of the wagon. "Any females?"

Stasha's blood ran cold.

"One," Lukas replied. "Human."

The rasp of a throat, followed by a snort and a spit. "Won't touch them. Okay, move in."

He wasn't even going to check the cargo? Averin and Boa were right—getting in was easy, but whatever awaited them in the camp had to be dire if the guards didn't bother with basic security. She flicked out her hidden blade and braced herself for the worst.

The horses moved forward. Darkness sucked into the wagon as they rolled into the tunnel beneath the mountain.

The wagon slowed, then stopped. The second portcullis?

Someone called. "Get your ass off that bench and open the back."

"Got it." Averin's light steps fluttered around to the back of the wagon. The lock turned, and the door opened. He grimaced. "We're about to find out what happens to invaders. Be safe." He was gone before she could reply.

Chains rattled. The wagon lurched forward through the open portcullis. Stasha grabbed the doorjamb to stop from sliding out.

Harsh light flooded the tunnel. She blinked back the glare as choking heat poured in around her, bringing the stench of death—and magic. The sheer force of it rocked her back and tumbled her onto her backside. She flicked her finger to retract her blade before it struck the floor—but the blade had gone. Breath coming in gasps, she patted her arm.

The sheath had vanished, like it had never existed.

She clawed for her dagger. It had gone, too. From the panicked searches going on among the six fae, she presumed their weapons had also disappeared.

What magic was this that could override schorl to destroy weapons?

Had the spell affected Averin and Lukas too? Or, as her guards, would they have been exempt?

No way to find out.

A whip cracked. Someone cried out.

The second portcullis clanked and slid shut behind them. Cogs clicked and snapped into place, locking it.

They were trapped inside Angharad Death Camp.

She probed her ears to check her glamour. Perfect points. Heart racing, she pulled her hood up to cover the evidence. All she could rely on now to seem human were her gray eyes.

In the flickering torchlight that pooled around the wagon, Averin and Lukas appeared at the door.

She hissed in a breath. Their glamour had gone, too. Would it be noticed, or would the capes be enough to pass inspection in the gloomy tunnel?

Behind them stood three Pyreack guards. Stripes on one of the guard's shoulders denoted rank, but she wasn't sure what it was. He scanned her and the other "prisoners."

"Weapons!" he snapped. "You let them keep weapons? And where are the rest of the slaves? This wagon should be full."

Clearly, their magic had detected their weapons, but he didn't seem aware of Averin and Lukas's arsenal. Perhaps it all blended into one.

"Sergeant, we were attacked coming in." Lukas spoke slowly, as if he were none too bright. "Lucky we even got them. Rebels must have left weapons in the wagon."

The sergeant lashed out a fist. It caught Lukas on the cheek, and his head snapped to the side.

Averin stood stoic, as if it didn't matter.

The sergeant strode to the wagon doorway and glared at her. "You one of those rebels?"

Fear, visceral and real, coursed through her. "No. I—I'm human." Angry with herself for that fear, she forced herself to drop to her knees for show. Her voice came out timid. "Sir, don't hurt me."

The sergeant shoved her forehead, stared at her eyes, and then spat at her. It hit her chin and dribbled down her neck. "Human trash."

Writhing with revulsion at his spit, and a sudden longing to set him alight, she ramped up her act. "Please, sir, I beg you. I'll do what you say. Just don't hurt me." She buried her hands in her cape in case they betrayed her.

A harsh laugh. "Should have thought about that before you got yourself captured." A bell sounded. The sergeant scowled. "Another load coming in." He shoved Lukas. "Get your wagon out of the tunnel." To his soldiers, he snapped, "Take the fae to Sector G." He lashed out at Averin but didn't hit him. "Take the human bitch to Sector H."

Lukas, Averin, and the two Pyreack guards saluted.

Averin shouted at Stasha. "You heard. Get down from there." He grabbed the chain between her manacles and yanked. She slid across the doorjamb and tumbled feetfirst onto a stone floor.

The rest of their team followed her and were quickly rounded up by the guards. Although Lukas couldn't have known where to go, the wagon clacked through the tunnel toward the light. Averin shoved her in front of him. They followed the wagon and the two guards herding their six fae into a cloud of crows. The birds were almost too dark to see against the blindingly white sunlight. She squinted to focus.

The crows cawed and flapped around a wooden archway at the end of the tunnel. Bodies. Human bodies. At least a dozen of them dangled from the top beam. They swayed in the burning wind on taut ropes, bumping into each other like macabre puppets. The wind pivoted one around to face her and Averin.

A hauntingly familiar face set in a mask of hopeless pain. One eye was gone—pecked out by crows. The same crows that tore at blistered ribbons of scorched flesh—

Stasha blanched and collapsed to her knees.

"Stasha," Averin whispered urgently. "Talk to me?" Out loud, he shouted, "Move, trash." He yanked her back onto her feet and whispered again, "None of them are Klaus. So who—"

"Hathrine," she gurgled. A firebird crest had been branded on Hathrine's left breast. Over her heart.

Hathrine, the gentle girl who had silently grieved for Lenka but had still cared for Stasha when she'd selfishly climbed into bed without fixing the dormitory for the other girls. Fire borne of rage and sorrow surged through her. Hidden by her cloak, her manacles pulsed.

Averin jumped back. "No!" he hissed. "Control yourself."

Control herself? How could he even suggest that?

His hand shot out and connected with the back of her head. He shoved hard, sending her sprawling onto the stony ground. The air oomphed out of her.

Boots strutted past her and stopped.

Her fire quelled as she lay in the dirt cringing. She could have blown everything.

The jagged end of a whip hovered above the ground an inch from her face. Would the fae notice Averin's blue eyes? She had, the moment she'd seen them.

The whip bearer spoke. "Trash giving you a hard time? Maybe she'd like to hang up there with them."

Averin stepped between her and the Pyreack guard. "Nothing I can't handle. Taking her to Section H as the sergeant commanded."

"Well, get a move on, then. Scorch her if you have to. They're opening a new stope in there today." The guard moved on with the band of six. Perhaps he hadn't expected Averin to be different than everyone else, so he hadn't really looked at him. That worked for her.

Averin pulled her to her feet. "You heard. Any more trouble, and I'll burn your ass."

Face hidden in the folds of her hood, she let him drag her down a narrow walkway wide enough for one wagon to pass through at a time. Where Lukas was, she didn't know. But he knew what to do— free enough fae to help with the diversion. She wasn't going to worry about him. Much.

She glanced back the way they'd come. A fortified stone building squatted above the tunnel. An archway and a single set of stone steps seemed to provide the only way into the building. Through the grimy window, she counted at least a dozen Pyreack soldiers. From the building's position, she guessed it was the control room from where they opened the portcullises. The control room she and Averin would have to capture if they were to let Boa and her soldiers into the camp.

Averin pushed her roughly. "Keep moving."

She stumbled forward. As she regained her footing, she hissed, "Where in all the darkness is Section H?"

"Read the signs."

She looked up. The walkway had opened into a huge amphitheater carved out of the reddish-gold mountains. On each level, dark tunnels yawned in the rock face—entrances to the mines, she assumed. Each had a faded white sign marked with a letter of the alphabet pinned to the wall.

At least the Pyreack believed in order.

Her boots gritted against red sand as Averin shoved her between piles of golden rock dumped next to a line of handcarts. A string of fae males shoveled the rocks into the carts.

A whip cracked, and someone screamed.

She turned her head. An overseer loomed over a fae female. The prisoner lay on the ground next to her abandoned shovel. Hunched and bleeding, she had schorl chains manacled to her ankles.

"Get up!" The whip cracked again. It sliced into the fae's back.

She groaned and tried to force herself up, but her skinny arms buckled, and she slumped back down. Every bone in her body jutted at painful angles through her thin clothes.

"I said get up!" The guard lashed down with his whip. Blood sprayed, splattering his already blood-soiled uniform.

The fae didn't move.

The whip struck again.

Still no whimper escaped the fae's cracked lips.

The guard kicked her over. Her head lolled back, sightless eyes staring into space. He swore. "Someone clean this mess up."

Stasha vomited on her boots.

Averin hurried her past as three other slaves dropped their shovels. They lumbered to the fae, picked her up, and carried her to a hole in the ground, at least twenty feet wide. They tossed her in as if she were rubbish and then plodded back to their shovels. Crows burst out of the hole, cawed, then vanished back into the open grave to continue feasting.

Bile rose in her throat again. She pressed her scarred palm to her mouth. Eliezar had been right. All she wanted was to let the fire boiling under her skin explode out to destroy every Pyreack soldier in this camp. And then she'd hunt down King Darien Pyreaxos and burn him too.

"Time enough for all that," Averin muttered as they headed down a winding track to Section H.

How well he knew her if he'd guessed her thoughts.

Averin propelled her through a rock opening marked H. She almost fell down a flight of steep steps carved into the rock. He grabbed her arm to steady her. "Manacles, pit princess," he whispered. "Now would be a good time to ditch them."

She fumbled for the key, and he helped her unlock them. While she rubbed her sore wrists, he laid the manacles gently on the floor to stop them rattling. She grabbed his tunic, pulled him close, and whispered, "How do we know this is where Klaus is?"

"We don't. But they think you're human, and they've sent you here. Good chance he's here too."

"I guess," she grumbled as she followed him down the stairs. The deeper they sank, the hotter the stifling air became. She longed to throw off her cloak but resisted the urge to do more than flick back her hood. Even then, sweat coursed down her temples and dripped on her chest.

They stopped in a circle of torchlight on the landing, which was nothing more than a long, wooden platform held up on iron hooks and chains.

Ten or so rickety rope ladders cascaded down into a cavern lit with hundreds of burning torches. They merely added to the oppressive heat. Carved from the rock, narrow walkways circled the walls, spiraling down until they vanished far below. Each walkway was connected at intervals by similar wooden platforms and rope ladders.

Ropes tethered to buckets hung like vines off each platform. In some, human slaves balanced precariously as they chiseled away at the rock. Swarms of others crawled like ants along the winding walkways, carting full buckets of rock to the handcarts. Whips at the ready, guards patrolled. She craned her neck, looking for Klaus, but from her height, it was impossible to make out details on people's faces.

Footsteps clattered on the stairs above her and Averin.

"We can't wait here," Averin whispered. "We'll draw attention."

They had just started for the nearest rope ladder when a guard exited the stairs and joined them on the platform. "Hey, she's fae. Wrong section, you idiot."

Mouth bone dry, Stasha froze, now furious with herself for not just enduring the discomfort of her hood. Hand waving, Averin spun to face the guard. A strangled gurgling made her turn.

Face puce, the guard had fallen to his knees and was clutching his throat. Another gurgle, and he tumbled over and rolled onto his back. Stasha didn't need to check his pulse to know he was dead.

"You—you killed him? How?"

"I ripped the air out of his lungs." Averin's face was as hard as his voice.

That answered the question about whether his weapons had been vaporized. He scooped his hands under the guard's arms and dragged him into the shadows. She hurried over to help him. Averin waved her away. "I've got this. Start climbing. I'm right behind you."

She stumbled to the closest ladder and gulped. It was a long way down to the next platform. The ladder, wooden slats lashed together with frayed rope, didn't inspire confidence.

But if Klaus was down in that terrible place, she'd climb a thousand such ladders to reach him. She knelt, backed to the edge of the drop-off, and gripped the top of the ladder with both hands. Her feet dangled over the edge, fumbling to find the treads. They connected just as Averin crawled over to join her.

"Today, pit princess," he coaxed.

She started to climb. By the time she landed on the next wooden platform, the rock face had grazed the skin off her knuckles. She wiped the oozing blood onto her grimy cloak. Averin hopped down next to her. As silently as any captor and prisoner, they walked together along the narrow walkway.

It teemed with slaves. Some hefted baskets of rock into carts, while others dragged full carts away. Coated in a layer of dust, and slick with sweat from toiling, their clothes hung in strips on their scarred, emaciated bodies. Chained in long lines, the manacles had rubbed the skin off their ankles.

A few looked up as they passed, but their eyes were empty. Mere pits of darkness, which gave no place even for despair. They barely flinched when guards cracked whips across their backs.

Fire blazed through Stasha's skin, but she kept it hidden under her cloak and hood.

With Averin leading, she plodded down the spiraling walkway. There was no sign of Klaus or anyone else from Askavol. She was beginning to despair of finding him when they finally reached the bottom of the cavern. Unlike the rest of the space, it was only lit with a few torches.

A sharp voice rang out of a side tunnel. "When one of you human filth step out of line, you all get punished." A whip cracked.

Stasha and Averin loped to the tunnel opening. They stopped in the shadows.

"Step out of line again, and I won't kill you," the voice barked. "It'll be them that die while you watch. Then you'll bathe in their blood."

Heart pounding so hard it gave her a headache, she slipped around Averin and padded deeper into the tunnel to see who the guard was shouting at. Averin followed her so silently that if it wasn't for the brush of his hand on her shoulder, she wouldn't have known he was there.

Through the flickering torchlight and dust clouding the air, she glimpsed a burly fae standing with his back to her, a whip curled in his hand. A young woman knelt before him. He grabbed her neck and pulled her head up.

Stasha's stomach dropped.

Acolyte Inna.

Tears streamed down Inna's face, leaving trails of dirt over the fresh wounds from her recent scarification. Her robes were tattered and bloody.

The impulse to rescue Inna almost made Stasha break cover. Instead, writhing with fury, she stood still and assessed the situation.

Two more guards watched over a crowd of slaves huddled against the far rock wall. The slaves' hair hung in their dirty faces, and some of them had bloodied mouths. While she recognized some of them, she couldn't see Klaus in the throng.

They each held a pickaxe. Why they didn't attack the two guards, she couldn't imagine—until she remembered how terrified she'd been of Averin that far-off night when her old world had ended.

"I've got this," Averin whispered. A breeze fluttered the stifling air. He stepped into the light. "Hey, you with the whip. How about beating up on someone your own size?"

"Who the—" The guard spun.

Stasha's flaming hand shot up to fling fire at him, but she stopped herself at the last second. If she was to convince the humans to help her, they couldn't see her as a threat. Better to let Averin deal with the swine.

Averin twitched his fingers to say come hither.

The guard swore and tossed down his whip. His other hand shot out a tongue of flame. The fae gagged, and the flame spluttered. He dropped to his knees and clutched his throat. Averin must have ripped out his oxygen, as he had with the other guard. Face blue, the soldier slumped to the ground.

"Pit princess," Averin said languidly, "are you just going stand there gaping, or are you going to find Klaus?"

She spun just as a second overseer broke away from the prisoners and lunged for Averin, fire blazing from his fingers.

A gust scooped up a rock and crashed it against the guard's

temple. The momentum threw him at the wall. He hit his head with a crunch and folded to the ground.

That left one guard. Hands raised defensively, he backed into the crowd of prisoners. "Touch me, and I swear, I'll burn them all."

She—and Averin—paused.

"Hurt them, and I'll boil your blood." Stasha tossed back her hood so he could see her fae ears. In deference to the humans, she kept her fire hidden.

The guard blinked, then frowned. "Why should I worry about you? I could kill you with a snap of my fingers."

"Don't even think about it!" a familiar voice yelled. The cry was followed by a sickening thud. The guard stumbled forward and fell face-first on a pile of rocks. He had a pickaxe embedded in his skull.

Stasha's stomach knotted, and she swallowed yet more bile. Her eyes darted from the guard to his attacker.

Klaus faced her. His new clothes were filthy and ragged, his face caked with blood. "You came." He spoke earnestly, as if he hadn't doubted that for a second.

"I did." She broke into a run.

He stumbled to her, dragging his damaged leg. His twisted ankle was manacled to his other leg on a short stretch of chain, which rattled as he lurched.

They connected with a thump. He wrapped his arms around her and buried his face in her neck. A sob threatened to break from her as she hugged him. Tight. Against all odds, he had survived. Boa had been right. Miracles were possible.

He flinched. Her fingers had pressed into something warm and wet. Blood.

The fire she'd suppressed since entering Section H burst through her skin.

Klaus yelped. He let go of her and staggered back. His feet tangled in his chains, and he tumbled to the ground. Eyes wide, he gaped, then snapped his mouth closed. "You—you're on fire."

She dove to help him up.

Averin got there first. His strong hands closed around Klaus's thin biceps and hoisted him back onto his feet.

"She's one of them," one of the prisoners shouted. She recognized the voice: Ivan from the fighting pits.

Still supported by Averin, Klaus swung around on his good foot. "No, she isn't! This is Stasha. The same girl we all grew up with. Just ... different. Powerful." His eyes flashed at Averin. "And she's brought help, to get us out of here."

Averin bowed from the waist. "Name's Prince Averin Trysael of Zephyr. So very honored to make your acquaintance, Klaus."

Klaus blushed, brightening his deathly pallor. "Um ... you too. I guess."

Feral Fox, Ivan, and Goul pushed their way to the front of the prisoners. Blood trickled down the side of Goul's face.

Eyes smarting with tears, Stasha barked a laugh of relief to see them alive. "Never thought I'd be so pleased to see you all." She shot a special smile to Feral Fox.

Goul blinked warily, his pupils dilating unevenly.

Ivan scanned her up and down. She'd quelled her flames. "So you really are fae."

She gave a curt nod. "Yes. Yes, I am."

No one moved in the oppressive silence. If she didn't know better, she'd have assumed Averin had sucked all the air from the chamber. "I'm working with a group of rebels fighting against the Pyreack. We're here to get you out."

Ivan snorted. "You expect us to trust you, fae? You spent years lying to us. Why would we believe a word you say now?"

She balled her fists. "And you spent years being as thick as sheep droppings! Ivan, for once, *please* use your head for something more than keeping your skin together. I had no idea what I was. Now I do. And I'm here to help. So choose. Fight with me or rot in here."

Feral Fox stepped forward. "Tell me what to do," he said in his unfailingly calm voice. His sheepskin jacket had gone, but its loss did nothing to improve his smell.

Ivan glanced at Feral Fox, and his lips thinned. He closed his eyes for a second, breathing deep. On his exhale, he said, "I'm in. What Feral Fox said. Tell us what to do."

"Let's get rid of the manacles." Averin held out his hand for Feral Fox's pickaxe. "Everyone who wants in, line up, and I'll bust your chains."

Feral Fox thrust his axe at Averin. A shuffling line formed with Klaus at the head. Vlad was next. While it warmed her heart that he'd survived, she bounced on her toes impatiently while she waited for Klaus to be freed.

"Pit princess, how about you guard the entrance." Averin spoke dryly. "Last thing we want is Pyreack company."

"On it." Her face burned with embarrassment as she flitted to the tunnel entrance.

On the other side of the cavern, watched by Pyreack guards, humans hacked gleaming rocks out of the walls.

Klaus's gentle fingers touched her back. "I knew you'd come." He shuffled next to her. "What's the plan?" His voice was muffled by the sound of chipping pickaxes.

"It's very simple. Averin and I are going to open the portcullises to let in a small army."

Klaus blinked twice. He laughed hollowly. "That sounds like something you'd cook up. How can I help?"

She grabbed him. "By finding a place to hide and staying there until it's safe to come out."

"No." Klaus hefted an axe. "I'm done being protected, Stasha. I might have a bad leg, but I'm not helpless."

She bit her lip, then gushed, "I can't risk you."

"And I can't remain in your shadow. For once, just let me be a man." His anguish brought tears to her eyes. She brushed them away. How could she deny him something that meant so much to him? But how could she expose him to danger?

Footsteps in the tunnel told her that Averin must have finished hacking chains. She didn't have long to decide.

Klaus leaned in close. "Please, Stasha. See me for what I am, not what I was."

A sob hitched in her throat. What was the use of saving Klaus only to condemn him to a life that demeaned him? It was why she'd wanted him to flee Askavol with her—to free him from a life of slavery. If she refused him, he would be little more than a slave to her will. She swallowed her tears and hugged him. "Don't take unnecessary risks. Promise me that you'll meet me at the gate when we open it."

Klaus hugged her back. "Promise."

Trailed by a dozen prisoners, Averin joined her. The look he shot her suggested he'd listened into her and Klaus's conversation and approved of her decision.

She mouthed, "Busybody."

Averin flicked one of his pointed ears and shrugged, like he had no control of his superb fae hearing. Then, all businesslike, he spoke softly to everyone. "Your job is to free as many prisoners as you can while Stasha and I get on with our mission."

"Why?" Klaus demanded. "I thought we'd be fighting with you."

Averin canted his head and appraised Klaus. As much as she longed to know his thoughts, his expression betrayed nothing. His brilliant eyes swept the rest of the crowd. "Stasha and I have to open the two portcullises. We're counting on you and your army of prisoners to create a diversion in here to give us the space we need to move freely above ground."

Goul swallowed. "You want us to draw more guards in here?" He threw up his hands. "That's insane."

Stasha appreciated his concern. She spoke quickly. "Relax. We have soldiers releasing the fae. They'll fight the Pyreack above ground. Just keep the guards in here busy so they don't join the fun up top."

"We can do that." Klaus looked at the other humans with such confidence, it made her beam with pride for him.

A few of them nodded.

Averin continued. "You'll be tempted to go for the weakest to help them. Don't. Pick the strongest you can find."

A few of the humans shuffled, as if they were about to protest.

Averin held up his hand. "Cruel, maybe, but the weak will slow you down. And they're easy targets for the guards. Pick the most agile to help you wreck this place." He gestured to Stasha. "We'll come back with an army to rescue you all."

"What about the guards?" Goul whispered. "They shoot fire. Or haven't you noticed?"

Goul showing such blatant fear? It was unheard of. Stasha ached with sorrow for him.

Averin wagged a firm finger. "You're not to fight fae head on. You won't stand a chance. But nothing stops you using stealth to take them down." He pointed into the cavern at one of the guards. Eyes closed, the brute slouched against the wall. "Look for idiots like that. Move quickly and silently. And aim for killing blows. Fae heal fast, and they get mighty angry when humans attack them." He smiled, showing a mouthful of pointed teeth.

Some of the humans hefted their axes.

Averin chuckled. "That's the spirit. Turn all that hate and rage on those bastards and their camp, and you'll do well."

Some of the tension drained from the group. It impressed her that they'd been willing to fight even though they knew how hopeless the odds were.

Hope. Tarik had been right. It *was* a powerful thing.

She threw her arms around Klaus. "You're my hero. See you soon." He was bright red when she pulled away. She offered Averin her hand. "Ready to go?"

Averin took it firmly in his. "Lead the way, pit princess."

It was time to change the world.

CHAPTER TWENTY-SIX

WHITE HEAT

Klaus was alive! And so strong! The words rang through Stasha's head as she and Averin scrambled up the stairs linking Section H with the rest of Angharad. Harsh sunlight spilled into the stairwell.

Averin stopped and held out his hand in warning. From the tilt of his head, she guessed he was listening. Trusting his ears far more than her own, she stopped on the stair below him and waited.

Even she heard the sound of fighting in the courtyard. And then she caught a familiar smell. She leaned into Averin and whispered, "Lukas."

Averin raised his eyebrows and mouthed, "Are you sure?" When she nodded, he shot her a bloodthirsty smile. "Then what are we waiting for?"

"Absolutely nothing."

As they took the last couple of steps, a shadow crossed the tunnel opening. Lukas loomed, his bulky body almost blocking out the light. He had lost his Pyreack cloak and was covered in blood, and by the smell, none of it his own. "Get to the portcullis!" he rasped. "We'll hold them off for as long as we can. Just get to the portcullis!" He stepped aside to let her and Averin sprint out of the stairwell.

At least a hundred fae prisoners fought against twice the number of Pyreack guards. Freed from their chains, some of the fae wielded pickaxes, while others tossed magic.

On her way to the control tower, Stasha dodged a fireball and skidded across a line of ice thrown by a fae prisoner.

Averin reached the stone archway covering the stairs first. He grabbed the banister and hit the first step running—only to cata-pult back as if hit by a battering ram. He tumbled head over heels before landing in a heap at her feet. Still running, she stumbled over him.

Someone above her laughed.

Her blood chilled as she fought for balance. She knew that laugh. Had heard it in Ealvera War Camp.

Shaking with rage and—she wasn't afraid to admit—fear, she looked up.

Radomir stood at the control-room window.

"You bitch," he shouted down. "Thanks to your escape, I'm here in this dump guarding prisoners. And if you think you and your rebel scum are getting into this control room, then you're even stupider than I first gave you credit for."

Behind her, Averin rolled over and creaked to his knees.

Eyes fixed on Radomir, she hissed to Averin, "Are you okay?"

Averin groaned. "I've never felt anything like that." He shook his head. "Now we know why no one ever gets out of Angharad."

"A spell?" she whispered.

Nasty smile twisting his features, Radomir watched them and the battle raging behind her—a battle now futile if they couldn't get into that tower.

"Must be," Averin muttered. "Spells that override schorl. And now this. Wonder what else they've got stashed in this death trap?" He still hadn't stood. That worried her more than the pain leaching into his voice.

She had to act. Right now, before Radomir sent down troops to slaughter Averin while he was weakened.

"Move back," she commanded. "Well back."

Averin staggered to his feet but didn't move. "What are you planning?"

"Just do it." She walked purposefully to the archway.

A second familiar voice called from the control room. "Stasha. No!"

Suren had joined Radomir at the window. Radomir punched

Suren's jaw, but Suren's head merely bobbed. He shouted, "The force will kill you! Averin got lucky. Don't step into the archway."

"Then disarm it," she shouted back.

Suren pounded his fist on the window frame. "I can't."

"And I won't," Radomir yelled.

"Then you leave me no choice but to do this." She raised her arms and sprinted for the archway. Despite everything, laughter ran like fire through her as blue-green flames rolled in waves from her body toward the stairs. Radomir would never let her die. As it was, he'd landed here as punishment for letting her slip through his fingers. She could only imagine what Piss Swill would do to the captain if he incinerated her.

She was still three feet away when the archway exploded into flame. Head held high, she strode through the flames and leapt up the stairs, taking them two at a time. Whatever had affected Averin seemed to have vanished. The door at the top of the landing slammed shut.

As if a plank of wood could stop her.

She spread fans of flames from her fingers and was about to slap them on the door when the wood crumbled to ash and sloughed to her feet. Startled, she pulled her hands back to rein the fire in. The flames retracted.

A long, narrow stone room with a bare stone floor opened before her. A semi-circle of fae armed with crossbows faced her. She guessed their quarrels were made of schorl. Behind them crouched four huge spiked wheels, wound with chains.

The mechanism to open the portcullises of Angharad.

She grunted. If she managed to get past the weapons, even with her fae strength, she'd never be strong enough to open even one of them herself, let alone all four. She would need help.

Her eyes fixed on Suren, standing next to Radomir.

Her pretty fae was going to open those gates for her. But first she had to get past the archers.

"Stasha, it's over," Radomir shouted. "Stop, or I'll give the command to shoot you." But his shifting eyes betrayed fear.

It fueled her confidence. She sauntered closer. "Stop? But I'm just getting started." She reignited the flames in her hands. They crackled and burned merrily across her skin. "Drop the weapons, Radomir, or I'll burn this whole place down."

Suren scurried closer. "Stasha, you don't understand magic. I've told you that before. Burn again like you did coming up the stairs, and the fire will consume you." He sounded genuinely terrified.

"Scared for me? How sweet of you." She took one step closer to the archers.

Sweat glazed their faces. One of them twitched a finger on the trigger of his weapon. She thrust her hand at him. Sparks shot in his direction but didn't touch him.

Still, he dropped his crossbow and screamed—a sound totally out of proportion to the fire she'd shot at him. It was so chilling, her hand fell limp to her side.

But on he screamed.

She stared at him in horror. What had she done? No flames burned him, yet he contorted in agony. He clutched his head, his chest, his abdomen—his head exploded, shooting scorching blood and gore across the room.

Stasha staggered back, retching. Had she boiled him from the inside? Was that white heat?

Crossbows clattered to the flagstones, and fae scuttled away from her.

Radomir swore—and then vanished. He'd spirited to safety, just like Averin said he would.

Suren wailed. "Darkness curse you, Radomir! You've left me here to—"

"To open the portcullis," she yelled at him. Her whole body shook with terror and shock, but to quail now was to lose everything. She would deal with the horror of what she was and what she'd done after she'd freed the prisoners.

Face twisted, Suren clutched his head. "Stasha," he moaned. "You're still burning. Stop. No one can handle this much magic. Not even someone who can shoot white heat like you do. It will kill you. It *must* kill you." She'd never heard or seen him more desperate.

She fought back tears. "Then open the portcullises."

"The portcullises are not what's important." Suren yelled at the top of his lungs. "You are."

"So you can give me to your king to bleed me dry of my magic." Hysteria spiked her voice. "Never."

"No! So you can *live*."

Suren really thought she would die? Apart from her self-loathing for her heinous crime, she'd never felt more alive. Yet if it forced him to open the portcullises to make him believe that she was dying, then so be it.

Hand held high, she vowed, "I will burn until I die unless you open those gates." She pushed more fire out of her body. Great swaths of flame streamed out across the stone floor, only to die with nothing to burn.

Still Suren hesitated.

Desperate and running out of options, she fell to her knees and faked a cough. It wasn't her best performance—at least *she* didn't think so—but Suren shouted to his fae, "Open the portcullises. Now."

The fae jumped at his command. Probably only too eager to be gone from here, they peeled off to the wheels. Obviously practiced, they heaved, and each wheel turned. Chains creaked, and Stasha imagined the gates opening to let Boa and the rest of the team into the camp.

Unless Suren was toying with her.

To ensure his compliance, she collapsed prostrate on the floor and let her flames splutter.

"Hurry up," Suren yelled. The wheels groaned as powerful hands clawed them around. Suren dropped to her side. A tentative hand touched her in spite of the flames still licking her skin. "Stasha, speak to me."

It hurt her to burn him—he really did seem to care, but she couldn't let the act fold until the chains stopped rattling.

"Are you okay? Please tell me you're okay."

It took all her self-control not to answer. She didn't want to think of what Piss Swill would do to him after this failure. Suren was a decent fae in a terrible situation. She wished she could relieve him of his worry, but the portcullises weren't open yet. So she lay still and burned.

The rumble of chains ceased.

"It's done," one of the fae yelled. "What now?"

Still on his haunches next to her, Suren spoke. "I suppose we surrender the camp." He sounded desperate.

A raven cawed from the window.

Stasha peeked at the window through her fingers just in time to catch a flash of blue-black light and a whirl of claws and feathers.

"Good choice." Averin stood in the room.

A flurry of air scooped up the crossbows. Two flitted into Averin's hands. The rest landed at Stasha's head. "Burn those, pit princess. This lot won't be needing them anymore."

Not wanting Averin to see her misery at the destructiveness of her power, she sprang to her feet.

Suren staggered back. "You—you tricked me! Again."

She flashed him her brightest smile. "Wouldn't happen if you were on the right team." She shot a handful of flame at the cross-bows. The wooden hilts smoldered, then the fire caught hold.

Suren snorted and kicked a burning crossbow across the room. "I knew you were powerful. But this?" His eyes drifted to the dead guard.

Her face fell. Was this what Eliezar had meant about her power setting her soul alight? Her ability to cook people from the inside out? No wonder soldiers burning with white heat chose a quick death in a normal fire over what she'd done to that guard.

"Don't know how you're getting out of this room, pit princess," Averin said. "You obliterated the stairs and all their wards. This place is wide open for the taking." He kept his voice light, but she knew him well enough to recognize his concern.

She loved him for trying to ease her pain. Like her, he must have realized that now wasn't the time for grief and self-recrimination.

She walked slowly to the doorway. The archway and stairs had gone. It was as if they'd never existed. More white heat?

She wanted to sob.

A shout from the tunnel entrance below the gruesome arch of bodies where Hathrine hung pulled her eyes away from her destruction. Boa, Trystaen, Eliezar, and Frea sauntered into the camp at the head of Boa's occupying army. She must have had three hundred rebel soldiers following her. Boa shouted a command to her army to hunt and destroy the Pyreack guards.

Guards in earshot, who had been fighting fae prisoners, took flight into the many tunnels leading into the mine. Some even scuttled into Section H. Freed fae prisoners and fresh troops pursued them into the darkness to carry on the fight.

Her stomach knotted for Klaus. She had to trust that he wouldn't do anything stupid to get himself harmed. She shook her head, impatient with herself. If anyone was dumb enough to be harmed, it would be her, not sensible, wise Klaus. Still, she clutched her belly with both hands. "We've actually taken Angharad."

"Now we hear the doubt." Averin joined her at the gaping doorway. "You've taken Angharad, Stasha." But instead of looking out at Boa, he held his hand up, palm facing the Pyreack guards behind them. She turned. Suren and his fae were pinned against the wall.

Reeking of failure, Suren looked at his feet.

She called to him. "You could still fight us. Why don't you?"

"Why?" Suren's voice was a mere whisper. "I've lost. Everything."

"Everything except a fresh start."

Suren gave a strangled laugh. "You mean death?" His eyes rolled in the direction of his soldiers. "At least let them go in peace."

"I'm not in charge here. Princess Boa is. That's for her to decide."

"Then we all die," Suren said matter-of-factly.

Stasha shook her head. "I make the decisions about you. And I've decided that you're coming with us." She nudged Averin. "Release him."

Averin scowled. "Something you aren't telling me, pit princess?"

Averin jealous? Not something she ever thought she'd have to deal with. But since he'd told her that he didn't want her—even if his actions belied his words—she said sharply, "He's my friend. Sort of. I want him with us."

The wind pinning Suren to the wall died. Exuding menace, Averin strode to him. His sapphire eyes bored into Suren. "First sign of trouble, and you stop breathing until I decide you're trustworthy."

Bemused, Suren shrugged. "I'm in your hands."

Stasha grabbed the back of Averin's tunic. "Big Bad Fae, it's time to get out of here. I need to find Klaus."

Averin took her hand. "Yes, ma'am." He offered Suren his arm.

A hesitation, and then Suren clasped Averin's tunic.

They spirited into the courtyard below.

CHAPTER TWENTY-SEVEN

HOARFROST

Overwhelmed by the carnage in the courtyard, Stasha struggled to balance when she, Averin, and Suren landed next to Boa, Trystaen, and Eliezar.

Bodies—fae and human—littered the sand, sand wet with blood. Drawn to the bounty, the crows of Angharad skipped across the corpses, fighting for sightless eyes. She covered her nose and mouth to block out the reek of blood, guts, and burnt flesh, but still the stench of death seeped into her like insidious smoke.

On the other side of the courtyard, Frea tossed over bodies, sending crows cackling into the air. Who was she seeking? From Frea's wild eyes, the missing fae meant a great deal to her.

Stasha looked around for Lukas. He was nowhere to be seen among the bemused and wounded fae prisoners wandering the battlefield as if they hadn't yet grasped their victory. She assumed he'd followed the Pyreack into the mines.

Suren clutched his head in his hands.

"Get used to defeat, Pyreack," Boa said harshly. "The tide in this war has turned." Her tattoos danced across her hands. "And why isn't he in schorl?" she snapped at Averin.

"Because he's not a prisoner," Stasha said firmly. "He's coming with us."

Boa, Trystaen, and Eliezar glared at her.

Boa spoke for them all. "Are you crazy?"

Not in the mood for arguing with Boa when all she wanted was to find Klaus, she started walking toward Section H. She called over her shoulder, "Suren, you better stay with me."

Suren followed her.

Boa grabbed Averin's arm. "You're permitting this?"

Averin shrugged Boa off and quickly fell into step with Stasha. None too gracefully, he shoved himself between her and Suren. "The pit princess knows what she's doing, Boa. And if Suren so much as hints at trouble, I'll kill him."

"If I don't do it first." Boa slid into the spot on Stasha's other side, effectively pushing Suren away. His shoulders hunched as he walked, reminding her of a whipped puppy.

Averin called to Eliezar and Trystaen. "Find a way to close the portcullis. We don't want any Pyreack coming in here. These mines now belong to Zephyr." Almost as an afterthought, he added, "And Ocea, of course." He shot Boa a cocky smile.

"Lucky save, wind boy." But Boa's tone didn't carry the sting Stasha expected. Boa clenched her sword. "Keeping the mines for Ocea might be more difficult than taking them. I can't rely on my wards. Not while Piss Swill controls my magic."

Averin bumped Stasha's shoulder. "Now you know why she didn't try to brain me when I said I was claiming the mines for Zephyr. I just failed to mention that I'm also taking them for Atria."

Stasha wished she understood what he meant, but she didn't.

Averin must have seen her confusion. "I can set up wards with air magic that no one will breach." A self-deprecating smile. "Well, perhaps not quite *no one.* My brother, Rican, is somewhat more powerful than me. And my father, of course. But apart from them, no one will ever undo what I toss over this place. Not even King Darien himself will ever set foot in this mine again."

"How humble of you," Stasha said dryly. "And Atria? Not claiming all power over that magic, too, are we?"

Boa chortled. Even Suren cracked a smile.

Averin's hand swept to his chest. "Wounded, that's what I am." His grin belied his pain. "You forget that Trystaen answers to me. His magic is not too shabby, either."

Boa's snigger morphed into a sigh. "And that, Prince Averin Trysael of Zephyr, is why I still deign to speak to you on occasion. You sometimes manage to save the day ... after irritating me close to death."

Averin gave a mock bow. "I aim to please."

A high-pitched wailing jarred Stasha—and everyone—out of their post-victory euphoria. It sounded like an animal in pain.

Boa swore and spun to the sound. "Frea? Who?"

That was Frea?

Stasha turned slowly, dreading what she'd see.

The archer knelt on one knee beside a fae built like a mountain. Blond hair fell across her face, pressed against her bow.

Stasha flushed with cold.

Lukas.

Frea looked up. Her twisted face echoed the agony of her keening. The bow jerked up and pointed at Stasha. "You did this," Frea wailed. "You killed him. If we hadn't come here, he would still be alive."

Boa stumbled. Her face resembled sun-bleached bones. The living tattoos danced erratically across her skin. "Not my Lukas. Not him. Please, no."

Averin bowed to Boa, low from the waist. "I'm sorry. So very, very sorry."

Stasha opened her mouth to add her shocked sorrow to Averin's words—she hadn't known Lukas for long, but she had liked him— but Boa brushed her away.

The same hard, beautiful mask worn on the night Stasha had met Princess Boadicea of Ocea dropped over Boa's dark face. "Stasha is not to blame for this," she barked at Frea. "The Pyreack are. Like always." Boa stomped ahead of them and reached Section H first. By the time Stasha, Averin, and Suren reached the top of the stairs leading into the mine, Boa had vanished into the darkness.

Chest tight, Stasha took the stairs at a leap. Boa waited for her on the wooden platform. No one looking at the princess would ever guess that she'd just lost one of her closest friends and comrades.

Stasha wanted to say something—as much as she disliked Frea, Lukas would have been alive if she hadn't brought them here to free Klaus—but Boa's posture did not invite condolences. Wracked with guilt, Stasha stared out over the cavern while she waited for Averin and Suren to join them.

Averin had said to destroy the place, and the humans had taken him at his word. The hundreds of wooden platforms and rope ladders had gone. Broken ore carts littered the narrow pathways. The web of ropes holding buckets had been cut. But it was the black scorch marks that chilled her. That, and the absence of human slaves. Only Boa's fae ran and fought against Pyreack guards with unerring speed and deadliness on the narrow walkways.

How many humans had died to achieve this mess before the battle had shifted?

Had Klaus survived?

Stasha scrambled to climb down the rickety rope ladder, one of few to survive.

Averin grabbed her hand. "Let me go first."

She blinked in surprise. "After everything, you don't trust me to take care of myself?"

"I don't trust you not to bring the roof down on us if ... if things are awkward."

If Klaus was dead.

Heavy with revulsion at her white heat, she didn't trust herself either. She moved aside and let Averin go first, then followed. She wasn't halfway down the ladder when Boa snapped, "Pyreack, not on your life am I letting you near her. She may trust you, but I don't."

Suren sighed. "I told you; I won't harm her. I know exactly who she is."

"Yes. A weapon to sell to your king."

"No, actually," Suren said indignantly. "She's a girl who's been cruelly and unfairly yanked into a war that didn't concern her until a week ago."

Suren defended her? Her ears burned. She wasn't sorry she'd rescued him.

"Pretty words, Pyreack," Boa snarled. "But I'm sure you had no problem helping kidnap her."

Averin offered Stasha a hand to help her off the ladder. She took it and let him pull her to his side, only to have him whisper, "As much as Boa and I respect your judgment, Stasha, Suren is going to have to prove himself."

She looked up into serious blue eyes. "He will. Just give him a chance."

"Not everyone turns out to be what you want them to be. You have to pick your friends carefully."

"Really? I don't actually remember picking you. Or Boa. You kind of got thrust on me."

Averin grinned. "And aren't you glad we did?"

"Fishing for compliments now?" She stomped out of his circle of warmth before she became too comfortable in his delicious-smelling personal space. "Klaus is waiting. Let's go. Boa and Suren can catch up."

Averin grabbed her tunic and pulled her back to him just as Boa and Suren reached the bottom of the ladder. "And just how are you going to find him this time?" he whispered.

She shrugged. "I expect they're hiding. It's what I would do."

"That's what you'd do when you were human," Averin said quietly. "Now you have to think like a fae."

Aware of Boa and Suren watching their intimate murmuring, she asked, "So what do you suggest?"

A typical Averin head tilt followed. He pointed across the cavern to where one of Boa's soldiers crashed swords with a Pyreack guard. "The buckle on the guard's boot is loose. I can hear it rattling." He glanced at the walkway to the right of them, where two Pyreack fae tossed fire at each other. With bigger fireballs and better accuracy, the prison guard seemed to have the upper hand. "The rebel just farted. If he isn't careful, he'll soil himself."

Her eyes threatened to pop out of her head. "You can't hear those things!"

Averin's eyebrows rose. "You sure about that?"

She wasn't. "Okay. Your point?"

"Your nose is my ears. Use it. Sniff the air as we walk. Lead us to the humans." But instead of letting her go first, he held out his hand to Boa. "Air magic will brush away the scent. Toss me one of your swords so I can clear a path for us."

Boa grabbed Suren's collar and dragged him past Stasha. The princess shoved him away from Stasha and Averin and then hauled one of the swords off her back. She held it out to Averin. "Return it, not like the last time I lent you a sword."

Averin grabbed it and hefted it. "Right. One of the other times I stepped in and saved the day." He and Boa started walking, forcing Suren to trot ahead of them.

Nose twitching, Stasha followed. A thousand discordant smells hit her. Fire. Smoke. Death. Rot. Human waste. Her stomach lurched, and bile rose in her throat.

It drowned out everything else.

She swallowed angrily. Why did her body choose now to betray her? She'd get down on her hands and knees and sniff like a dog if that's what it took to find Klaus.

Stomach roiling, she gritted her teeth and sniffed in breath after breath. The smells rolled over her senses like sour wine, soon all merging into one indiscernible mush.

"Anything, pit princess?" Averin shouted as he and Suren manhandled a broken cart out of the pass.

She shook her head. "Working on it."

It didn't help that Boa, Averin, and Suren had to clear the path of rebel soldiers and move dead bodies before they could cross. Most of the torches had been ripped off the walls, leaving cloying darkness.

They were halfway down the cavern, and she was beginning to despair of finding anything definitive in the air when, above the reek, she caught a memory.

The pine forests back home. Crisp, cold, and sharp. Freshly baked bread, dripping with hot butter and honey, stolen from the Kňazer.

She skidded to a stop.

Averin paused. "What you got?"

"Home. Klaus was here." She stepped forward. "Definitely." She walked on. "They came up from below, but then—" She frowned. "Where did they go?"

Suren tapped her shoulder. "Check here." He cupped a small fire-ball in his hand to light the path for them. She followed the glow and, when the familiar smell sharpened, hissed with relief. Unsure of where she was, she looked around. Another tunnel, one they never would have seen in the dark.

"Is this right, Stasha?" Averin asked.

"Yes." She skipped forward. "Where does this lead?"

"The rock crusher, where they extract the gold." Suren's eyes were hooded, betraying none of his thoughts about his defection from his own kind.

Stasha bounced on the balls of her feet. "Then let's hurry." She darted down the tunnel, smelling not just Klaus but some of the other humans who'd been with him earlier.

A thick wooden door blocked her path.

She grabbed the latch and rattled it. Locked. "No key," she said to no one in particular.

"Burn through it," Averin suggested.

"I suppose that's what magic is for." She slapped her hand on the door, determined to use nothing but her blue-green flame.

Before her fingers began to glow, Suren shoved her out of the way. He glared at Averin. "No. Magic comes at a cost, Stasha. You've burned enough today."

She glanced at Averin for confirmation that she could be at risk.

Averin glowered at Suren, as if he didn't agree. "Stasha isn't like the rest of us."

Suren turned his back on Averin. Golden flames spilled from him. He rolled them into a ball the size of his head and tossed it at the door.

The ball exploded on contact and rippled through the dry wood. Seconds turned to minutes while the door burned.

Stasha resisted the urge to tap her foot on the stone floor. Compared to how quickly she'd ashed the door into the control room, this felt like an eternity.

It proved yet again how much wild power she had. Averin and

Eliezar were right—once Klaus was safe, lessons on fire control held the highest priority on her to-do list.

Averin paced like a cat.

Unable to bear his restlessness, she grabbed his arm. "What? This isn't like you."

"I can hear burning."

Boa rolled her eyes. "The door *is* on fire."

Averin gave her a withering look. "Beyond the door. Something big. I can't believe you can't hear the roar."

Stasha—they all—shook their heads.

Averin wrapped his hand around her head and tilted her face to his. "Burn this door down. Now."

His urgency decided everything. She lifted her hands and willed fire into them.

Nothing happened.

Not sure if she were bereft at the loss of her killer magic, or thrilled to be free of it, she clawed for the heat under skin that had become so familiar.

"Hurry," Averin pleaded.

"Schorl," she stuttered. "I can't access it."

"There's no schorl here," Boa said. "If there was, Suren couldn't have thrown a fireball."

The charred door tumbled off its hinges. Heat hit her like a punch. She shivered, suddenly icy cold with fear. She was about to dash to the shadows at the end of the tunnel, but Averin pushed ahead of her.

A flash of blue-black light, and he took flight, flapping silky black wings faster than she, Boa, or Suren could run. He rounded a corner and vanished.

Dreading what she'd find, Stasha pumped her legs harder. Now, all she could smell was smoke and charred metal. She careened around the corner and skidded to a halt with Boa and Suren at her heels.

Liquid gold oozed across the stone floor. It spilled from a fire easily twenty feet high and twenty feet broad, which roared down the middle of the long, narrow cavern, where slaves had crushed the rocks in Piss Swill's gold mine.

Manacled and tossed in a heap on the floor, Ivan, Goul, Feral Fox, and Vlad lay perilously close to the gold. Their bodies glistened with sweat.

Stasha swore. While she and Suren dragged them away from the gold, Boa sent a deluge of water over the fire.

Ivan lifted his head and moaned. "We tried, Stasha. We really did. Bastard got us."

She planted a kiss on his forehead. "You did famously. Thank you. For everything." She bit her lip, then blurted, "Klaus? Where is he? And did you see a raven fly past?"

Feral Fox's eyes flickered in their sockets. "The raven that turned into a fae?" He gulped. "He chased the guards." He twisted his head to look down the narrow passage between the wall and the rapidly diminishing fire.

Wrought with concentration, Boa still spewed water. Steam clouded the air.

"And Klaus...." Ivan's voice hitched. "I—I'm sorry."

Stasha froze solid. "What are you saying?"

"There." Goul rattled his chains. "He's there."

She spun on her haunches. A crumpled shadow lay in the corner of the cavern. "Klaus!" She skittered across the floor to him. Not daring to even breathe, she rolled him over—and screamed.

The skin on the right side of his body had melted away, leaving nothing but blistered, charred flesh. On the left side, his clothes hung in ragged strips. She touched his tunic, bought with such hope for a new life, and sobbed.

What was the point of anything if Klaus wasn't in the world? And she didn't even have fire to burn this mine and everything Pyreack in it to the ground as punishment.

Suren and Boa fell on their knees next to her.

Boa touched Klaus's neck. "There's a pulse." Boa slapped Stasha hard across the face. "Stop that wailing. He's alive. We can still save him."

Stasha snagged in a ragged breath. Boa expected her to follow the example she had set when Lukas fell. Boa had walked away from Lukas to carry on as if nothing had happened. But, perhaps, one night over dinner in the far distant future, Boa would find the will to open her heart to talk about her loss. Her stoicism grounded Stasha.

When she faced Boa, her tears had dried, replaced by desperate hope. How she wished that hope would shift the icy dread in her core. "How? Tell me what I must do. Anything." She clutched Klaus's charred tunic as if her life depended on keeping him close.

"I need to cool him with cold water and then get him to the healers." Boa lifted her hands. But then, her eyes widened, and she sucked in a breath so sharp, it whistled between her teeth. Her hands dropped to hang limp at her sides.

"Then do it," Stasha pleaded. "What are you waiting for?" Her fingers were colder than they'd ever been. Stiff and aching, she flexed them, but it didn't help. She looked down and gulped.

Hoarfrost crept across her hands.

By all the darkness! How was this possible?

Yet frost crackled up into her arms, turning them white. Crisp with ice, Klaus's tunic crunched under her touch. She jerked her hands away from him and tumbled back on her heels.

Suren swore. "Sta—"

Boa flew at him. Her hand clenched around his throat. "Tell anyone what you've just seen, and I *will* kill you." She looked over her shoulder at Ivan, Feral Fox, Goul, and Vlad. "Same applies to you. No one says a word about that ice. It never happened."

Suren's arms flew up and knocked Boa's hands away. He croaked, "As if I would. Stasha's my friend. Sort of. I know what will happen to her if this gets out."

Transfixed, Stasha stared at her hands, and then at the jagged ice crystals clinging to Klaus's tunic. Surely ice was as dangerous as fire for someone burned as badly as he was? But ice was nothing more than very cold water.

"Not good enough." Boa looked at Stasha with a mix of horror and awe. "No one should have two powers. If Suren's foul king finds out—"

Not interested in Boa and Suren's argument, she placed a tentative hand on Klaus's burnt flesh, willing water and not ice out of her fingers. Instead, hoarfrost spread across his blisters.

He whimpered.

She was about to demand that Boa spirit him away to the healers when Suren hissed, "Princess Boadicea, you forget that I'm a mere conscript in this war. My mother and four sisters are back on our farm with no help to plant crops. If I go to them, I will be hunted down and killed for desertion. They have no magic either. My father made sure of that when he bound all of them to him and stole their powers."

Suren's bitterness reached Stasha. She dragged her eyes away from Klaus to look at him. His face was shadowed and brooding, and his body shook. "Not that it helped him. He still died in this endless war." Suren thrust a hand at Stasha. "She can change all this. I know it. You know it. So, if it gives you peace, I pledge you my sword. My magic. Everything I have. I will fight at your and Stasha's side. Anything to just go home to my family."

Boa's mauve eyes swirled. She blew out a long breath. "My army is made up of many such stories." She folded her hand over Suren's and gripped his wrist with her tattooed fingers. "I accept your pledge."

Suren dipped his head. "Thank you."

Stasha croaked, "That's good. But what about Klaus? We must find Averin and leave. Now." Her eyes flicked to Feral Fox, Ivan, Goul, and Vlad. "They need help too."

"Averin." The way Boa said Averin's name frightened Stasha. The princess leaned in so close that Stasha could see flecks of dirt in the pores of Boa's otherwise flawless skin. "You cannot tell him what happened here."

"But he's Averin!" she objected.

"Do you even know why he wants you in Zephyr?" Boa asked urgently. She looked down the passageway where Feral Fox had said Averin had gone, as if expecting him to reappear at any second.

"No. Not really." Stasha dug in her tunic for her amber, needing its comfort. "Do you know?"

"I have my suspicions." Boa grabbed her arm. "Shush. He's coming."

"But...." She wasn't sure she wanted to hide another thing from Averin. A frown creased her forehead. Maybe Boa had a point. With all the time she'd spent with Averin, he could have given her the reason he wanted her badly enough to risk his life and his father's disapproval by coming to Angharad. Yet he hadn't. She'd made him a deal she could not—would not—back out of, but that didn't mean she had to trust him if he didn't trust her—regardless of how much he made her pulse race. "Boa, get me and Klaus to the healers. Right now."

"Suren. Find Frea," Boa said. "Tell her to work with Averin and Trystaen to ward Angharad. Then she must get the word out. I want every fae in Ocea to know that we've taken Angharad."

"I heard my name." Averin strode in. Bloodied and dirty, he walked with a swagger that breathed success. Whoever had done this to Klaus had paid the ultimate price.

Stasha opened her mouth to thank him just as Boa touched her and Klaus. Averin and the room vanished in a blur of color and light. They were headed to the healers. She had no idea what Averin would say when he caught up with her, and right now, she didn't care.

Keeping Klaus alive was the only thing that mattered.

CHAPTER TWENTY-EIGHT

Stasha clung to Boa and Klaus as they spirited right into the heart of the temple in Ocea. Still holding Klaus in her arms, Boa stumbled and fell to her knees next to the tree. "Stasha, take him," she rasped, clearly spent from spiriting so far.

Klaus writhed and moaned, awake and in agony. Stasha laid him on the marble floor under the glowing tree's gentle light.

A serene-looking female fae she didn't recognize glided over to them. Eyes as green as grass assessed Klaus. Her lips pursed worryingly.

"Can you help him?" Stasha demanded, hardly daring to believe it was possible.

Without saying a word, the fae laid her hands right into the center of Klaus's burns. He flinched, whimpering.

"You're hurting him."

Green light spread from the fae's hands and covered the left side of Klaus's body. "To heal, we first have to ache. I'm not a restorer, so expect scarring." The healer's eyes drifted to the tree. "It helps that we have set up this animus here."

"Animus?" she breathed, watching in wonder as Klaus's blackened flesh softened and glowed.

"Place of healing." The healer lifted her hands, and the green light extinguished.

"Why have you stopped? It was going so well."

"He's human, not fae. He does not have the life force to support more work. Now he must rest." The healer ran her fingers over

Klaus's eyelids. His head lolled in sleep. She stood. "Follow him to his bed. I will visit with him later."

Flat on his back, Klaus levitated and floated slowly across the temple, past rows of beds to a pallet covered with crisp white linen. He sank down until his back settled on the sheet and his head rested on a pillow.

Stasha sat next to him on the floor and took his hand. She didn't mean to sleep, but she must have drifted off. A gentle touch on her shoulder woke her.

"You abandoned me, pit princess."

She jerked upright. "Averin." She blushed, conscious of the enormity of the secret she now kept from him. *Secrets*, she silently corrected, seeing as she had yet to tell him about the deal she'd made with the Tiyanak.

She clambered to her feet. Klaus was still sleeping, and she didn't want to wake him, so she whispered, "Klaus was burned, and I needed to—"

Averin brushed her face with a long finger. "You don't have to explain. I was never in any doubt about where your first loyalty lay." He knelt next to the bed. "How's he doing?"

"The healer did something with green light. I'm not sure what. He hasn't woken. I'm not even sure how long he's slept."

"At least five hours."

No wonder she was so refreshed, even if her legs protested the lack of blood supply as she knelt next to Averin.

She bit her lip. New, pink skin had covered Klaus's blackened body while they'd slept. As the healer had warned, it was as rippled as a pond in a gale. He would carry those scars all his life—unless he came with her to Zephyr. Maybe someone there could help him.

"Did I hear you mention green light?" Trystaen sauntered over and knelt on the opposite side of the bed. "Then he's in the very best of care." He swept his hand across Klaus's chest, trailing the identical green light.

"You're a healer? I wondered why everyone looked at you when discussing my multiple injuries."

Trystaen smiled. "From a long line of them. On my mother's side. Atria is famous for its healers." He smiled wryly. "I chose a different path, but I can still patch skin and mend bones if I have to. And talking of which, Averin brought your other human friends here."

"At least the ones we could find," Averin said grimly. "There were a lot of bodies."

She winced. "It has to end. This war."

"It will," Averin said. "Do you want me to take you to them?"

Torn between seeing who had survived and staying with Klaus, she hesitated.

Trystaen nudged her. "Go. I've got this. Feral Fox asked for you."

She allowed Averin to pull her to her feet. She hadn't taken more than two steps when a hoarse voice said, "I sailed in a boat, Stasha. A real one. Across the sea."

Her heart soared. She burst into joyous laughter and pirouetted around. "You're awake."

Klaus smiled up at her. There was a lightness in his tawny eyes she'd never seen before. "Last I knew, I was beating some fae with a pickaxe." He grimaced. "It didn't end well."

"Of course it didn't, you clumsy brute."

Klaus grimaced a smile.

Trystaen leaned in. "Are you still in pain? I'm Trystaen, one of Stasha's friends."

"Um...." Klaus sighed. "The truth? A little bit."

"Then sleep is what you need." Trystaen lifted a hand glowing with green light. "May I?"

"I don't know." Klaus grabbed her arm. "Should he?"

She kissed his cheek. "He should." She pulled away, awed with Klaus's trust as he lay back and let Trystaen brush him into a deep slumber.

Averin offered her his hand. "I'm sure your four other friends would like to see you."

"Is that all that's left?" She curled her fingers around his and walked with him to the section of the temple with the wall of prayers. Through the crowds of healers, rebels, and survivors, she spotted Suren talking with Boa. At least they'd formed an accord. The three children they'd saved from the prison wagon sat in a circle with other youngsters, slurping bowls of food. She'd visit with them after seeing Feral Fox.

"Most of the people we freed didn't get involved in the fighting," Averin said. "Or so Feral Fox told me. They waited in that tunnel where we found them. The Pyreack cut them down."

So much blood. So much waste.

She pulled Averin to a stop. "I know I have to go to Zephyr with you, but—"

"You make it sound like a hardship, pit princess." Averin smiled, clearly keeping things light.

Not willing to play along, she grabbed his tunic with both hands. "I know this wasn't part of the deal, but Klaus comes with me. If that's what he chooses."

Averin shrugged. "I think I figured that when we struck the deal, Stasha. You'd hardly rescue him and leave him behind."

"Will he be welcomed?"

"As my guest? Of course he will."

Would she be welcomed too? The question hung in the air. "And me? Why do you want me so much?"

Averin canted his head. "Chemistry, I think." His laughter bubbled as he pulled her across the room. "And a handful of compatibility thrown into the mix for good measure." Her stomach swooped. He was falling for her, just as she was falling for him?

Enjoying the touch of his skin and the smell of snow, sun-ripened oranges, and chai spices that summed up Averin, she let him drag her with him. There would be time enough to discover Zephyr's secrets when she arrived at the palace in Ilyseryph. Right now, she just wanted to enjoy being with him.

Ivan was the first of the four to spot them coming. He sat up on his bed and grinned. "Still got those awful ears, I see." He tossed a pillow at Goul, asleep on the bed next to him. Goul stirred and groaned. "Wake up. Stasha's here."

"Let him sleep," Feral Fox said sharply from his bed. Dried blood coated his bare chest.

On the bed next to Feral Fox sat Vlad, uninjured as far as she could tell.

His hazel human eyes bored into her.

She smiled at him. "We never actually met, but I won two silver coins off your first fight."

"Won!" Averin snorted. "Stole, more like it."

She smiled pertly at him. "You're never going to let me live that down, are you?"

Averin leaned in close and whispered, "Not even if we both live for two billion years."

A burning need to kiss him overwhelmed her. She was about to give into the compulsion when someone called, "Anyone hungry? We've set up a table behind the tree. Come help yourselves"

Stasha's stomach roared at her. "They don't have to ask me twice." She yanked Averin's hand and started walking. "Let's go."

Averin didn't move, and she jerked to a stop. "You and food."

"Yes, me and food. What are we waiting for?"

Averin gestured to Vlad and the others with his head. "An invitation maybe, pit princess?"

She gawped at her human friends. Hungry eyes watched her. Even Goul was awake and sitting at the edge of his bed.

She scoffed. "You're all orphans! Since when are you backward in coming forward when free food's on offer?"

Feral Fox looked around pointedly. "This isn't like any orphanage or fighting pit I've ever seen."

The others nodded, all looking equally as uncomfortable.

Feral Fox's Adam's apple bobbed. "And fae food...." He grimaced. "Is it—"

"Edible by humans," Goul snapped. "And what *exactly* will we be eating?"

A soft smile claimed her face. They were as unsure of themselves here as she had been in Radomir's tent.

At least they were amongst friends.

"The Martka and Kňazer lied about a lot of things. Salt doesn't keep fae away. And they don't eat—"

"Humans," Averin interrupted. He made a gagging sound, then swept his free hand out with a flourish. "Please, be Stasha and my guests at the meal." For a prince, Blue Eyes certainly knew how to make others feel welcome.

Vlad was the first on his feet. The others weren't far behind him. They followed her and Averin as they picked their way through the crowd of healers and fae.

They reached Klaus. He was fast asleep. When she hesitated, Averin said, "Let him sleep. We can rustle up food for him when he awakes."

She let Averin pull her along and almost fell over her feet when something small and warm barreled into her. Little arms encircled her hips. The fae youngling and his two sisters beamed up at her. Their brown Pyreack fae eyes were bright as sunbeams. All physical traces of their hardship had gone. She tousled each of their heads in turn. "Good to see you all."

"And you," the boy answered. His eyes flitted across the cavern to where a group of fae youngsters played. He squeezed her legs, and he and his sister bolted.

"The resilience of youth," Averin said, head canted to watch them.

"What will happen with them?" She had to know.

Averin shrugged. "Boa will take them in. She always does. In time, they'll be bearing rebel weapons and fighting their own kind."

Her jaw hardened. "Then the sooner we win this war, the better."

Averin leaned in to whisper, "Perhaps you haven't noticed, my pit princess, but we've already scored a major victory." He jerked his thumb at the youngsters. "They were all slaves just a few hours ago."

Warmth that had nothing to do with magic blossomed in her chest. "Let's eat and drink to that." Still holding his hand, she skipped to a trestle table on the far side of the tree.

Her mouth watered at the mounds of sliced bread, butter and honey, platters of steaming meat, and bowls of spiced vegetables that covered it from end-to-end. Earthenware jugs were jammed between the platters. Wine, she guessed.

"Darkness be damned!" Feral Fox whistled. "To think I've lived to see that much food in one place at one time." His eyes rolled back in his head. "Now I can die in peace."

Ivan shoved an elbow into Feral Fox's side. "Before eating some of it? That sounds pretty dumb to me."

"For once, Ivan is right. As astonishing as that may seem." She smiled and winked at Ivan to remove any sting. He had fought like a champion in the mine and would forever hold a special place in her heart.

Averin waved their four human friends to the table. "Dive in. Plenty more where this came from."

She stood to one side with Averin, smiling with joy as Vlad, Goul, Ivan, and Feral Fox loaded piles of food onto their plates. Only when they'd sat with their back against the cavern wall did she grab plates for Averin and herself. She tossed a pile of honeyed-bread on one side of her plate and meat and vegetables on the other.

Averin laughed. "Sure you won't still be hungry after that, my pit princess?" Her load of food was at least four inches higher than his.

"I'm just doing what you asked—putting some flesh on my bones so a stiff breeze doesn't blow me away once I get to Zephyr."

Instead of laughing with her, Averin's face clouded. "I think a stiff breeze is almost guaranteed." His face cleared. "But don't worry, I'll always be there to catch you." He joined their friends and sat, patting the space next to him. "Pit princess, sit."

Why did he have to make that comment? She didn't want to think about what life in Zephyr would bring. She sat, her knees brushing his—much to the delight of her stupid nerve endings, which zinged and danced. Once they eventually settled down and behaved themselves, she munched almost mechanically, while everyone else shared banter and jokes.

So much to think about. So many unknowns ahead of her. What would happen with Feral Fox and the others? There was nothing for them back in Askavol. Could they also join Boa's army? Or did humans need their own army? If so, could the four of them be the core? Would they want that? And who would they fight?

Fae?

No. That was crazy.

But perhaps they could be glamoured to look like fae for intelligence gathering.

And Klaus? What would he want?

The click of Boa's boots on the floor reached her. She put her half-eaten plate down and looked up at Boa.

"Averin, can I have Stasha for a moment?"

Averin's brow creased. "If you must." But he grabbed Stasha's hand.

Boa wouldn't have sought her out for no reason. She prized his fingers open and pulled her hand way. "I'll be back."

"You better be."

She waved at Averin over her shoulder and followed Boa. The princess led her across the temple, through the tunnel entrance, and out onto the side of the mountain. She drew in a shuddering breath of icy air. A thick layer of snow had frosted everything white. "Does Averin's legendary hearing have anything to do with this choice of venue?" Her breath clouded in the freezing air.

"You're learning." Boa sighed. "Averin. He and I are ... complex."

"I've gathered that." Turned out that she and Averin were also complex. Very. She waited expectantly for Boa to speak.

The princess was silent for a long while, watching her. Finally, she said, "We need to figure out why you have fire *and* water magic. It's impossible. Not even younglings born from a mixed sealing have two powers."

"I have to go with Averin."

"I know. But...." Boa huffed. "Will you permit me to do some research?"

"Of course. But I'll have to tell Averin at some point."

"Give me time, Stasha," Boa pleaded. "Say nothing until I make contact with you. It will be safer for you that way."

She rubbed her arms. "Are you saying I'll be in danger in

Zephyr?" Hadn't Averin implied something similar although he'd told her she would be welcome.

"I'm saying you'll be in danger anywhere your powers are known."

"I can defend myself, you know."

The living tattoos threaded around Boa's steepled fingers. "I don't doubt that. The question is ... will you? After Angharad."

Boa knew of her guilt and grief and pain at what she'd done to that fae. Boa hadn't been in the control tower, yet she knew. Had Suren told her? He must have.

She looked out over the snowy cliff. Even the waterfalls spewing from the mouths of the carved gods had frozen.

It reflected her mood.

She said dully, "I'll consider what you're saying. Now, if you don't mind, I'd like to be alone."

Boa nodded curtly and turned on her heel. She stopped and said over her shoulder, "I'm sending Suren with you to Ilyseryph."

Stasha frowned. "As a bodyguard?"

"No. As a friend. Someone you can trust. Someone who has pledged his loyalty to you and to me. A fae outsider, like you'll be in Zephyr."

She clawed at her leggings. "Will Averin's family accept him?"

"Probably not. But I can't see that worrying you, or Suren. He's already agreed."

"Can they refuse him entry?"

"Right now, our blue-eyed prince will do anything for you. Insist on it while he's in a giving mood." Boa snorted. "Averin can be as stubborn as a brick wall when it serves him. Don't let him pull rank and push you around."

"He's never tried any stunts like that."

"Good." Boa smiled thinly. "Freeze his leggings with him in them if he does."

Stasha sighed. This skullduggery and distrust only served to widen the chasm between her and Averin.

But it couldn't hurt to have someone on her and Klaus's side in

Zephyr. She nodded. "Okay. Now please give me a few minutes by myself to think about ... things."

Boa's boots crunched in the snow as she made her back to the tunnel.

Stasha tossed her head back to look at the stars. Peaceful and calm, they sparkled in the blackness. Brightest of all was the Sword. Would she ever know that kind of peace and tranquility, or would she spend the rest of her life fighting and running, merely existing and surviving, unable to really trust anyone?

And it would be a long life. A long *fae* life. While Klaus....

The breeze picked up sharply, blowing her hair from her shoulders, and bringing with it a familiar stench of blood and rot and dead things. Not Angharad. More like....

Her heart sank.

A Tiyanak towered over her. No glamour or pretense covered its hideous form. Worse, it wore a red ribbon tied in a neat bow around its wrist. It hissed, "My, my, the little fae has been busy. Has she found time for the Tiyanak's bargain?"

HE END OF BOOK ONE.

EPILOGUE

*D*ear Reader,
     Thank you for reading *The Fire Thief*. This book was born in Italy, where we got the idea for an exceptional heroine, who we now know as Stasha. She's been telling us her story for years now, and we couldn't be happier to share it with you.

But of course, Stasha's story is far from over.

What does the Tiyanak want with her? Will she manage to fulfil her bargain without sacrificing something she really values? Like Klaus.

And why is Averin so cagey about what awaits her in Zephyr? Will her deal with him lead her into more life threatening perils?

You can follow her adventures in *The Winged Assassin*, available on Amazon in ebook and paperback.

Cheers
Gwynn and Erin

56780164R00158

Made in the USA
Middletown, DE
24 July 2019